I0611966

Glass House Books
The Ship Wife

Anne Vines won the Boroondara Prize in 2014 and the Keith Carroll Award in 2020 for short stories.

She was shortlisted for the Alan Marshall Short Story Award 1987, The Age Short Story Award 2009, the Henry Handel Richardson Short Story Award 2011, and the international Wasafiri New Writing Prize, 2014. She was commended in the Varuna Harper-Collins Award in 2007 for her novel's "compelling, very exciting voice" and "character-driven unusual twists" which "build up a head of steam". Her novel, *A Good Killer*, entered in the Victorian Premier's Literary Award for an Unpublished Manuscript in 2008, was commended by the judges for its "fast-paced storytelling".

Anne's short fiction was published in *Word U Up* 2014, *Award Winning Australian Writing* 2015, *Wasafiri Magazine Online* 2016, *Ring of Words* 2018 and *Boroondara Literary Awards Anthology* 2020.

Anne has worked on her novels with Peter Bishop and Helen Barnes-Bulley at Varuna, with writers Lee Kofman, Toni Jordan, Sydney Smith and Janey Runci, and with editor Irina Dunn.

Anne Vines completed a Bachelor of Arts at the University of Melbourne, concentrating on Literature and the history of Australia and Britain. She taught at secondary schools in country Victoria, Melbourne and London and at the Council for Adult Education, Melbourne. She managed student welfare, English curriculum and staff professional development. She co-wrote the VCE English and Literature courses and was a public examination assessor of those subjects.

Anne has lived in England and Germany, and for shorter periods in Ireland, Wales, Spain, Italy and France. While traveling to UK, Ireland, Europe, USA, South America and Asia, she carried out research in libraries, archives and communities for her novels, including *The Ship Wife*.

Glass House Books
Brisbane

The Ship Wife

A novel based on a true story

Anne Vines

Glass House Books
Brisbane

Glass House Books
an imprint of IP (Interactive Publications Pty Ltd)
Treetop Studio • 9 Kuhler Court
Carindale, Queensland, Australia 4152
sales@ipoz.biz
http://ipoz.biz

This book was written on the traditional land of the Wurundjeri people of the Kulin Nation. The author acknowledges and pays her respects to their elders, past and present and emerging.

Printed in 12 pt Adobe Caslon Pro on 14 pt Avenir Book.

ISBN: 978192830241 (PB); 978192830258 (eBk)

A catalogue record for this book is available from the National Library of Australia

for Richard, Andrew, Laura, and in memory
of my grandmother, Catherine O'Shannassy Vines

Acknowledgements

Front cover images: *The East Indiaman Ceres off St Helena,* William John Huggins (1816), *Portrait of Emma Hamilton,* Angelica Kauffman, 1791, MET Museum

Back cover image: *Sydney from the Western Side of the Cove, 1803,* George William Evans, State Library of New South Wales

Cover design: Mark Droic

Book design: David P Reiter

Author photo: Laura Vines

I am indebted to Thelma Birrell (nee Bostock) for her generous sharing of information and for inviting me to write the story.

I thank my husband, Dr Richard O'Sullivan, for introducing me to Thelma Birrell, his distant relative. His understanding of Irish history, language and culture was a great assistance. I also thank him for his enthusiasm and very helpful comments on a late draft of the manuscript.

My thanks to my sister, historian Margaret Vines, who connected me to our many Irish relatives and to sites in Ireland and assisted my research. Thanks to Laura Vines for her very helpful comments, and to Andrew O'Sullivan for his support.

Thanks to Janey Runci, who gave extremely helpful advice and encouragement on an early draft; Toni Jordan for her astute, pivotal advice; Andrea Goldsmith for her generosity and wisdom; Sandy Jeffs for her insights about writing and for her constant example of creative courage, generous communication, and dedication to shaping art; Susan Pierotti for her skilled editorial assistance; the Lyceum Club Melbourne Writers' Circle for their support and advice; Irina Dunn for her expert editorial assistance; Dr David Reiter for his insightful editing and meticulous preparation and publication of this book.

Thanks to librarians in the National Library, Dublin, the National Archives, Dublin, the British Library, the Mitchell Library, Sydney and the Tasmanian Archives and Heritage Office.

Contents

1 Evanton Estate, Wicklow Hills

County Wicklow, 1792

Just after daybreak, sitting in the cart behind two men and a woman and wedged between portmanteaux and boxes, Elizabeth gazed intently at her street, which was all she knew of the world. She waved at her parents, grandmother, sisters, cousins and neighbours. It was hard to believe she would not see them for years.

The cart clattered into the wider street that she hardly knew and then along to the high street, past the green and the big cathedral. Soon they were driving out along the road to the country. Dublin Town took so little time to ride through and leave behind. Here, there were fields and scarcely a house or shed for miles. Cows she saw, but not people. She must get used to the countryside. In her new life as a housemaid, she would have country fields and hills all around. She unwrapped her small portion of bread and took a bite. It was cold in the wind; even in her shawl and bonnet she shivered. She must not eat too much at first or she would be hungry and too cold as night drew near. After a time, her head drooped, and she dozed. The wobbling of the cart had a rhythm that soothed her.

When she woke, the cart was stopped in a crowded village street. The driver told her to walk about.

Granny had told her this, too. "If a body stays on the cart the whole journey, the bones and all will be stiff for days."

"But don't go wandering out of sight," Da had warned. "Don't trust anyone in the villages, especially young men lounging about."

She pressed her nose to the window of the shop next to the inn and looked over the bonnets and ribbons. There was a statue of some nobleman in the middle of the street with steps around it. She sat on one of the steps for a few moments and looked to see if there was water anywhere. Her mother had worried about her not getting anything to drink. Granny had suggested asking for a cup of water at the inn, but Elizabeth feared she would be sent packing, like in Dublin Town.

She stood up and walked back and forth, trying and failing to ignore the jostling boys rushing past. Then she saw them grabbing something off a tree near the corner and running away. No one came after them to scold or whip them. She followed their path and saw a big pear tree overhanging the street. It grew behind a high stone wall. On the ground near her were two pears, one half smashed and one whole. She looked about her, stooped quickly, scooped them up into her shawl and scurried back to the coach. Though she could not eat them till she was safely away, they felt so soft and plump in her hand under her shawl that it was all she could do not to grin in triumph.

The pears made up for the cold wind. As the cart trundled off, she ate the soft smashed one – so sweet and running with juice – a taste she had not known, for it was only old apples that they ate at home. She pulled her shawl close about her and pressed her back against the wooden rails as the cart rocked back and forth. No one else was travelling on with her so she sang softly to herself and imagined her future life in the Big House. Granny had described the outside of the house, but not the grand rooms or the ladies' clothes, for she had lived in the outer region of the estate on her small farm and did not know the ways of the household.

They drove past so many streams that Elizabeth lost count. Twice she spied a castle and once they drove close to its gates. Who would believe such great high buildings, half-ruined but still so grand. Way off were such hills – no, mountains – they took her breath away, they were so beautiful. To think that she would have never seen them if she had stayed in Dublin Town.

She saw men and boys bringing in the cows. There were farms a way off from the road and when she saw the smoke wafting from their chimneys, she shed quiet tears at the thought of the little fireplace at home. How she wished Granny could have come with her, or Ma.

They stopped two more times. It was tiring to climb down but she had to find a spot behind the bushes to lift her skirts. When she climbed back the second time, the driver threw her a rug to snuggle under. When the gloaming came on, she loved her view of the sky and the rising moon and then the flicker of stars behind wisps of cloud.

She did not know she had fallen asleep until she heard the driver's voice. "Wake up, girl, the estate starts on this hill."

She saw gates and long meadows and then, hazy in the dim light, gardens that went on and on. In the distance, tiny farmhouses – one that was once Granny's.

Then the Big House. A lantern lit up the main entrance. The walls and roof were etched against the violet sky. Their lines were so straight and grand. The dark windows gleamed in the moonlight.

The cart rattled around to the back. She was shaking in anticipation and could hardly take in the courtyard and the smaller buildings. The driver helped her down, led her to a door and knocked.

An old, dried-up looking man nodded at the driver and then looked her up and down. He ushered them both along a corridor into a large room with a fire. She wanted to rush to it but did not dare. The driver sank down on a long bench by the fire. The old man handed him a jar and uncorked it. Then the old man handed Elizabeth a cup of something warm. She gulped it. He waved towards the table, and she saw a plate of bread and a little cheese. He nodded towards a chair, so she sat and ate. The driver stretched out on the bench. When she had eaten, the old man beckoned her and led her out to a passage at the end of which was a narrow staircase.

"Be quiet, child, as we go up to the room. The other maids are asleep. Your place is on the bed near the door. Do you require the water closet?"

She stared.

"Do you need to make water, child, to relieve yourself? There is a place here for the maids."

She nodded. He took her bundle, then led her to a small door and opened it. She walked inside and shut the door. She looked at the wooden bench and the hole. So well-scrubbed, a bowl inside to empty, and hardly a smell at all.

He led her up to her room and pointed to a bed, the closest of the three. The other girl on it was facing towards them but did not wake. Elizabeth took off her boots and her shawl and slowly slid under the quilt on the other side of the bed. She feared she might wake the other occupant with tossing and turning, but she slept at once.

A few hours later, the sun streamed in the windows and the girls were talking.

Maire, the tallest girl, had a wide smile, kind eyes, a broad face, and a noticeable bosom. Her hair was bundled up under her cap.

When Elizabeth sat up, Maire said, "Show us your boots – no, the soles," and the girls all laughed. "Brush them off." She handed Elizabeth a hard brush. "Over there in the corner where we won't walk in your dirt. You can't go bringing outside mud or dirt inside the house, see? Downstairs there is a boot-scraper and a brush for when you come in from the laundry or the garden. You will get your clothes from Mrs Ryan once we have the fires going and the breakfast ready."

Aine was smaller, not much bigger than Elizabeth, and her eyes were mischievous but a little sad too. "Come down with me," she said, and they ran down the stairs so fast that Elizabeth was laughing and panting to keep up.

She watched Aine and the others lighting fires, opening curtains, dusting and carrying in platters of fruit and bread that smelled better than anything Elizabeth had tasted before.

In the kitchen, she met Mary Hogan, the cook, who was calling out orders and who sat Elizabeth down on the end of a bench. The other girls rushed into an adjoining small room and brought back bowls of steaming gruel. One was banged down in front of her. She was so hungry she would have eaten it were it sour or bitter, but it was pleasing – and filling. Oats and other grains it was, with milk and hot water. Maire brought in a tray covered with slices of bread; was it the wonderful kind that she had smelt? Perhaps not, more like yesterday's bread, but thankfully not too hard or dry.

Maire said to her, "Don't expect butter or jam, except on Christmas Day."

Aine said softly, "Sometimes there are leftovers at lunch time."

When Mrs Ryan appeared, she was dressed like a fine lady, with no apron.

"You are neat enough, I am pleased to see," she said. "Keep that straight back, girl. Good posture is what we like at Evanton. Maire, fetch her uniform. Now, Elizabeth, go to the scullery, take off your things and wash your face, neck and hands. Wash the soap off thoroughly or you may get a rash."

In the scullery, she found a basin of cold water and a bar of soap on the bench under the window. She took off her upper garments but kept on her petticoat – surely that was what Mrs Ryan meant. She swished her hands around in the basin and splashed her face and neck. Mrs Ryan came into the room holding out a cloth.

"Dry yourself, now. And leave those clothes in the basket at the door."

She had scarcely put her clothes in the basket when Mrs Ryan was behind her again. The housekeeper lifted Elizabeth's arms and hair to

4

examine her for lice, but her family hardly ever had those. Inspection completed, Mrs Ryan swept a cloak over Elizabeth's shoulders and pulled her out into the kitchen. Elizabeth's garments were on the long seat. She found the dress fastenings were beyond her.

Mrs Ryan called Maire, who was stacking bowls into a dresser, to come to Elizabeth's aid.

"Tomorrow, you will fasten your clothes yourself," said Mrs Ryan. "You will need to change your clothes if they become soiled, but we try to keep the one dress for the week, so remember to use the apron at all times. Your payment will be kept for you till the end of the trial period and then all your payments will be kept by me to avoid you losing them. You may apply to me if you need ready cash. Most of our girls do not, not till the summer fair. You may attend Mass with the other girls on Sunday when I can spare you, and you are lucky that your master allows it."

Elizabeth nodded. "Thank you, Mrs Ryan."

"You will work with Maire today and all this week." Mrs Ryan dismissed her with a quick nod and walked swiftly from the room.

Maire was watching in the large silver-framed mirror she was cleaning. She winked at Elizabeth. "All of us are so tired by the time we get to Sunday, but we must trudge out to the field for the Mass and listen to the priest talking his foreign lingo, or who knows what might happen to us. The devil is always watching, isn't he? It is a comfort when the priest gives us the blessing to keep us safe from curses and the devil's tricks. Come here. I'll show you how to dust this cabinet."

"How do I know what my work will be next week if I'm not with you?" Elizabeth asked Maire.

The girl laughed. "Old Ryan will make sure you know, don't you worry."

Elizabeth wondered when she would meet Milady.

"Did you start here when you were my age?"

"What age are you? Twelve? Yes, that's the age that my lady wants her maids to be." Her voice changed to an old, slow, English one. "I need them young enough to be moulded and old enough not to miss their mothers."

Without warning, Elizabeth burst into tears. She hid her face in her apron and wished she could be anywhere else. How scornful big Maire must be.

An arm slid around her shoulder. "Never you mind, we all cry. Almighty God in Heaven, why wouldn't we? Here…"

Elizabeth found a piece of biscuit in front of her face. She gulped down her sobs, accepted the gift and stammered her thanks.

"We cry so much," Maire said, "that if the master or mistress ever came within earshot of the attic, they would hear a choir to harrow their hearts – if they had hearts." She sniffed. "They only hear the cries of their own daughter. Rarely, too, for that girl only cries when she is not off enjoying herself. Come on, you'll learn to like some things here. At least we eat, and the rooms are warmer than most, and though the work goes on too long, it doesn't maim us – so we're the lucky ones, aren't we?"

When her voice was back, Elizabeth said, "Do we ever see the grand rooms or the garden?"

"Sure, you can look out at the garden today. Do you like gardens?"

"I've never seen one. There are always high walls and gates to stop you seeing."

"Aye. This work lets you see how the gentry live, for what it's worth to the likes of us." She laughed and bent down to push Elizabeth's hair back inside her cap. "Keep that bright hair out of sight. They don't want to see it. As Mrs Ryan says, 'A maid must not draw attention to her appearance.'" She laughed again. "You can take it down at the fair one day and dazzle some poor fellow."

The second night, Elizabeth felt content and a little excited when she went to bed. She thought she would sleep at once, like the night before, but while the other girls' breathing became deep and even, she found her tears welling up. The night wore on; she heard Aine sob and peered anxiously at her. Then Elizabeth heard herself give a wail and Aine's arms were around her.

For the first week, this happened every night. Once, another girl woke and joined their crying. Maire got up and stroked their backs and told them to hush and never mind.

At the start of her second week, Elizabeth found that she could make herself stop thinking of home. In her bed at night, she thought of the future instead, of how she would grow big and strong, and how she might become more than a downstairs maid. As Maire said, here they had a warm bed, good food and work that would not steal their health and turn them twisted and old before their time. A position where, if they behaved well, no one beat them. Back home, there was not enough to eat some weeks, there were no positions for girls like her, nor any work at all most of the time; she might have been on the streets – begging, scavenging or, like some girls, stealing. She was a fortunate one.

Yet the lord of the estate owned her now, more than her father did. Her life depended on pleasing her master and mistress. One false step and out with her, back to Dublin Town to be a burden on Ma and Da.

One day that summer, she served Milady. In the garden courtyard, she carried plates of bread and fish and meat to the big, smooth stone table. She did not dare look at Milady except for a second.

Not till she was clearing away did Milady say, "And who is this swift little person?"

The butler, Mr Creggan, said her name and Elizabeth stood still.

"You may look up, child," Milady said.

Elizabeth had enjoyed her voice all afternoon. It was low, and sometimes sounded like singing. She looked up and took in the lady's curled, garlanded hair, her jewels and the soft sheen of her gown. Milady's dress was prettier than the Virgin's on the statue in St. Anthony's back home. Elizabeth felt a flush of shame for a moment, but it was true and why shouldn't she admire pretty things? When she was dismissed the next minute, she had taken in all of Milady as if she were a painting.

But the soft beauty of Milady was not a picture of her heart. Maire had said it: they had no hearts. When the next winter was ending, Elizabeth's cousin, Joe, came to tell her that Granny had just died. He asked to take her to Dublin Town in his cart, to the burial and the wake. Mr Creggan told Milady of the request and she refused. She did not look at Elizabeth after that, and Elizabeth felt a fury that did not abate. Never to see Granny again, the sorrow of it so much harder when she could not share it with her parents and sisters. Did Milady not know that the whole family must gather and pray and mourn together, and that Elizabeth would always remember that she, the eldest daughter, the one meant to support her mother the most, the one who had known Granny the most, had not been there at the wake, and that all the family would remember too? Would Granny's spirit be uneasy or be angry at Elizabeth's absence? Would something bad befall Elizabeth now? These rich folks must think she had no feelings. They must see their servants as no better than their horses, dumb beasts to do their bidding.

*

It had been easier not to draw attention to herself when she first went to Evanton Manor as a child with no bosom.

Two years later, her bosom had appeared. She was the youngest of the girls and so it pleased her to look more like them. Mrs Ryan trained her for the good rooms, for the upstairs parlour and even once for the young lady, the master's daughter, who was over from London. Elizabeth liked to listen to Mrs Ryan and to watch her preparing the washstand and the dressing table. Even more, she liked learning what to say and how to say it. Not that Mrs Ryan sounded English like Milady, but she sounded like gentry – soft, low and pleasant. Elizabeth could hardly bear hearing Mary the cook after the smooth tones of Mrs Ryan.

One day, Elizabeth had a moment to stop in the side passage upstairs and see her profile in the glass. It took her breath away – she thought it was someone else for a minute. The shelf her bosoms made jutted out so far and her waist was so little that she looked grown up, like a lady in one of those black drawings on white cards that she had seen on the library wall.

But she felt less glad of her new bosom when the master and the young master noticed, and the footmen too. The young master she could dodge and shake her head at, for he was still a child, but if the master spoke or touched, she must stand stock still and await his pleasure – no, really, surely, he would not, but she felt his eyes on her that day when she was helping the young lady.

Six months later, he was home for the hunting, and he looked at her again. She had shot up a half a head. He came upon her in the upstairs passage when she was dusting the paintings near the small parlour. He grabbed and pushed her into the doorway, his face against hers, his tongue in her mouth, his breath hot. She tried to stand still but his weight nearly pushed her over. It was well that they were in the smaller parlour and could back into the harpsichord, which was closed, thank God, and silent. It proved surprisingly sturdy. She hoped the master's buttons and rings were not scratching the pretty painted flowers on the wood. He cupped one bosom and squeezed her waist but if he left her alone below, she thought she wouldn't mind too much. Suddenly he laughed and left.

She realised she had not made a sound. How could she? He had taken over her mouth. And she was afraid. It was like she was struck dumb and unable to move. A mournful sadness swept over her, like a huge dark bird hovering above her, closing its wings over her head.

Wasn't it just as well she had not made a sound, just as well she had not resisted? What good would it have done? The mistress might have heard, or Mrs Ryan, and wouldn't they dismiss her? She would be blamed, surely. The master would not admit any wrongdoing. She had heard tales from Maire and the others of how they had been used so. "Even Eilish, with her holy face and pretty manners," Mary Hogan had muttered, but when someone mentioned that Eilish was Elizabeth's kin, Mary said, "Take no notice, Elizabeth. It was only the talk of the footmen, and you can't believe a word they say."

She stood up straight. She still felt the hard imprint of the harpsichord lid on her back. She tried to get her breath. It was not till the blood stopped racing at her temple and her throat that she could focus on the painting she was facing, of a beautiful, serene lady in a shining pale blue gown, bright pearls in her hair and at her throat. Did such things happen to ladies like that? Wouldn't they be treated to charming poems and promises, not grabbed and pushed like hens in the yard?

Next day, she had to dust in the upstairs corridors just the same, and the master pounced again to clutch and push. She thought, *thank God, the business below isn't happening*, but it was a trick because he pressed her against the wall of the corridor and it was all she could do not to scream. So fast, she was astonished, though cousin Meg in Dublin Town had told her that men were in and out and off they ran. The pain inside was stinging. She felt hot smarting liquid spill out of her. She sped up the three flights to the maids' room and grabbed a rag. There was blood. She tied the rag ends onto her petticoat waist and hurried back to work.

Her legs and arms felt heavy as she waxed the wooden floor in the library. She kept hearing the words, purity, virtue, virginity – now they could never be said of her. She was pure no longer, a virgin never again. She remembered her mother and her aunts whispering about a girl in the street who had lost her virginity. With mournful, disapproving faces, they said "lost" over and over, and their tone was scornful; the girl was lost – from God, Heaven and the Church, and from the respect of men and the friendship of women. A bad girl. Fallen. Elizabeth put down her work cloth and put her head in her hands. Should she pray? Would God or Christ or St Brigid help her – or the Virgin Mary?

Why had it happened? Why had the Holy Ones let it happen to her? What had she done wrong? She thought of Mass last Sunday – she had fallen asleep and not even heard the blessing. She had not said "Amen". Or was it because she had not properly mourned and sung for Granny? Or had she smiled too much at the master?

He found her again on the morrow and it hurt again, though she shed not a drop of blood. She felt pain there for days. Would the footmen and Milady smell something? The footmen did, or else they knew from her face or her demeanour or the master's, for they smirked at her. But they would not touch her now. For a week, she worried till her monthly bleeding started around the usual day. She tried to warn off the master when next he found her at the height of the bleeding, for she thought it would stop him, but he took no notice, though he let her be for the next few days. Soon after, he went away to his town house in Dublin and then over to London. So she was safe for now.

He might take his pleasure when he willed, but she could keep her heart free. Maire told tales of girls who lost theirs to gentlemen or even footmen. But then Michael, the boy in the stables, started giving her the eye when she went outside to the laundry and to the kitchen garden. And truth be told, he had already caught her eye – such shoulders on him, and legs. A tall country lad, the like you never saw in the smoky streets of Dublin Town. The way he stared at her was lovely compared to the master who looked her over like she was a horse or a cow. The way Michael waited, and then only wanted to talk, was lovely, too.

So was the way he walked out with her twice before he even tried a thing. When he did, it was a kiss so sweet and light, no slobbering at all. Michael didn't know what had gone on with the master. He didn't know the indoors people. He didn't mention them at all. She wanted to tell him, but it was hard to find the right moment, and the words. If she told him, she would not feel this heavy dread, and she would not be treating him falsely. Soon she would know when and how to tell him.

That summer, she turned fifteen. The master and the family went to their English house, so life on the estate became easier. When she had an evening off, she could stay out till late. Michael could, too, when his stable duties finished early. One clear evening, he took her to a place he had talked of often, in the nearby hills. She was longing to see it, for it was the place her grandmother had spoken of with such love.

They walked along the valley and up the hill to where you could look down over the glen. It was as beautiful as Granny had said.

Swathed in mist, the greens of the glen were rich and varied. Streaks of flushed sunlight were thinning; the world grew dimmer and softer. In the distance, she could see the green hills turning blue-grey. She watched the trees become blurs of brown then black, while the birds whirled and sang their hearts out before they vanished, and the white moon hid behind soft cloud.

He was surprised at how thrilled she was. "What a town girl you are," he teased.

All that evening her heart was light and full of love for this long-limbed, carefree boy whose eyes were hot and joyful. No greed or cruelty dwelt in him. The other feeling she knew that day was one she could barely name. Freedom was not a word her people threw about. It had a strange, foreign sound. Her uncles who had fought over the sea might say it, but not her parents or cousins or the girls she worked with now. Yet much of the happiness she felt that day was the absence of fear.

For though his mind was made up, like any man's, she could say things to him, ask, and tell even. So when they rolled in the grass, he only caressed her and he was so gentle it was no hurt, but just what cousin Meg said, the best of anything in the world.

They clung together in the beauty and the cooling air and when they could stay no longer, they walked quickly back to the edge of the estate. Michael ran to the stables to tell some tale to the head groom about his wanderings. She walked swiftly to the house, into the kitchen for a cup of water before bed. She never told where she went on her few afternoons off; planting a story about visiting her mother's cousins, Joe and Nora, in the nearby countryside had been enough lying. It brought her close to blushing, thankful that no one knew her family. Maire guessed, she knew, and probably others, but no one said a thing.

The next time they walked out, she was determined to tell him about the master. Once he knew, wouldn't he see that they should make their courting known to the head groom and to Mrs Ryan and Mr Creggan, and wouldn't everyone think that they should marry soon? Then wouldn't the master move from her to someone else?

It was late and night had fallen. They did not go further than the meadow beyond the Big House. Across the foothills, the high dark outline of the Great Sugarloaf Mountain overshadowed them, blocking out the moonlight. They sat down, and she could hardly see Michael's face. How could she begin? What words should she use? Although she had thought of this moment for nights and nights waiting to go to sleep, she had not found an easy way to tell such a story.

"Michael, you know that the master has everything his own way in the house with all of us, and there is nothing we can do, whatever he decides?"

His eyes met hers. "What is he going to do to you, Bessie? He's not about to send you to the house in Dublin Town?"

"No, not that." She waited. How she wished he would guess. When he started to speak, her heart lifted.

"Does he order someone to beat you?" His eyes were kind and concerned.

She stroked his cheek. "No."

Was it something in her eyes that gave him a sense of horror? He stared with a look almost of fear, a look of dread.

She could bear the tension no longer. Her voice came out in a sob. "Oh, Michael, you know he does own the bodies of us, of us girls. He has used us all most shamefully..."

She stopped, halted by the tension in his look and the sudden hardness of his grip on her arm. His face turned into someone else's. A sneer twisted his mouth. Hatred darkened his eyes. "Those who flounce about like Maire or Eilish, to be sure he grabs them. But why did you catch his eye?"

"All of us upstairs, he looks us over—"

"You could have dodged him; you could have told the housekeeper."

Her tears were streaming now. "How could I? There is nothing she can do."

"How do you know? If she told the mistress—"

"I would be dismissed."

"Would not that be better?"

"How could it be? I would have to go home. I would have no wages, no reference, no chance of another position."

"Your family would help you."

"They could not find me work like here – probably no work at all."

"But to just let him, how could you? Did you tell him no, did you bid him to stop, did you struggle?"

She wept and gazed at him, unable to say a word. Could he not see how it was with the master? What did he think had happened? What did he imagine the master would do if she protested?

He pushed her away onto the grass. She fell onto her back, looking up at him. He leaned over her. "You just let him, didn't you? How many times?"

He sounded like the priest.

She shook her head and sobbed. Then a hot feeling came over her; she sat up and said, "But he hasn't had me, Michael. That's not what I'm saying. I am afraid of what he *might* do, I worry about how to dodge him. I've managed it so far. I told the other girl, Aine, to come in when I give a loud sneeze. She knows to race along the passage and into the room, so he stops touching my cheek or sliding his hand around my waist."

She watched his red colour fading and his eyes calming down. What if someone told him tales later? They would never tell the details, and he would believe her still.

"Aine and I have protected each other so far and we will continue, but there's only the other girls to talk to and I wanted so much to tell you and for you to understand."

She stood up and there was but a wisp of air between them. She smiled and tried to make him see, to make him keep loving her. She started to shake; it was so risky. What if he shouted, struck her and spurned her? But the shaking she felt was pleasurable too, as if she had run down a hillside in the summer night breeze. How easy it was to change his thoughts and his mood and his face. Why should she lose him because of the master? When she and Michael were married, then she might tell him, but probably not for the idea riled him so much. Thank God, she had the gift of the gab a little, like Da. She understood now why Da's eyes sparkled when he buttonholed someone and talked at them.

Michael said, his tone still aggrieved and hot, "Can't you work downstairs again so he doesn't keep looming up at you?"

She put on a look as hopeless as his idea.

He was breathing fast again. "When we are a little older, I can wed you. Then you would work elsewhere in the house."

"Oh yes, Michael, I hoped you would say that. I am longing to marry you. I am hoping to be a ladies' maid. Mrs Ryan says I have the makings, the face and hands and voice too."

"But in Milady's or the young lady's rooms, you would be near the master."

"Yes, but Milady might see. I don't think he tries it with the ladies' maids, only with the housemaids."

He looked unsure. She wasn't sure herself, but it was the best she could think up on the spot.

There was anger in his eyes. "The master does what he likes with all of us. Don't you know that he throws families out to starve, raises the rent, or pays less for the crop if he has a mind to? My brother is afeard we will lose our farm. But there are some folk who have ideas about how to help us." He stopped and stared at her.

She gave him a smile and he flushed. She leaned on his chest, and he put his arm around her, but it was not quite a caress. There came a booming noise from a way off and a sound of shouts.

"Come on," he said. "I have less taste for kisses right now. Let's see what the row is."

He strode off. She struggled to catch up to him but he walked too fast on those long legs of his.

She could almost have rejoiced at the sight of the huge cloud of smoke rising from the Big House because it made him stop in his tracks when they came over the hill. He did not look surprised or worried. He did not run to assist Mr Creggan and the group of men carrying water to douse the fire. He stopped on the side of the hill and watched, so she stood beside him. She wished he would hold her hand, for no one would have seen. She wondered how she stood in his eyes now. Had she kept him? Surely she had, but she would have to take pains to keep his feelings waxing hot and his doubts cooling. It had taken half the joy from their courting. Yet she felt less at his mercy now that she knew she could talk him round.

The stables were alight. The head groom drove the carriage out of the coach house along the path to the other side of the house.

Michael counted the horses that followed, herded by the other groom. "They're all out, thank the Lord."

She saw Maire and Aine run out of the house, and behind them Mrs Ryan and Mary Hogan. What of the scullery girl? Had she run away or burned to death?

A crowd of men and women, strangers, came running out of the side door, laden with candlesticks, silver and cloth. They began to run up the hill, chased by a small group of farmers from the estate. Were they thieves, tinkers, or a gang from the town, or folk from the hills? Mr Creggan sometimes spoke of rebel gangs in the hills, but she had never seen any.

When horses' hoofs rumbled a way off from the road behind, she did not fear, even when they thudded closer. But Michael turned, stared behind and shouted, "It's the militia. Flee, flee!"

He took her hand, and they ran along the hill path after the thieving folk. She had no breath to ask him why. Soon they were amidst the panting, cursing, shouting crowd of thieves. Then horsemen wheeled in front of them, blocking their way. Folk tumbled over each other. A shot rang out. A boy fell. A volley of shouts erupted from the crowd. A horseman with shiny things on his shoulders hollered orders to them all. A soldier seized Michael and dragged him away. She held fast to him and felt her feet leave the ground. When Michael struck the soldier, she pushed the man too. He batted her off. She was ripped away from Michael and watched the soldier take him into the gloom.

Strong arms from behind pinioned her arms, crushing her chest. Large hands reached down over her arms, grabbed her between her legs, held her hard. Her feet were in the air. Some man's legs beneath her were running her forward. To her death? To ruin? To prison? Who had her?

She opened her mouth. No sound came out. How could it have helped?

The man turned her around. He was a soldier, young, breathing fast. His eyes were on her hair. She tossed it back. When he hoisted her up as if she were a child, his buttons grazed her breast. He threw her into a cart. She struggled to find her footing. More women were thrown in.

Where was Michael?

She strained and twisted about.

The wagon of screeching, cursing women lurched off. Where was Michael? She saw a line of men marched under guard. As her wagon passed, she spied him. She called, but the air was full of women wailing. He did not look up. She passed him and kept her eyes on him till she was too far ahead.

The side of the wagon kept bumping her. She could see little in the gloom. The Big House and the estate were long gone. She stared at the Great Sugarloaf Mountain until its dark bulk was too dim to see. The path became a road of bumps and holes that made the women curse and cry out.

There was little talk on the wagon. She knew no one. None of them was from the estate. All from the hills, she guessed. The butler always sneered about such folk and the other maids said they were wild and half of them rebels, so she wasn't ready to give much away to any of them.

For wouldn't she be sent back to the estate, to Milady – or would she be arrested? Was she arrested already?

If only they had gone home early. If only she had joined the other maids. If only Michael had been with the groom and the horses, hurrying from the smoke and the noise.

She couldn't wait to see him, run to him, feel his warm arms around her. Now he would forget what she had said. Because what she had told him didn't matter anymore.

2 A Prison

Kilmainham Gaol, Dublin Town

At the end of the next day, when she walked into the dark cavernous cell of the gaol, there were women like figures of stone, wrapped in shawls, sitting or lying on the floor. None made a sound. She told her name to two of them and they muttered. She retreated to the group from the cart.

There were men in the room too, all thrown in together. She had not expected that. Surreptitiously, she scanned the faces of the men. Michael wasn't there.

She slumped onto the floor that was hard and ice-cold. She kept her head down and her shawl close about her head. The men had better keep their distance.

Her fears and worries would not let her sleep. She bit her lip and tried not to sob. How the floor hurt. She thought back to the soft grass of the glen when she and Michael sank down upon it, entwined. Her tears set in, thinking of how his mood had changed. Had she been a fool to tell him about the master? It had seemed right; he shouldn't be ignorant of what all the inside staff knew. And wouldn't he have heard it anyway from someone? Better she told him first so he understood.

But he hadn't. Ma and Aunt Kate were right. Men had to own you, from the first and always.

Her thoughts were stopped all at once. A turnkey was speaking loudly at the entrance of the cell. Another laughed. It wasn't the fellow prisoners she had to fear most; it was the new masters she would have forever now.

She hated the eyes of the turnkeys upon her, staring right through her clothes, waiting.

If she died in here overnight, no one would know. If she screamed, what saviour would hear? The walls were six bricks solid. Knowledge like that raced around the cell when they were herded inside – "the door is as thick as your thigh". She felt wetness on her face and stifled her sobs.

No one would come to her aid. No one cared about a girl in gaol. Proper folk and decent working folk would think she was on the game, on the streets, or a thief.

And her mother, her father – how she had hurt them. What would they think she had done when they first heard where she was? To bring them shame like this. She tried to stop picturing their faces and hearing their voices. Around her were such groans and cries that she could not sleep.

In the morning, she stared up along the heavy stone walls. The high roof was dim. Narrow windows, high and barred, let in only thin beams of light. Rare bright rays of sun showed in stripes across the dirty rough floor.

On her second night, Michael had still not appeared. The gaol held none of the men from the crowd that had robbed the Big House. She had no idea what had become of him.

The darkness and chill drew down upon her, and the younger turnkey's stares made her afraid for her body, her life and her very soul. She had hoped to marry before God and everyone and be a good woman, but the master had sinned against her, and she had lost her virginity. Now, she would never be wed. Here in this dank cavern, she would become one of the others, the bad women, the lost women, lost both in this world and the next. She was like vermin. How did such women escape damnation? They were not to be among the blessed at the right hand of God.

When that turnkey stomped in, his boots rang on the floor, a sound she came to know too well, one she never forgot. She felt a stiffening of the women beside her. His face appeared in the gloom inches from hers. She smelt tobacco and brandy or such on his breath, and the odour of rotten teeth. His leering face was illuminated by the burning torch he held. He thrust it at her, and she cringed back, though she was already against the wall. She pushed her hair behind her shoulders, lest it catch on the torch flame. When he placed the torch on the stone floor, its low crackle was like a warning. Her head was smacked down on the floor, her skirts were pulled up, his weight pressed her breathless. She felt pain worse than she feared, force and roughness like to tear. Her voice screamed and echoed.

Then the turnkey knelt up, set his clothes to rights, stood up and spat on her. But it was no goodbye.

She pulled down her skirts, tied back her hair, and wiped away her tears. A stinging wetness crept down her legs. She moved back to her spot on the wall near Molly and Peggy, who had been her fellow sufferers from the cart.

Now they pushed her away. "Find another place, you filthy cow; you're his doings. Get you gone. It's to hell with you now."

She tried one look of appeal, but they gave not a flicker of softness.

She gathered her shawl and her skirts and crawled away, half-crouching, feeling in the darkness for a small empty space on the edge of where the lone women sat, the old, ugly ones with no friends, and the rough ones who thought they needed no protection.

She sat, numb and half frozen. Now she was just fair game.

*

A heavy-set man lurched across the room and fell on her. "Come on, my young bitch, you're loosened up, ready for me."

She struggled and fought, shouted, hit and bit. What was there to lose? She should have known – he hit her hard across the face. She heard herself gasp and cry out.

"What are you moaning about? Who do you think you are, lady muck?" He hit her across the breast, and all at once there was another man pawing her legs.

"Wait your turn," the first man said.

She half-shut her eyes, but before he could throw himself down, he was wrenched off.

A new voice said, "It's poteen I'll give for her, and it's a broken head you'll get if you refuse."

Her two assailants hesitated, and she peered at the man offering the liquor. His voice was not so rough at least. He was blocking the light, and she could not see his face. A smallish man but with shoulders on him. The posture of command. A soldier perhaps at some time. Not so young.

The small jar of poteen accepted, the assailants gone, her new master sat beside her. "I'm James Brannan. I'll not be bothering you. Don't give them a thought, or the turnkey. Cockroaches, all of 'em. It's just what happens to the prettiest girls. Nought you could have done. And I'm sorry to say, nought I could have done either."

She caught his eye in the dim light.

"I can't help you against a turnkey. But I can stop the rest of these rogues, so that's something, isn't it?"

He looked away. Thank God, he didn't expect a grateful look. What did he expect?

"Do you have aught to drink?"

She shook her head. The cup of cloudy water given her earlier was all gone. "No. I'm sorry."

He gave a sigh and laughed. "Sure now, girleen, I don't mean for me. You need a little yourself." He handed a flask to her and unrolled a cloth with a flick of his wrist. "Here's brandy and cheese will do you good. Go on. You don't know when the next will come."

She ate and took a draught.

He pushed a sheaf of straw at her. "You should sit on this. Take the coldness from the floor."

She placed it down. He packed it firmer and patted it. She slid onto it, her insides hurting so much she wept. She started shaking and couldn't stop.

She felt the warmth of his arm around her shoulders.

"Never mind, girl. One day, all these sad times will be over."

He leaned back on his bundle against the wall and drew her on his breast. He must have loved some woman, maybe still did. She thought she would stay awake all night, but later she woke and found herself lying on her side, her knees drawn up to her stomach. The warmth along her back was him.

In following days, she learned of his status among the men, especially the ones gaoled for attending meetings of the rebel group called the Defenders. He had come down from Armagh, one of the leaders of the Defenders. Did he know Michael? she asked. When he shook his head, she wondered if Michael would have known him or his name. Not that Michael had ever said that he was in the Defenders – but would he have told her, or was that what he meant when he spoke of the folk who offered help against the masters? James asked who Michael was and how she had become involved in the crowd that was rounded up. She explained and tried not to sound like a foolish girl running after a boy.

He smiled. "Sure, we would never have got you caught up in this trouble but for the smile of your sweetheart."

She laughed. "I cannot deny it, yet after I started to work in the Big House, what I heard in the kitchen about the landlords' evictions and their armed men led me to think that you Defenders had some rightful grievances, though my mother and my uncle here in Dublin Town would never agree." Her voice trailed off. He was looking a little surprised. She looked back at him apprehensively. The talk in the kitchen had been of how fierce the Defenders were, how they saw you as for them or against them, and you wouldn't want them to see you as against them.

But then James smiled. "It's good to meet a person who can see more than one point of view. You keep that way about you, Elizabeth; it will hold you in good stead in these times." His lively face gave her a vision of what he must have been like when he was young.

She dared to ask, "Why is it that you are with the Defenders? I don't see what the Defenders think they can do against the landlords, the masters."

He met her eyes and his had become sad. "Aye, the masters with all the firearms. But since the law let us Catholics have arms again now, we can fight to keep at least some of the land that our families have farmed for so long. We can fight to stop our families and our friends from starving – we can't turn our backs, we can't bow down like oxen, we must fight like men."

She nodded. She knew that way of thinking from her Da and some of her uncles. But were all the firearms making things worse? Her Ma would say so. Elizabeth felt confused, the way she always did when older people talked about these things. James sounded brave and generous but look where his action had landed him. She wriggled and didn't want to talk about it anymore.

"Do you have children back home or are they all grown up?" she asked.

"I am the father of the two most beautiful little girls in the land, nay, in the world."

His face brightened at the mention of them but then fell. She wondered what his sentence would be and whether he feared he would never go home.

"Betsy, you are not too old to remind me of my wee girls. I will watch over you and the younger girls in this place."

*

He had visitors first of anyone in the gaol. Men of means, some of them looked, in collars and coats with no holes, men who brought newspapers to show him. She hadn't realised that he could read. He saw in the newspaper that Michael had been brought in straight to court along with the men from the hill near Evanton. The militia alleged, James said with a sneer, that Michael was one of the rebels. His denials had got him nowhere except in the first group to be sent to Cork and onto a convict ship.

The one she had loved on the yielding grass of the glen for a few short afternoons was banished forever. Lucky not to be hanged, he was instead transported for fourteen years to New South Wales. It might as well be life, for everyone said that no fourteener gained the freedom to return. She had barely heard of the place where he was going. Even had he been innocent – and he surely was – he was doomed to leave Ireland forever.

As was she.

It was only a matter of time before they sentenced her too. They would transport her. Nothing was surer. No matter that she had done nothing. She wriggled and rocked to keep warm, and her anger rose. How cruel of the judges to stamp out her future. How heartless to lock her away for her best years. How could the English King banish her? For she would never return. Only the rich could come back across the world. But then her hopes rose; she couldn't help it. She had heard tales of America. It was a land of flourishing farms. Nowadays convicts didn't go there, but surely New South Wales must have land to farm too. No one even knew where it was. Somewhere on the bottom of the world. How much harder could the work for women be there than at home? Did some convicts become free once they had worked out their sentence? She would be one of those. She would marry Michael.

Would she see him in New South Wales?

James Brannan admitted that he didn't know, but he said gently that they would probably meet.

She tried to imagine their first sight of each other. But she couldn't slide into a daydream when she felt so angry about all that they would suffer on the ship and in the colony before they could be together.

Why was she being punished? Granny would have said it was a punishment for lying to Michael about the master. But she had been right to lie. She needed to lie. She had to make him like her again. And it was what he needed to hear from her. Surely God did not play tit-for-tat with every nobody from Dublin Town? Da would not think so. Ma might not either, despite her belief in God and the priests. It wasn't good to lie, but sometimes you had to. The lying brought her sadness because she had always thought of herself as honest. It was the first big lie she had told. What harm she would have done if she had told Michael the truth. Had her cousin Eilish told her farmer before their marriage? Elizabeth bet she hadn't. The kitchen was full of stories about Eilish and milord, but her husband out on his farm would never know.

Ma had said sometimes with a funny smile, "And we don't have to tell your Da, all right, Lizzie?" when they had bought some sweet morsel and gobbled it up on their way home. They loved Da, but they had to look after themselves. And he lied too, not just about his drinking but about Mr Barker, the head blacksmith.

At home, Da was always railing about Mr Barker, but one day she and Da came upon him in Baggott Street and her Da was so polite and respectful that Elizabeth stared. When they passed him, Da shrugged and gave her an odd look, half-ashamed, half-cheeky. Further along the street, he said, "Ah, Lizzie, you need to put on nice manners sometimes for the man with the whip-hand. I wish I could tell him what I think of him and the way he runs things, but then we'd never eat, my love, would we?"

If she never saw Michael again, hadn't God given her beauty? He couldn't blame her for using it. She would find some other man, down there on the bottom of the world.

3 Shame

When her mother and father came to see her at the gaol, Ma cried while she told how Father Mulvaney had come to their house. How he had come at dusk so that Da would be there too. Elizabeth felt her face grow hot as she pictured it: the priest sad and earnest, choosing to tell the man of the house, not trusting Ma to pass on the whole or the exact truth of the daughter's calamity; her mother shocked into silence, struck with dread; her father's face falling; his hopes for the future crashing into a lifelong shame. Did the priest pray for her, pray for all of them? A family of trouble now.

Father Mulvaney hadn't visited the gaol but there had been a priest in the cell one day, a priest she didn't know. He hadn't spoken to her, only to James and a few of the men. Before he left, he said loudly to the room that he was coming back and any Catholics from any parish could speak to him. Did he tell Father Mulvaney? The priests in Dublin Town would all share the news, especially of prisoners from local families.

Did Father Mulvaney know how she was used by the turnkey? Would the strange priest know those things? Would he tell? Would Father tell her Da? She couldn't imagine that, she told herself, no, it couldn't be. Thank God, her parents would not know that added, almost worse, shame. If the priests knew that she and the others were so ill-treated, wouldn't they stop it, or complain to the head warden or to someone? Were they powerless in the gaols and in the courts? She knew they weren't listened to by those in power, not the way the Church of Ireland ministers were. It hadn't occurred to her to tell the priest. She couldn't speak of the ill treatment and she had no confidence that he could stop it.

James had said there was nothing to be done, that the warders could do whatever they wanted. James hadn't told her to speak to the priest; he had not made any approving comments about him. She gathered from what James and Connelly and Boyle said that the priest was unable to understand how things were, how so many had ended up in the gaol and why they had to fight.

She stared at Da. He said nothing. He hardly looked at her. His face was different. No smile, no soft look.

And then Ma shouted. "Why did you not find the housekeeper and the others? Did you not know that the militia round everyone up these days?"

Da scowled. "How could she know? Stuck out there in that house, how would she hear news from Dublin Town? Serving folk are told nothing by the gentry."

She smiled gratefully at him, but he did not smile back.

He looked away, his face stiff. "We will bring you what we can, my girl, but the times are still hard."

Ma said, "What were you doing out in that crowd? Why were you away from the house?"

"I was walking with Michael. He is…was the groom's helper. You would have liked him, Ma."

"How long were you walking the countryside with him? No wonder you did not worry; your thoughts were full of him. What was his name?"

Her father looked up when she answered. "Flaherty? Was he among the Defenders?"

She saw out of the corner of her eye that James was in earshot. She hoped Da would not say anything more. "No, Da. He's just a stable boy."

Da looked relieved.

She said quickly, "You must ask Uncle Peter to try to get an appeal for me. The ones in here who know the way things work say that you need a letter from a lord or lady or a Church of Ireland bishop. Uncle Peter could ask someone at his church, perhaps the lady who is the patron of the concerts for the poor."

Da had a glimmer of hope in his eye, but Ma began to weep.

Da's face changed. "Lizzie, if only he would help, but the shame, the shame of telling him – and I fear he will not wish to know you now or even us." He sounded beaten.

"It doesn't matter if we feel ashamed," Ma said, but she could not stop her sobs.

Elizabeth said, "He only has to ask the lady, then she will write a letter, and then my sentence could be changed to one here in Ireland, or to less time at least. And he or the ladies he knows can ask if my mistress will speak for me."

Only Ma and Elizabeth's youngest sister, Ellen, came to the gaol to tell her of the conversation. It took time for Da to ask Uncle Peter. Elizabeth pictured Uncle Peter looking down his nose far more than usual. How Da must have suffered.

Uncle Peter had said no. He had given them good advice before, he said, but all to no avail. Lizzie might have made a good marriage to a steady servant or farmer. But Michael O'Flaherty was clearly not that sort of man. He shook his head, and Ma reported his exact words. "No good ever comes from consorting with Catholics. In those parts, they are all Defenders."

Elizabeth sighed. She could hear his stern voice.

When Ma had told him that all Elizabeth had done was to stand outside Evanton Manor in the crowd, he threw up his hands and said, "Joining a riot, threatening property, oh my heavens, Elizabeth is ruined. You'll never see her free in Dublin Town again."

Ma sighed, "He told us that he must sever all connection with us, because we're so bad for his business and his standing in the Church."

She felt tears spring up as Ma went on, "And your Da said, 'But can't you ask Milady to appeal, because Lizzie didn't know none of it, and none of those people. She was only waiting for the young man to escort her home. It wasn't safe for a girl to walk among that crowd.'"

"What did my uncle say to that?" Elizabeth feared she already knew.

"He said, 'That crowd set fire to Evanton Manor. Men and women ran in and stole silver and linen and plate, anything they could run with.' And I said, 'But not our Lizzie; she didn't take a thing,' and Peter said, 'Is that so? I hope it is true. Standing in that crowd shows a rebellious attitude.' And he said, 'Why didn't she go back to the household instead of watching like a vulture?' He blames us for not warning you against boys like O'Flaherty. He said, 'There's nothing to be done now. She must take her punishment and you must forget her.'"

Ma's face wouldn't stop trembling and she broke into weeping.

"Just go now, Ma," Elizabeth said. "I'm sorry."

She looked at dear Ellen, whose small face was tense with worry. "Ellen, I'll look after myself." She got a smile from her sister, but Ma shook her head.

Elizabeth touched her mother's hand. "Ma, can you bring me some herbs and some water or spirits so that I can wash my face and neck. And some clean rags."

Above all, she would keep herself fresh, whatever the young turnkey did to her some nights, dragging her away from James or gesturing at him to go out of sight. Her bleeding was about to start and to stain her dress, when she might be taken off to the ship at any moment – no, she wasn't having that.

Her mother grasped her hand. "Oh, my poor girl, it is hard to say this, but I thank the Lord that your grandmother is not here to see your disgrace and our shame." She burst into wails and ran out of the dim room.

Elizabeth felt a new hardness closing around her. She would not think of how Granny might judge her. She would hold fast her hatred of Milady for refusing to let her go to Dublin Town to mourn Granny, for keeping her in the country for her husband to use.

Ellen hugged her. "Lizzie, it wasn't your fault. I don't blame you. I'll never blame you."

Elizabeth wiped the tears from her sister's face. "Nellie, my love, bring me Ma's blue dress and her second-best bonnet, and a pretty shawl of Susan's. I'm going to need clothes on the ship to the colony. Ma and Susan can get more. Hide the things in a thick shawl and don't tell anyone. Bring them one at a time if you must. But don't come here by yourself. It's a long walk, and in this part of town I fear for you. Bring one of our boy cousins and tell them not to snitch to Uncle Colm."

*

Of course, she had expected it. She was a goner just like the women standing next to her, but, even so, when the judge said seven years and whacked his piece of wood down – crack – she wanted to shout, plead, sink to her knees and clasp her hands to him. Such useless, foolish instincts. Men like those judges had no hearts. She kept her head high and tried not to stare at him the way she wanted to, as if he were a drunken tramp at a poteen hut door.

It was hard going back to the cell not knowing when she would depart, glancing away from Ma's agonised stare. They never told you when you were going. Even James's visitors had no idea. She hoped it would be months. Seeing her sister every week made things close to bearable. Ma's visits were not so pleasant; she wept so. Da never came; she did not need her mother to explain why.

Winter drew on, and they shivered in their stone prison. She realised she had not bled that month.

It crossed her mind that she might be expecting a child, but she cast the thought aside. More likely, she was so badly fed that she couldn't bleed. She had heard Ma and her aunts talk about how that happened when food was short. But the weeks dragged on, and then she felt a difference, hard to find a word for, a new feeling in her insides, in her breasts and her skin. Then one morning, the sickness came, and she knew.

Poor babe, you would hate your father, she said to it silently. *Just as well you'll never know him. We'll be far over the sea. One reason to be glad I'm going.*

When she grew bigger, the turnkey moved on to another girl. James tried to give her what food he could, but his visitors had mostly stopped calling. Many of them, indeed, had joined him here in the cells. Those still outside were now afraid to come and show themselves as his friends. He had pored over the Dublin Town and county newspapers and quivered with anger about what they said about him when he was tried. He told her that landowners in the counties were even more afraid now of the Defenders and were desperate to see them hanged or transported. She didn't dare ask what his sentence was but from the way he and his friends talked, she was sure it must be life.

Her belly started to show, and she dreaded the next visit from her mother and even from Ellen. This was yet another shame, perhaps worse than being a convict. Would they understand at all? Would her mother dissolve into tears or turn on her heel?

When her mother saw, she glanced at James across the room and then said softly, "But he's married."

Ellen was frozen in distress and confusion.

Elizabeth said quickly, "James is not the father. He hasn't touched me, or any of us here."

Her mother looked partly relieved. "I am glad of that. Your Da says James is a good man, despite all his fighting and killing. It's hard for me to believe that, but I suppose he must fight against what he sees happening to the folk he knows. But your Uncle Peter, now, he blames the Defenders, well, you know that…" she paused, her face troubled.

"It was the warder, of course, Ma," Elizabeth spoke more roughly than she meant to.

Her mother's eyes filled with tears; her hand clutched at Ellen's. "Oh, my God, to think a daughter of mine – to think my first grandchild should come like this."

It felt like a winter wind when her mother shrank away, so Ellen's embrace was even more welcome.

"None of it is your fault, Lizzie," Ellen said. "What can we bring you? We have little spare food, but I will bring some potatoes and bread when I can."

Her mother pulled Ellen away and quickly left the cell. She did not visit for some weeks, and even then, stayed hardly at all. When Ellen came with bread, she could not stay for long.

Elizabeth was hungry to desperation. Some days she grabbed the green parts of the weedy flowers in the prison yard. Once or twice, she scraped some whitewash off a wall and licked it down. It wasn't sugar or salt, but it had a grainy feel, a sort of taste at least. The slop the prison doled out was a chore to eat and so soon gone, in a gulp. She felt herself getting thin and scraggy, while her belly poked out taut and hard. The one good thing was the warmth it gave her, the child inside. She crooned softly to it some evenings, and James patted her shoulder. Even old Molly gave her a softer look.

She wondered if it would be a boy, but she didn't mind at all if it wasn't. A girl might be more company in New South Wales. Maybe a daughter could work alongside her and not be sent away as a son would be.

When pain came in a stab one morning in late spring, she sat up stiff with shock. The stabbing turned into a strong ache. She began to fear. It was too soon. Just over six months, she guessed. Her auntie at home had lost babies, and some women had died of the childbirth. She was scared. What did it feel like? What should you do to hold the baby fast?

She stayed in her straw bed and sat with her back to the wall, her bundle behind her. The ache kept on and on. All at once she felt wetness seeping from her. No, dear God! What happened when something went wrong? She didn't know at all. Did you bleed then? Did the baby move out or fall or did you have to push it out when it was ready? Did it get stuck sometimes? She thought she had heard tell of that. She found some clean rags in her bundle and shoved one under her skirt, between her legs.

"Are you all right, Betsy?" James sat beside her, his face concerned. "Is it the child?"

"I'm afraid," she said. "I don't feel the same."

"Is the babe moving like before?" he asked. How he had smiled when he felt the kick through her dress.

She looked at him. "I cannot feel it moving. There is only pain."

"You should rest," he said. "Take a sip of this, dear girl. It may settle down. Maybe it's those pains women often get along the way. Nothing to be done, Betsy. Think of a beautiful hillside or the sea. Take your mind off it and away from here."

She had watched his face with that faraway look most nights and sometimes in the day too. She tried to see the glen in her mind. The blue of the hills, the green below, the soft, shadowy, feathered trees. She went to pass water and was so afraid that the baby would fall from her. A little blood passed but not a lot. She went back to her place, her back and insides aching. The pain kept on, but later she slept a while.

When she woke, James was asleep next to her. She slipped her hand between her legs; even in the dim light she could see the blood on it. She put another rag down there lest her dress be dirtied; she had only one warm dress for the nights. She hoped it wasn't touched with the blood. Horrible to ask Ma or Susan to wash out that stain.

Four days and nights she bled, until it seemed thick. She ran out of rags and tore up an old underskirt. The fifth morning, it felt like she was being kicked in her stomach and torn inside. Holding her side, she staggered to the outhouse. There were no doors. It was filthy as always. No – to drop her child there would be the worst place. She sobbed and fled to the cleanest part of the passageway near the outer door. She sank down. She felt a grinding and scouring inside and then a cleaving asunder – oh, God. She pushed her skirts aside and felt a swelling surge, and there it was, solid in her hands, blooded over, shrivelled, small, but a child in the making. If he only had breath, if she could but breathe the life into him. Her face ran wet.

She pressed her ear to his tiny warm mouth but there was neither sound nor wisp of breath. She breathed into his tiny open mouth and rocked him, again and again. Could she give him breath? Did that happen ever? He did not move. He looked grey, almost blue. She pressed him, pushed his back gently. Air did not seem to stay in him, nor come from his little chest. She stilled the rocking, stared down at him. His eyes were barely open. They had no sight. She held him close, greeted him with the name she had chosen – Michael – and said farewell.

Two women came, peered, shrieked at her and left.

She wiped him till all the blood was gone. Then his body was even colder. His little face, all closed, no breath, no gaze. His tiny hands, stiffening. Her tears flowed. She drew her shawl about him. There would be silence out here for a short time before the others came to wash or drink or walk. She fell against the prison wall and clasped her son's body so cold.

When James came to her, she couldn't speak, couldn't let the tiny one go.

Later, when the guard was due to come, she realised that James was still there. He was holding a small knife.

He said, "Can you…do you want me to cut it?"

She took the blade and cut the child from their joining cord, cut him from her body.

She asked softly, "Can we bury him?"

"Oh, my dear girl, there's nowhere."

"They'll take him. Where will they take him?"

He turned away. "A grave, Betsy."

She stared at his drooping head. "They throw these children away, don't they?"

He turned. "I can bury him near where I work, in the garden plot."

"Let him lie down deep. At peace. I will wrap him in a cloth."

She wrapped him in a kerchief, he was so small, and she would never see where he went, but he would not be thrown into the prison waste. James hid him under his coat when he left to work.

Just before he walked away in the line, James asked if she needed a surgeon or midwife. He was sure there was someone the gaol could send for. It hadn't crossed her mind.

"I will be better in a day."

He looked at the women standing staring across the prison yard.

"For God and Jesus and Mary, will you help the girl? Every one of you has been where she is right now." He turned on his heel.

She took a rag to the trough and washed her face. She doubled up at a sudden sharp pain, so like those before. She remembered what had horrified her watching her aunts and her mother, but now she barely felt the searing, then the afterbirth fell at her feet. It should have been larger. It wouldn't have fed a bird.

She was unaware of anyone as she washed her legs. What did she care if they watched like ghouls?

Molly came near and said softly, "The fairy ones have delivered you early and taken the babe. It's for the best. What chance did that creature have in this world?"

*

The seasons passed. A full year and more she had spent in Kilmainham. Of her family, she saw only her sister Ellen, and rarely. Then, one day, among the new folks in the cell was her cousin Meg.

The cousins hadn't been close friends, for Meg was by far the elder, but now it was a relief for them both to find each other. Then Meg was sentenced: seven years for sedition, just like Elizabeth. They prayed they would be on the same ship.

4 Elizabeth's Decision

As winter drew near again, James said, "The ship will be better than this gaol. We might have more food and a bit of sun if we are lucky."

"Not if our ship is an old slave ship," a man muttered. "Those vessels carried poor Africans shoved in one atop of the other. The spirits of those tortured souls will hover about us."

James said, "There may be Irish spirits too. Our ancestors were sent to the Caribbean, you know. Poor Irishmen who were homeless and had commmitted no crime at all were seized on the street and sold as slaves."

Another man said, "And then Irish folk, men and women, were sent to America to work for masters on the land."

"Aye," James said, "It was lucky for our people when the English decided that the Africans would bear the heat better on the sugar plantations. They sent our folk to America as labourers. But we are better off than those ancestors or than the African slaves. We may be convicts, but we are not slaves: we can work out our sentences and be free again. Our treatment on the ship will be better than for those wretched blacks."

A man said, "But we'll be shoved down into the bowels with no headroom, no space to move."

"Chains on our legs, if not our necks too," a fourth man's voice boomed out of a dark corner.

"But not for us girls," Meg said, looking urgently at James. "They don't put the women in chains, do they?"

Sounds of scoffing and derision came from the rougher men.

James looked down. "Women are chained, too, I am sorry to say."

Meg slumped back against the wall, but Elizabeth felt anger rising and her breath grow faster. To be chained like savage slaves. To be chafed and bruised by hard iron. To be stopped by heavy bonds from walking freely or moving at will. She could not find words for her fury.

One of the more recent female arrivals, the street harlot Sue, shook with laughter. She said loudly, "Not me, sweetheart. I won't be in chains in a shelf down in the hull with the rats and the water and the rest of you putrefying dregs. It's in a sailor's cabin I'll be, or in an officer's."

James threw her a black look. "Aye, women like you will service them with a smile, I have no doubt."

"And why not," said Sue, "if it will get me a full belly instead of a few spoons of slops, and a soft bed instead of a plank of wood? And a better man? The likes of you lags wouldn't leave me alone. You'll all have your way with us girls. Well, not me! I'll pick me a handsome sailor or a man with brass on him."

Elizabeth felt the shock of truth in the harlot's words. She could barely heed what Meg was saying to her. "If the sailors pick out the pretty ones, it's the likes of you they will grab, Elizabeth. I will be lucky to hold my own with the hags below."

Elizabeth met her cousin's eyes. Meg was undersized, her skin papery, her hair dull, her teeth half gone already. She had worked for a clothing maker in Dublin Town in a cramped dark room for long hours, constantly underfed and calling it a lucky day when she avoided beatings from the overseer.

"You have a good heart and a good temperament, Meg," she said. "Some fellow will want you. Keep a smiling countenance and a bright eye."

Meg sniffed. "As if I would sleep with an English gaoler who sends us to the bottom of the world."

James nodded. "Good on you, girl." He turned to Elizabeth. "It will be a sad time for some girls, but I pray you will not be the slave of a sailor or officer. Keep your head down and your hair covered, and we'll hope they don't notice your beauty."

Elizabeth flushed. For the first time, she felt disappointed in James. Her beauty was hers to use, not his to hide. She felt more keenly than before an anger against her countrymen, who could not protect her but still thought they owned her and would despise her for taking care of herself.

They were so set on sacrificing themselves. She had heard this way of thinking since she could remember – fight, fight, never give in, hate the English to the death. Of course, it made sense; they had reason to hate. But how they rushed to bare their throats for the sword, or the rope. Her Da and uncles sat around the fire recalling who in the family had fought the English Protestant King and died long ago, but what had their deaths won for their people? She didn't know or understand it all, but she certainly couldn't see how those deaths helped the mothers, sisters, wives and daughters.

Sue glared at Elizabeth. "Don't worry, darlin'. You won't have a hope next to me and me friends who know what to do with a man." She cackled. "They want a good time, them sailors, and they know the girls who can give it to 'em. They'll choose me and send a prim little miss like you down to the hell below. Don't even try, redhead. You'll never keep up with what they want – you'll be black and blue inside and out!"

Elizabeth held her tongue and hid her resentment. As if she couldn't get a sailor if she wanted one! And wouldn't the men do the choosing? Sue and the rest would do what they were told.

She turned to James. "What will happen to you and the men?"

He looked down, his jaw tight. "It won't be easy, not like here in the cells."

She felt a chill. "What do you mean, because you will be chained?"

"Aye. And I won't have supporters like here. How men are treated depends on the captain, what sort of a man he is, and if the officers are decent and trained. And if they think we are all revolutionaries or the enemies of England."

She hoped that English officers would know little of his past. Yet wouldn't he be marked on their records? Wouldn't they single him out for worse treatment because he was a rebel?

What would life on the ship be like for her? How could she deny the horrid truth in Sue's words: it *would* be less frightening to sleep with an officer than suffer below. Some of the older women in the cell said that many a sailor took a woman as his "ship wife" – chose a wench and kept her in his cabin. Wasn't that better than being used and starved and chained down in the hold? Wasn't it her best hope? She was bound to be one of the best looking and youngest. Why not use it? Catch a good one as she walked on board. Treat him like a master of a big house. What did it matter what she had to do to get through the voyage? Someone would take her, and if she didn't make sure it was an officer or a sailor, it might be a pack of convicts, together or one after the other. She would aim for a man with power to keep other men off her, just as James had done here. She might make a useful friend. It might help her in the colony afterwards – God knows, she would need help there.

She looked at James talking earnestly with his friends and Defender fighters. How he would despise her if she slept with a sailor – or worse, with a soldier or an officer. But he would be down in the depths, in chains. Wouldn't he be among the most punished? He would not be able to help her or anyone. Perhaps even his followers would not heed him. In recent months, they had started to argue with him and dismiss his words. The way some men looked at him had changed.

And, in the colony, men like him would be the last who could help her. Wouldn't he be among the ones sent off to an island for worse punishment? It frightened and saddened her to peel herself away from him, but wasn't it wise, and weren't they going to part anyway?

Was there any sense in doing what he thought was right when it would be so much worse for her? She looked around the room. None of them would weep for her. They had shunned her when the turnkey assaulted her. None but James had helped her when her baby died. Why should she give a thought to what they would say or think of her? Even Meg, who already blamed her for being the type of woman a sailor might want – how was that her fault? Her pleasant face and frame were gifts from God. Why not be happy if her looks could ease her time on the ship?

She spoke sternly to herself. When she faced the sailors, she would not be shy. She would show them she was no whore, but she wouldn't act like a foolish girl. She mustn't be squeamish; she must play up to them and look after herself.

Would Meg come to understand? If Elizabeth found herself a sailor or an officer, would she be able to help Meg on the ship and perhaps in the colony afterwards? Meg might come to thank her.

What did sailors or officers do with their women? Were they things the master would never have done? Would it hurt or disgust her? Surely, it could be no worse than the turnkey in his drunken harsh handling? She tossed her head and got up to walk in the yard. As she passed the sneering group of streetwalkers, she caught Sue's nasty stare. She thought *I'll snare me a redcoat, you watch me, Sue,* and found herself choking back a laugh that was more of a sob. *God help me.* The faces of her mother and father rose before her. And Susan and Ellen. And Granny – was she looking down from Heaven to see, the way the priests and the serving girls at Evanton said the old folk could do?

Granny would loathe every plan Elizabeth was making. So would her parents. They would be heartbroken to think that she could act that way; they would believe that she was damned for eternity. Her sisters would be terrified – and shamed even more than they were now. They would be shunned: they might not find husbands.

But her family would never know that she had chosen to be an officer's whore. If they heard her fate, they would think she had been seized, forced, given no choice. Only Granny would know, with her Heavenly vision.

But *she* would know, for her whole life. She would know what a sinner she was. No longer would she be a good girl ravished by evil men; she would be a whore, seeking advantage by sinning with a stranger – doing it for food and a better bed and to avoid beatings and casual use by convict men. Sinning, because she was a coward. Because she would not leave it to chance – probably a sailor or officer would choose her if she did nothing to draw attention to herself, but she was too scared to take that risk.

Headed for Hell. For all eternity. Unless St Brigid or the Virgin helped her at her death, or St Patrick took pity on her when he judged the Irish on the last day – but how could she count on such special help? She was damned. Dead or damned – if she didn't become a whore, she could die or be beaten into disfigurement; if she became a whore, she gave her soul to the devil.

Her thoughts ran on far into the night. She was ruined already. Wasn't her soul already in the devil's grasp? Why else would she be having these thoughts? He was putting them into her mind like rats running round and round, agitating her till she lost her serenity, and her ability to think and pray. Too late to turn back; her mind had sinned already, making such wicked plans.

She would never see her dear ones again. If she took protection from an English sailor, how would they ever know? She would need her health and good looks in the colony to find Michael again or some other man like him. He hadn't given a thought to her fate that night when they were arrested. If it hadn't been for him, she would have rushed down to the house, to the other servants. So now she would get herself above deck with proper food if she had to strut like Sue and the painted girls along Dublin's Royal Canal. But she would do it with more grace, like Milady and the fine ladies at Evanton.

One morning when it was barely light, the door of the cell was scraped open with its ear-splitting noise and four soldiers appeared. There was a moment to exchange a look with James before she and other women were bustled out into the cold street, grasping their small bundles of clothes. A cart awaited. She clambered up and found a spot to wriggle into with hardly space enough to stand in, let alone sit. She grabbed Meg, hoisted her up, and they got their hands onto the outside rail to hold themselves steady when it rattled off.

A short time later – though long enough for her to feel bruised – they reached the North Wall of Dublin's seaport and were herded off the cart onto a ship. It lurched off. The word went around that they were bound for Cork.

And the men?

They walk, someone said.

Of course, marched in chains with an escort of soldiers. The relief of being only with women was dampened by the loss of James.

*

The Cork gaol was like a pig pen. No light, little air, dirty straw on the floor for bedding. No James – the men were squashed onto aged hulks in Cobh harbour, waiting to board their transport ship, the *Britannia*. A haggard old woman rolled her eyes and said the hulks were where you caught your death. But Elizabeth didn't see how you might not catch it here in the Cork prison. She yearned for the voyage; the ship would surely have some air and there would be something to see sometimes instead of mouldy walls. The guards took their pick of the women. She kept her face and hair hidden; she was still thin from losing the baby. They missed her and went for the harlots and the very young.

December, 1796

It took some weeks till the women were walked down to Cobh harbour to board the *Britannia*. A wearying walk but to Elizabeth, the fresh air was worth it, and the long view. The harbour was huge, and the ring of high cliffs was like a painting in the Big House. The water was full of ships and boats. The sails and masts soared so high. There were men everywhere, and boys, and livestock. She had never thought that goats, cows and chickens sailed on ships. Some old man in the cells had said sailors lived on hard biscuit. Great casks and chests were hauled up the side onto the deck. Where would it all go? How would the convicts fit in?

The *Britannia* reminded her of the ships in the paintings on the master's walls. Folks said some convict transports had been slave ships. Didn't that make you laugh – weren't they still? She remembered James saying that Irishmen had been sold as slaves. She reached the plank leading up into the ship and stared up.

On deck and on the bridge were sailors of all sizes and colours, but also men in fancy uniforms, officers and such. Some of them were staring down at her. She attempted to put a pleasant, lively look on her face. Just as well she had worn her best dress. She had been afraid to leave it in her bundle – who knew if they were permitted to take anything onto the ship? – and she was afraid of Sal and her friends' thieving hands. Better to wear the best she had. She straightened her back, raised her head and spread out her bright hair. Mrs Ryan at Evanton had said that the English didn't share the Irish fear of red-headed women as the harbingers of bad luck. So, look at this, my fine fellows, she laughed to herself, despite the fear that almost had her shaking. She couldn't stop imagining – so strongly that she felt it – that moment when she would be pushed down into the bowels of the ship: no space, air or light, like falling into darkness, into the grave, into Hell. She dreaded it. The gaol had been full of tales of how slaves and convicts alike were shipped out on their backs on shelves, like dead fish.

Down the ladder they all went, not pushed exactly but herded so fast. Only a few thin lines of light broke the darkness. There was not much smell yet, though the odour of sweat and worse that she had almost come to think of as normal assailed her as she turned and peered into the low-roofed space. The beds were planks of hard wood but – she could hardly believe it – each convict had a heavy big blanket. She and Meg found places alongside each other.

The worst moment was when the chains were attached by a rough sailor. The irons were so heavy, and at once dug into her flesh however she wriggled and moved.

She tried to tell Meg that it was not so bad, when there was a sudden lurching, and they banged their heads on the posts beside their beds. The ship rocked only a little. So, they hadn't left yet. Would they know when they left the harbour? They could see nothing. Not to see the shore receding – it was too mournful. No look of farewell.

It was hard to sleep, tired from walking though she was. The space had seemed cold and dank when they first entered but as night drew on, the air grew foetid and humid with so many of them packed in there. At least they could swaddle themselves with their blankets and then, when the air became hot, lie on top of the heavy blankets to avoid the hard, bruising plank.

In the morning, they would not have known day had broken if the officer had not unlatched the hatch above them and let them see a glaring light. They were to eat the provisions they had been given last night on their cots. Elizabeth had eaten hers already; Meg had no appetite at all.

Before noon, there was a muster. They climbed up onto the main deck and their chains were examined. The women were brought up after most of the men. She looked about. They were still in the harbour.

She had kept on her own clothes, had not used the thick, hard, shapeless garment they had given her. If she were forced to stay down below, if no officer or sailor chose her, then she would have time enough to wear such drabs.

She was cheered to find the officer motioning some of the women forward, apart from the others. She caught his eye. He looked her over and his eye sparkled. She tried not to shudder, tried not to think about being a whore. It was her only chance. Whore, wife, slave.

Another officer with more braids on his shoulders came and examined her face and figure and hands. He nodded to the first man, who motioned her to stand over the other side of the deck.

An older woman tittered, "Out of the frying pan."

Elizabeth tossed her hair, squeezed Meg's hand and stepped as gracefully as she could to where the officer had pointed. Several girls were there already: all pleasant, some good-looking, but none with her fine features or the bright abundance of her hair. Though a few giggled, Elizabeth stood silent, trying to look her most poised and refined.

5 The Selection

Who would choose her? She couldn't stop picturing what he might do, what she might have to do, what it might feel like, and how long till it stopped feeling painful. She must accept him as her master. She could do that. The longest she would have to bear him – them – was six months. Surely these officers and sailors would be less rough and repulsive than the Dublin gaoler?

She shuddered, watching Meg disappear down the hole again. If she got herself established, she could ask for Meg to be up on deck some of the time. Couldn't they be maids to the officers' women?

Another group of men emerged from below and were hustled into lines. She looked out of the corner of her eye for James.

There he was. She didn't dare smile, but he caught her eye – a moment's affection quickly supplanted by surprise and then a shadow of suspicion and disappointment. She knew what he was thinking: *why are you in that finery?* It cut her, that look of accusation from him of all people. Couldn't the man be glad that she might be spared some of the squalor? Would her Michael understand? Alas, probably not. Yet surely people would die down there, beaten and starved, while she would survive.

After their chains were examined, most of the male prisoners were forced down the steep, narrow ladder into the dark bowels. She looked away. Tried to smile a little. Like a lady.

Two male convicts were hauled down the back of the ship. Word travelled – some holes had been discovered in the wooden partition between the males' and females' cots; these men had been found guilty. Who had betrayed them, under what threat or for what reward?

The whipping started. Each lash cracked – so loud, so sharp. She quivered, imagining how it must feel as it cut the flesh. How deep? A woman in the Cork cell had said it cut chunks out of a grown man's back. Elizabeth counted the lashes – twelve. Each lash was followed by a piercing bellow or scream. It sounded fiendish, worse than pigs being slaughtered at Evanton. There was a pause and then the next twelve cuts.

The officer who had caught her eye came up beside her. He unchained her and took her arm. The relief – almost free again, she thought for a second, though of course that was nonsense. But she breathed deeply and strongly for the first time on the ship. The difference between chains and no chains was the biggest difference a body could feel.

"This way, me dear. How d'you like this, eh?"

He opened a small door and ushered her along a tiny corridor into a cabin where she had to bend her head till she sat as directed on a bench along the wall.

"Now, me pretty one, you're going to be nice to Charlie, ain't you?"

"Oh, yes, sir," she smiled.

His grin broadened, then he lurched forward and squeezed her breast before he turned his back and vanished through the low door. She felt a sick taste in her mouth. She breathed in hard and thought, *what's one more touch of a stranger?*

A moment later, the other selected women came pressing into the little room. Some chattered, but she kept aloof. Her thirst was fierce. The room was airless. She calmed herself, relieved that she had avoided getting filthy down in the hold and had not lost the advantage of her good dress and her almost clean face.

The ship lurched, tipped, then steadied into a rhythmic rocking. She peered out of the tiny porthole on the outer wall. They were leaving Ireland. She stared back at the receding cliff and the wharf. The ship pitched and rolled at the mouth of the harbour. One girl fell from the bench and others laughed. Elizabeth said a silent goodbye to Cobh Harbour, to Cork, to Ireland, to land. She looked out of the window opposite, out to sea, the grey-green moving expanse below and in front of them. Above, the clouds were thick, dark and swift.

After a time, she found the rocking was rather to her liking. She had seen children and young ladies at the Big House on a swing in the garden and it had looked exciting. She pretended for a minute that she was on a swing like that. Around her, several women were retching into the buckets on the floor. The sounds and smells were hard to bear. She kept her eyes to the window and imagined that swing, her on it and Michael pushing it. She felt no sickness, thank the Lord. She let her body roll with the ship.

They sat for hours. The day passed and the little room began to darken. A sailor climbed into the cabin and handed out tankards and hunks of hard bread. She nodded thanks and downed the drink. It was beer. The taste and tepid warmth of it make her grimace but it was liquid. She gnawed at the bread, then silently scolded herself and broke pieces off, eating them daintily despite their toughness.

The doorway darkened. An officer she hadn't set eyes on – older, small of stature, with a sallow, closed face and a look of indifference, if not distaste – surveyed them. He walked up to each and peered at their skin, eyes, hair and figure. He opened their mouths wide with a spatula of smooth wood. Elizabeth felt her face flame with anger – it was like the Master and the groom checking the horses. The officer came up to her, peered hard, fingered her cheek, jaw and hair, opened her mouth, and felt her waist and – Good Lord – her haunches.

"What do they call you, girl? How old are you? Have you given birth? Carried a babe? Lost any?"

She held her tongue about the last questions. What good could it do to confess?

"Married? Catholic or Protestant? A follower of the Defenders or the Peep o' Day or Break of Day agitators? Is your young man a Defender? Your father? Your brothers? Do you have any relatives on this ship?"

She couldn't deny Margaret. Perhaps some good could come to Meg from her better position.

"Other relatives in gaol? Relatives in New South Wales?"

At the end of the quizzing, he motioned her into the corridor and nodded at the boy. "Take her to the Surgeon's room."

She wondered which of her answers made the sallow questioner choose her. At least he seemed quiet. Not a beater or even much of a bully. She couldn't even imagine him being energetic enough in the act to hurt her much.

She waited in the small room with its shelves, cupboards and slab table. It was some time till he reappeared. He ordered her to undress. Her fingers shook. He nodded at her to remove even the undershirt. To stand stark naked before a man! He looked with a little more interest than when she had been clad but still with a weary lack of enthusiasm. She wondered if he had seen many girls as slender and shapely. For an instant, she had an urge to laugh and toss her head, but she was too wary. Then fear struck her – could he see signs that she had borne a child? Her stomach was flat again, but her breasts had changed; would that tell him? She was so thin. Her breasts were less round than they had been: was she a shape to please a gentleman now?

The room was not cold, yet she felt herself shivering. To stand naked with him made her uneasy. But she thought, *this is nothing.* When he ordered her to kneel, she presumed he would take her. She felt afraid, recalling snippets of talk in the cells about being taken behind or being near choked by the man's hard piece. Looking up, she fixed her eyes upon his face. Would he be telling her to unbutton him? But he gestured to her to put her hands on the floor in front of her. She almost laughed in embarrassment to have to stick out her bottom like that. She felt fear too; she didn't want to be taken like a dog, the way they said whores did it. Surprisingly quickly, he moved behind her and put his hands on her buttocks. She froze, then craned her neck to see what he was doing. He had bent over and was looking in front and behind – right up her!

What do you see, my fine gent, she felt like asking, but she made no sound except when he put a cold hard piece of metal up her. She gasped and gave a quick cry, not really a scream. Would he do that behind, too? Thank goodness, he didn't.

He started a new volley of questions. Did she itch, ache, smart, get her bleeding regular, heavy or light, did she hold her water or wet herself without control, did she wet herself at night, did she soil herself, did she rid herself of waste regularly, did she ever have a rash, did she hurt when a man took her, did she want a man every day or all the time, did she have a lot of men, did she have more than one at a time?

She gasped and forced out her voice. "No, sir."

He smirked. "Stay," he said and, to her surprise, walked out.

She stood up but dared not dress. There was a kind of daze upon her but, even so, she wondered if what was happening to her now was at all like what happened to the painted girls along the canal in Dublin Town. Or even the dancing girls in the music hall her father went to once with Uncle Bartholomew and came home red-faced and laughing. "Oh, Molly," he said to her mother, "I won't forget those bosoms and legs for the rest of my days. But you would have stood up well beside them in your youth, my love."

Her mother had smiled and flushed but muttered to Auntie Peggy, "I hope he has enough spirits in him to make him sleep or I'll never get any rest tonight," and the two women shook with silent laughter.

When the door opened again, the officer was with another one. She trembled for a second. Was he going to see how she coped with two?

She saw the broad shoulders of the other man, and then the gold on them – the captain! Was it? It couldn't be. Without thinking, she bent her head in a sort of bow and tried to smile – a lady's smile, not a child's, she hoped.

The captain looked her over but did not meet her eyes. "Elizabeth," he said. "You *are* young but a full woman. I like a full-bosomed woman, a full-bottomed one, too." He turned to the other officer. "Yes, very promising." He laughed, and in a step, had a hold of her bottom in one large hand. He stroked and kneaded, and his laugh grew heartier. "Oh, yes, m'girl, you'll do."

The other officer said, "She seems healthy, no virgin of course, none of those among this refuse, but she's pretty fresh and not on the game that you'd notice."

The captain harrumphed and waved his hand, and she heard the officer leaving and the door shut. The captain was holding her waist with one hand and unbuttoning the front-piece of his breeches with the other. She bit her lips and tried to take a deep breath. She was breathing fast already from apprehension. He wasn't looking at her face, but she felt herself almost smile. She half-liked and half-hated herself for that.

He was not as large as she had feared and not rough, though he entered her forthwith and jumped her up and down with a vigour that belied his balding pate, which she could see now that he was bending his knees and heaving her upwards. She didn't know whether to tense herself down there or to relax. She tried both. Both hurt, but not more than she could take. She concentrated on relaxing. He didn't pull her down on him very hard – thank God, she wouldn't ache too long after – but how her skin hurt. At least she could breathe; he wasn't all over her, not touching her face, not looking at her. She stopped herself from making grunts of revulsion or wails of pain. He caressed her breasts and hips and kissed her throat and face for a few seconds before he shouted with his pleasure. She felt relief. It hadn't hurt like in the gaol. She would be able to bear this. He slumped a little on her and kept feeling her hips.

"Wait till I have you in my cabin, Bess," he said and slapped her rump, hard enough to hurt. He did not exchange a glance with her though she was watching his face every second. He stroked her hair, held up a long curl and admired it as one might a horse's condition.

After he left, she put on her clothes and stood holding her bonnet. As if he had been watching all the while, the officer she now realised was the surgeon opened the door and motioned her out. She expected to go to the captain's quarters but found herself back in the room with the other women who had been chosen with her.

Was it a brothel they were in? How sickening. How infuriating. What power would she have among so many? She clenched her fists inside her sleeves. She stared around at the others. They were less pretty, and less strong than she was. *She* would be the only woman that the captain would keep, she said over and over in her head.

The night grew dark. Though they followed the coast for a time, soon the land became smaller and smaller, farther and farther away, just a line in the distance and then out of sight. Nothing. The sea was a moving sheet of grey, spreading out forever. She couldn't speak, though she tried to keep a friendly manner and listen to the lively Polly who sat next to her and spoke non-stop. All she could think of was what she was leaving – her mother, father, sisters, their little house, Dublin Town, the river, her cousins, the neighbours in the street, the girls at Evanton – her people. She would know no one where she was going. Who would be worth knowing? Who would deign to know her? Not the soldiers whose duty was to order her, enchain her and beat her. Not the other convicts who would shun her now. Not the free ladies and gentlemen who would never consider what she wanted. There was Meg, but she would resent her for being with the captain and officers. Perhaps she and Meg would stop being friends, or family, in the days to come. James would call her an enemy – would not care to know her.

Never to see Dublin Town again, never to set eyes on her family again – she could not believe it. Surely there would be a way, after many years? Even if her parents were gone by then, she would see her sisters. She found tears on her cheeks before she knew they were falling. She rubbed them away. The other girls were drinking and getting rowdy. She vowed she would not hit the drink.

Her mother's warning voice echoed strong: "She drank so much she couldn't keep a decent man. She took to the drink and that was the end of her."

Outside, the sea was a black glimmer. The girls pulled the portholes shut for the wind blew hard. Sue and Sal, the loud, hard-faced pair of Dublin Town whores, stretched out on the bench seats. No one challenged them. Elizabeth dossed down on the floor with the others. They each had a blanket, and the cabin was so much warmer than the gaol. She hadn't thought she would sleep, but the ship's rocking was a comfort, and it was the warmest bed she'd had for so long.

Next day, she felt dread and excitement. A world made of water and sky. No land. It had seemed safer when the shore was in sight. The women were ushered out to the deck. Elizabeth walked unsteadily to the rail, her thin, ragged shoes slipping on the scoured wood. Hanging on tensely, she stared at the ever-moving waves, at their shades and sparkles of colour. It was pretty, the water. You could stare at it for hours. The sky was partly clear, and the clouds were so big and moved faster than she was used to, except in the country near the Big House where they raced sometimes. *Forget that*, she told herself, and then, *no, remember. Picture everything that you loved every day, so you don't forget.*

She practised walking without hanging onto the rail. She and Polly burst out laughing at how silly they felt and looked. A couple of the officers' ladies were walking. They gazed above the convict girls' heads and did not speak to them. Elizabeth took note of their clothes, their complexions, their hands and shoes. Though they wore ladies' dresses, only one of them moved with the grace and restraint of gentility. She recalled Milady's way of standing, holding her chin high, then dipping it and looking to the side at the gentlemen. She tried to walk like Milady – and had to smile because the rolling of the ship fought against her efforts. How could you put one foot daintily in front of the other? You'd fall on your backside. But she managed Milady's gliding motion and mostly she could keep her head up. The ship let her roll her hips and arch her back. She knew she looked to advantage; sidelong glances let her see the officer on deck eyeing her.

The captain suddenly strode into view from some door she hadn't known existed. He was above her, and with him an officer and a sailor. She slowed down and separated from Polly and the others. Only when she was certain that he had looked at her did she retreat to the rail and rest for a moment. She set off once more, but he vanished into a cabin.

In the early afternoon, they were given food again and then told to clean the officers' cabins, but not the captain's. Before sunset, all the convicts were mustered on deck. She and the chosen girls were told to stand apart. It was horrid watching everyone climbing up fettered, hobbling and stiffly straightening their backs. She spied Margaret and smiled, to no response. She saw James at once, standing shoulder to shoulder with men she recalled from Kilmainham. She nearly cried. Her chest felt tight. He looked away when he saw her.

The captain stood above on the top deck. His officer checked the chains. The surgeon looked closely at some convicts and made remarks which a junior officer wrote in a book. She felt relieved. James was right; he had said that the health of the cargo was important for the colony. After the last line of men was checked for their chains, the convicts were sent below again. She breathed deeply and looked out to the now darkening sea.

Night came down, and the chosen girls sat in their room again. The door opened and the officer called Charlie burst in. He walked straight up to her and, seizing her hand, pulled her up and began to lead her to the door.

The surgeon appeared in the doorway. Shaking his head, he motioned her back to sit near the window.

"Not that one," he said to Charlie.

"You've got good taste, too, sir."

"Not me, you fool."

Charlie's face fell.

"Take one of the others when he's made up his mind which ones he wants."

Ones! Her face flamed. How stupid she had been, imagining she might be like a wife. It was a whorehouse she was in.

Later, the captain appeared. He surveyed the room of expectant faces, the smiles of invitation, seduction or resignation. She smiled too, but not too much. She was afraid he wouldn't choose her. When he beckoned Polly, Elizabeth slackened her upright posture and did not disguise her disappointment. The captain glanced at her, a teasing, pleased, almost vindictive look. She cleared her face of resentment or pleading. She hoped he was intrigued by her disappointment, if fleetingly, before he turned back with enthusiasm to Polly whom he pulled out of the room.

Would he sample all of them? He chose the more buxom of the two Dublin whores the next night. She expected he would sample the other one the day after but, to her surprise, she was summoned; he didn't come to choose.

She was taken to his cabin. She couldn't help but look about, even while she told herself to concentrate on him, to show her gratitude, to do her best to excite him, to make him feel sure that he had made the right choice. Meeting his eyes, she saw that he was pleased at her curiosity.

"Is my cabin what you expected, Bess?"

"It is ever so nice, sir." She hoped her Dublin accent didn't annoy him. At least her voice would sound gentle after the Dublin whore.

"Let me look at you, girl." He motioned her to stand, and he sat on his bed gazing at her, head to toe. "Now," he motioned in a circle with his hand.

She blushed in confusion. Did he mean turn around, undress, kneel? His face became amused. She said softly, "What would you like me to do, sir?"

"Put your clothes on the chair. Turn right around for me."

She removed her clothes and told herself to feel excited. Told herself this was admiration, and from gentry, from a man who'd seen more women than most. She raised her hands to her head, like the statue in the oval parlour at Evanton that she'd seen a few times. Now she understood the pose: it let men see it all, didn't it? She turned around slowly, thinking of the beauty of the smooth statue and of the ones in the fountains in the gardens.

As she faced him, his eyes were glazed. He pulled her close, stroked her, followed her outline, stood and held her to his body.

He removed his own clothes so fast she could have laughed. He leaned over and let her sink onto the bed. He was gentler than the first time but more intense, more demanding. She forced herself to relax and breathe. He wasn't squashing her chest much and her face not at all. Her skin hurt down there at first, but her body seemed to help her with some kind of liquid – or was it his? He didn't look at her in the eye, but his admiration of her body was there in his face. It wasn't long till he got to gasping and half-shouting but then he lingered, caressing and exploring her. She couldn't tell if he wanted her to be excited and if so, how much. *He's a sea captain*, she thought. *They are men of the world and men who know how things work; of course, they expect women to like what they do.* But she would not let herself go for long or be loud like the Dublin whores. She gasped and clung to him and smiled.

His eyes were still young. Clear, not unkind, joyful. He put his hand between her legs, gently, as if he knew how she felt. She responded so fast she surprised herself. It was like something for herself, for once. Why shouldn't she? She thought all the while of Michael's blue-grey eyes. The captain smiled. He seemed not so much older then, this man who knew how to choose the sail, when to set off, how to find his way across the world – without falling off, as her mother used to say. This man who could keep them all alive on the vast sea, in this creaking, groaning set of rough timbers and straining canvas, this man who could read books, follow maps and understand the stars and the heavens – of course he knew how to steer her; he had steered so many women all over the world, maybe even black and yellow women.

Elizabeth wriggled and quivered and felt it strong all up her stomach, heard herself yelping and screaming, heard him pant and groan again, felt his hands caress and his lips kiss gently and then his tongue. She could taste his brandy and tobacco, not stale like the turnkey, but rich and sweet. She could like him enough, she knew. And why not? Most girls anywhere didn't get a gentleman to take them with style.

If he was really a gentleman, she couldn't know. Of course, he wasn't one like the master, who was a nobleman, but compared to the other men she had met, this captain was the next thing to a lord. He knew so much, he had been educated, perhaps not like a lord with fine music and Latin books, but no man she had met before possessed an inkling of his knowledge.

Afterwards, he wanted her close alongside him, naked, and he wanted to look at each part of her again. She hoped he would not soon know her too well and be tired of her. But she could hardly stop him. She couldn't get up and get her clothes.

He said, "You have never undressed for a man before, have you? And never enjoyed having one inside you, either? Have you not had a sweetheart, a lover?"

"I started walking out with a young man, but then we were taken to Kilmainham one night soon after, sir."

"So, you never – but someone had you. Your employer?"

To her surprise, she hardly had to tell the story of the master. He nodded before she said the whole of it. He asked her to describe Evanton and what she liked there. She found herself talking about the fountain and the parlours and the gardens. She stopped herself mentioning the swing. She would not share that dream of pleasure with him. He smiled and stroked her hair.

"I have a big house in County Cork."

"In Ireland, sir?"

He laughed at her surprise. "Yes. A lot of Englishmen do."

"Oh, yes, sir, those who have lived in Ireland for generations. Have you lived in Ireland a long time, sir?"

"Only for the last two years. I grew up in the south of England. I like the Irish countryside and the game, the hunting."

She wanted to ask about his family, his wife, his children. But she didn't dare.

He drew up the blankets. "If you need a chamber pot, it's in the next room in the low locker. The heads for me are at the front. Use them, not the crew's."

She had to think for a moment – in the Cork gaol, convicts had talked about the heads, where the crew relieved themselves; they didn't have to use buckets, like the convicts, but sat on poles of wood sticking out from the ship over the sea – it sounded frightening, but it would be better than the reeking, filthy buckets.

His arms encircled her. He was not too heavy. So, she was to stay. The Dublin whore hadn't stayed all night.

She couldn't sleep. He was off like a baby, as her mother used to say. She stared out of the high small window at the stars.

When she awoke, he was fully dressed at the door.

"Ah, sleeping beauty. The day is afoot for me. You rest a little here and have some ale or milk or what you will and then go back to your companions." He stared down and his face was softer and younger. He stroked her breast and her face.

She leant on her elbow and smiled. "Thank you, sir."

He laughed for a second. "Good morning to you, Bess."

He was gone before she could decide how to farewell him. Surely, she would sleep here again? Would he want the others back, or the rest to sample? Had she got him? How was she to do that? She sank back into the comfort of his bed and slept a little.

When she had dressed and washed at his washstand – so much handsomer than any she had used at the Big House – she drank a little milk and walked out on deck. The air was cool and fresh. Birds were wheeling and screeching. The sun was bright and sloping down across the deck. She saw some officers looking at her. Perhaps that was good – let them know that she was the favoured one.

Sometime later, she went back to the room where her fellow convict women were waking. Polly gave her a wink, but the Dublin whores cast dark angry looks at her. She turned away, trying not to show any vanity or triumph. Perhaps she was not number one yet.

"Think you're smart." Sue dug her in the ribs harshly. "But you just wait. He'll come pantin' for me." She filled her small pipe and went out on deck. Sal flounced out behind her, shouldering Elizabeth aside on her way.

Polly smiled at Elizabeth. "Isn't his cabin comfortable?"

That night, Elizabeth was sent for again. She waited in his sleeping cabin quite a time till he appeared. He was a little less friendly and attentive, but he did not hurt her, and she needed no acting to respond. He was a little more tired, she suspected, and went to sleep quickly. She stared out the window at the clouds. The ship was pitching, but she fell asleep soon.

In the morning, she sat up to find him buttoning his coat. He farewelled her pleasantly. Nothing was said about her staying or going, so she went back to the others.

That night, Sue was summoned instead. Elizabeth turned to the window so that her disappointment and embarrassment would not show. For the rest of the week, the other girls were called in turn. Then no one for two nights in succession. The weather was unsettled, and the ship rocked alarmingly. She wished she could ask the captain if this was safe, if they were in danger and how he was going to steer them out of the way of that storm in the distance.

He didn't. As the storm raged, the other girls screamed till she covered her ears in exasperation. Many of them were vomiting into the buckets. She knew they could not help it, but she felt like shouting at them. It was too bad that they could not go to the railings outside because of the rain driving down so fiercely. The sour, decaying smell in the small room was intolerable. She opened a window on the sheltered side for a moment till someone shouted at her that it was freezing, and the blasts of wind would kill them. She shrugged in contempt but closed the window.

When the weather calmed and the sailors and officers stopped shouting and running about, there was a muster of convicts on deck. From the ranks of the chosen whores, she strained to see Meg and James. Meg looked disconsolate and stood slumped among the women. He stood tall and straight, staring ahead, ignoring the officer who checked chains and hit at legs whenever the whim took him. James received a whack but made no movement and no sound that she could hear. The officer moved on. A few convicts were taken aside by the surgeon and not sent back down.

Elizabeth walked with Polly around the mid-deck, enjoying the fresh air. It was a little warmer than when she was last outside. Were they close to Spain? She heard it was a hot country, though no doubt not in December. She looked for the captain, but he was nowhere to be seen. Some officers' wives walked near her and Polly but did not deign to speak.

She hoped he would send for her, but it was Sue who was called. Next night, no one. Then her.

He was sitting on his bed when she arrived. He motioned for her to undress. It was like the first night, but not so much talk. For a moment before he went to sleep, she wanted to clasp his hand and stroke his face and tell him she loved to be with him. Indeed, she took his hand and gazed deep into his eyes with a smile, for perhaps he would see what she could not yet dare say. Though he barely smiled back, he instantly drew her head close on his breast. She felt his arms big and warm around her, such a comfort. It seemed so long since she had been held in a sort of loving embrace.

The touch of someone, anyone, was something she couldn't live without. For a moment, she wished that she had stayed with Meg in the hold for she would have seen James. It would have been better. What had she done? It shocked her that she would settle for anyone rather than no one, and that she would use this need for her benefit. Yet every animal needed its mother or its mate to snuggle with. Loneliness was a heartache and body-ache; she was learning that fast. She thanked James for his friendship, even though he would despise and condemn her now.

The next morning, she did not see the captain and went back to the cabin where the women were. That evening, a group of officers and sailors suddenly swarmed in, eyeing the girls, but not her. She sat in triumph – they knew she was the captain's. She had won.

The selection occurred in order of rank. The third officer chose Polly, and Elizabeth shot her a gleeful look. The first mate looked for a time and then picked the demure blonde from Tipperary. When young Charlie's turn came, only the Dublin whores and the nervous little factory girl were left. Elizabeth was glad he chose the factory-girl who summoned a sweet smile, and Charlie rushed her out. Three women were left. The gunner scratched his chin and went for Sal. Did he surmise that the captain might have a yen for Sue some nights?

Sue hooted with laughter and lit her pipe. "So much for you, Queen Bessie. I'll wipe the floor with you. I know how to wind our captain up. He wants to have us both. See how you cope with that, Miss High and Mighty."

Elizabeth did not look at her. Her fear and disappointment ached to the bone, but she would not let anyone see that, least of all one of the whores. She seethed with anger. How could the captain have so little taste, so little appreciation of her innocence, her cleanliness, her beauty? She half-wished she had not even tried. How could the coarse woman next to her have won, too?

6 Captain Dennett

It was only a few minutes before the door opened and a tall black sailor strode in. He mock-bowed to Sue. "I'm to have you, m'darlin'. Don't give me no sour looks. You be gettin' the best man on board." He swaggered. "Wait till you see me, gal."

"But where will I sleep?" Sue wailed.

"In my hammock, darlin'. More space, more comfortable."

She looked him up and down. "I never had a black man afore. You're plenty big enough." She tittered, "Where are you from?"

He took her arm and led her out.

Elizabeth leant back, relieved but exhausted and depressed. Nothing but slaves, they were. She sat for what seemed like many hours but was only two, she knew from the watch. The cabin boy came to summon her. Until he took her to the captain's cabin, she was afraid that it might be to someone else's. The surgeon had not chosen a wife. For a second, she feared that they planned to share her, but then she recalled Sue jeering that the surgeon wasn't the type who liked women. Perhaps the harlot was right again, or perhaps the surgeon drew the line at convicts.

Captain Dennett was sitting in his chair in what she later learned was called the great cabin. "Let's have a draught of wine, Bess," he said.

She gazed in delight at the large table, the chairs, the padded window seats, the mirror, the desk and the gleaming metal cups. If only Ma could see it. Perhaps she would have a letter written to home one day when the disgrace of it was long gone. She would pretend that she had seen a captain's cabin in other circumstances.

"Are you happy to spend the voyage with me, Bess?"

She assured him with a smile "Oh, yes, captain, I am very happy to be with you, sir."

He said, "Do you know what being the captain's woman means?"

She swallowed. "I will be loyal, sir, and try to make you happy so you enjoy your nights."

His face was half-pleased, half-amused.

She added quickly, "I will not embarrass you, sir, by low-class behaviour or any talk with the convicts."

"You have a relative among the felons. What was her crime?"

"Sedition, like me, but she didn't do much more than I, sir; she just stood with a crowd."

"With the wrong crowd, Bess. Traitors, rebels, enemies of the Crown and of the Irish Parliament. Do you understand that?"

"I do, sir."

"You agree that what you and Margaret did was wrong?"

"Oh, I do, sir." She had a flash of James' proud face and warm arms and stopped herself from trembling.

"You agree that the rebels, the Defenders, are traitors and deserve to be transported?"

She took a breath. How could she! As her father said, Englishmen were fools. "Yes, sir."

"That is the truth. If you are asked, you must denounce all the traitors to everyone. Even your cousin Margaret. And the men from the Kilmainham cell whom you knew. What were their names?"

"Oh, there were so many." She stopped, but his look was stern. "I cannot recall but a few, sir."

"You were close to some. Their names?" His face and voice so cold.

She started to see what he could be like to men under his command.

"Peter, Timothy, James and Christopher, sir."

"Christopher Connelly? James Brannan?" His face was like a judge's.

She felt afraid of him for the first time.

"I don't know, sir. We just used our first names."

"Nonsense. Irish men often use the family name."

She kept her eyes wide and clear. One more minute and she might tell.

"They are Defender leaders and traitors with long records. Some should have been hanged in my opinion, and in the opinion of many Irish judges."

She lowered her head. "Yes, sir." He looked away. Tossed down his liquor. Poured a little into her glass.

"You will try to get on with the officers' women. Not the convicts, the ladies. The so-called ladies." He snorted. "Only Mrs Martin is what you Irish call gentry. You make sure you learn who she is."

"I can see that she is from quality."

"How can you see that, Bess?"

"By her countenance, sir, and by her posture and her walk, and the soft clear way she talks."

"Good. Imitate her if you can." He looked amused.

She felt a flash of anger. *Oh, I can, fine sir,* she thought. *Just watch.*

"You weren't a lady's maid, were you?"

He said it without the slightest hint of a doubt. It got her goat.

"No sir, but Milady told the housekeeper that I might be trained as her maid if they could get no more girls from France."

"Hmm."

"She said I was pleasing in my manner and appearance and cleanliness, sir. And my speech. Mrs Ryan, the housekeeper, was teaching me and the head upstairs maid the fine words to say so that we could help when there were guests and so that we might be ladies' maids, or even housekeepers one day if we didn't marry."

He looked amused. "But you wanted to marry, didn't you?"

"Oh yes, sir."

"The stable boy," he laughed. "Well, I'm a good rider, Bess. Can you imagine that?"

"Oh, yes, sir."

"How so?"

"You walk so fast and steady, and you stand so still in the wind and the pitching and rolling."

He laughed and took her hand. "You like me a little, Bessie." It was not quite a question.

She let her dimple work and tried to blush but put a little fire into her glance. "I do, sir, more than a little."

"Hmm. What do you like?"

"You know how to be with a girl so much more than most men, I am thinking, and you are a gentleman, and you know almost everything, and you have seen London and the world, sir."

"A good part of the world, and now I'm going to see the rest of it. We both are."

"I am glad, sir, that you like sailing so much and seeing new places and being captain."

"Hmm. You think being captain is jolly?"

"Yes sir, but difficult too, far too difficult for most men."

"Ah. That's true, my girl. Work rarely stops for a captain. Sometimes there will be problems with the ship or the sea or the weather and I will have no time or patience for you."

"That's all right, sir."

"I will have bad tempers some nights."

"Of course, sir."

He laughed. "And you, Bess, will you have bad tempers?"

"I will not, sir."

He laughed more.

She almost laughed too. "I will try very hard not to, sir."

"You know that once the ship reaches the colony, you will not be the captain's companion or his problem. You will be a convict subject of the colonial governor. You will most likely have a master or a mistress again."

She nodded, trying hard not to show any disappointment or resentment. So he promised nothing?

He stroked her hand. "So soft. You were fortunate to work in a big house indoors and to avoid the spinning machines or farm labour. I may be able to assist you a little in the colony, but I cannot say so now. Even the fact that you were in my cabin will help you somewhat, of course."

He stood and embraced her, felt her haunches and buttocks. Squeezed too hard. "From now on, do not converse with the felons, even the officers' women. You will be alone a good deal."

"I don't mind, sir."

"I notice that you like exercise. That is excellent. Walk outside whenever the weather permits. You may look at the animals and tend them, and the plants, too, if you wish. Never talk to the prisoners below. Do not go out for the muster. You may sit in here if I am not here meeting with officers. I will tell you to go if I need privacy. You can sew here – your own clothing. I have my young man to maintain mine. Are you hungry?"

He produced cheese and some dark cake. He ate a little, and she as much as she dared.

When they repaired to the small sleeping cabin, he wanted her to undress and turn round and round. He took her like before except that this time he pleasured her. She heard herself cry out. Was he pleased, or did he think her common? The former, his face told her, thank God. Ah, but didn't the very word "God" send her spirits down?

For she was lost now. Damned. She had chosen earthly comfort, not virtue. Worse still, she was delighting in sins of the flesh. She was a fallen woman, well and truly. She would spend her middle and old age doing penance, praying for forgiveness and hoping for mercy.

He pulled her close under the covers. "We fit well, Bess. I am glad you are on my ship."

She smiled. "Oh, I'm glad you're my captain. I mean, the captain, sir."

He laughed softly and kissed her cheek, as if she were really his sweetheart. She felt her eyes fill with tears and hid her face on his chest.

*

She had thought that she would now eat with him, but, the next day and night, her meals were brought to her, and she ate alone. At each meal, she rejoiced that she had snared a place above the hold; it was worth it for the food alone, the beef, the potato and cabbage or greens. She knew she was getting more than the poor folk below, and the food better kept and better cooked by far. They would not be seeing cheese or cake at all. She went out after her supper onto the shadowy deck and walked to the end. A sailor tipped his hat to her. She almost gasped. When she returned to the captain's sleeping cabin, she could hear that the captain and the officers and the real ladies were dining in the great cabin. She peeked for a minute through the spyhole and then sat on the bed and waited for him.

The sketch on the wall was of the house he owned in Ireland. She stared at it for a long time. It was not grand like Evanton, but big. His wife lived there. He had grown up in a large house but not a grand one, he said. His mother and sisters still lived in England. He alone liked Ireland and the house and the land he could buy there.

The next morning, the captain's steward brought her a wooden chest and opened it. Inside were clothes.

"Whose were these?" she asked before she thought about whether such a question was wise.

He almost sneered. "Ma'am, they are from ports in the Orient mostly. And from England. Perhaps some from Belfast." He left her. He never bowed the way some of the sailors did.

Many of the fabrics were lovely. She spread out the ones she liked on the bed. It was like playing when she was tiny. She wished she could fetch Polly, talk with her about the colours and give her a dress or two.

Several dresses looked like her size. As she held them against herself and admired the effect in the mirror, she smelt sweat or perfume of roses and some smells she could not recognise, whether of spices or flowers she could not tell. Who had worn them? Ship wives like herself? Slave girls? Blacks? She threw the dresses down, cursed him and the courts and the judges. How many wives had the captain chosen on how many voyages?

She sat and stroked the dresses. Did it matter in the end? What was the point of not wearing the best of these costumes? She sifted through again, discarded the brightest ones that had first taken her eye – folks said natives and whores loved lurid colours – and selected delicate muted shades like Milady's in the evenings, and stylish, subtle stripes like those she wore by day.

The dress she liked most was a soft shade, like a pale rose; it shone, and next to it, her skin glowed. When she put it on, she looked a different shape and outline. The feeling of the fabric on her skin was pleasing; the soft way the cloth clung to her gave her grace and elegance. Even the length was right. She stared at her image in the glass; she could have been a cousin of the young lady of Evanton Manor. She searched for some lace that might sit at the neckline and found a cream, openwork piece that she could sew on at a few points and take off to wash. She put it in place around the low neckline and smiled at the lady in the glass.

Next, she tried the shoes. Some would fit her if she stuffed paper or cloth in them. The soft boots with buttons were snug and warm and the evening slippers were worth keeping too. She selected a soft pair of day slippers. She would sew ribbons at the sides to tie and make them more secure.

When the steward reappeared to tidy away any unwanted clothes and to offer needle and thread, she asked in a lady's tone, "Who wore these things?"

He stood silent, his head turned away and his eyes scornful.

"My betters?" she said. Then she took a breath. She must not provoke a complaint from him to the captain. She said, "To be sure, who is lower than a convict woman, if not an Irish one? Aren't all these females my betters?"

He disguised a laugh with a cough and then he glanced at her pile of chosen garments. "You have chosen well. Some of these things were from blacks, slaves and natives; I'd say they are lower than you."

She smiled. He could be a useful ally. Was he even a year older than her? He had hardly any beard. "Thank you, Simmons."

He shouldered the wooden chest but not before he half-bowed. She sat in triumph and opened the window to listen to the whooshing of the waves.

*

Her days were solitary except for Simmons. The weather improved later in the week as they sailed further south. On the finest day, she walked on deck and peered across the waves and into the sky. She had never seen such distances, such brightness and so much sky. She wore a scarf around her bonnet and shaded her face almost entirely.

Polly happened to be walking, too, so they spoke for a while. Elizabeth explained the captain's orders and Polly's face fell.

"I hoped we would be companions. I hardly see my lieutenant."

"And when you do?" Elizabeth smiled a little.

Polly blushed. "He's amorous, not rough much at all."

"I'm glad. He should realise he has a gem in you."

They stood a short while at the rail, before Elizabeth excused herself and went inside. She was aware that the first mate and some sailors had seen her conversation. They might report on her or be questioned by the captain. The surgeon often watched her when he walked or examined the chained convicts who were on deck, most of them incapacitated with dysentery, seasickness or other illnesses. She kept her distance from them and was relieved that they did not include James or Meg. She wondered how Meg was faring. James could look after himself, but Meg had become so thin in the gaol that she had lost much of her strength. Elizabeth wished she could send her some food; of course, that was impossible. She must stop wasting time worrying about things she could not make better. Why should she care? Meg begrudged her any ease she could find.

She looked up to the sky. The birds were different from those in her country. Large pale birds circled gracefully. Flocks of birds flashed past in lines. How did they keep the pattern? How did they fly so far? Did they fly wherever they wanted, these wild birds? Did they fly to

61

where the air was warm and the water or the land offered fine food and shelter? The birds were better off than girls like her.

When she walked on the deck in the afternoon, she encountered the officers' ladies, Mrs Martin and Mrs Peters. They looked past her. Mrs Martin's face was blank but the other wore a look of disdain. Elizabeth tossed her head. After the ladies retired to their cabins, she scolded herself. So much for imitating a lady – at the first test, she had reacted like a strumpet. She would do better. The next time her path crossed that of the ladies, she would lower her head in deference; indeed, she would bow to Mrs Martin. It would stop her feeling a misfit or a failure. She would look like a lady if it drove her mad.

But it was lonely being a lady. Milady had invited her maid and Mrs Ryan to converse with her often, for she spent most of her days alone. The master was forever off hunting, fishing or visiting in town, and the young lady was mostly away. Elizabeth had envied her ladyship but now she realised the drawbacks of a lady's life. Ladies couldn't walk across the fields or play at the river or wander off to gaze at the glen. They could only pace about the paths of the orderly gardens near their house. They could only visit one or two other ladies, and that necessitated an uncomfortable, bumpy carriage ride, sometimes a long one. In the colony, it might be lucky that Elizabeth would not be a real lady, for she might keep the few freedoms of common women – if she could find a husband or even a good master.

As she sat in the sleeping cabin that evening, staring out the window, she began to sing:

> Siuil, siuil, siuil a run
> Come, come, come, oh love,
> Quickly come to me, softly move;
> come to the door, and away we'll flee
> And safe for aye may my darling be.
>
> I wish I was on yonder hill:
> 'Tis there I'd sit and cry my fill
> And every tear would turn a mill.
> May you go safely, my darling.
>
> I'll sell my rock, I'll sell my reel,
> I'll sell my only spinning wheel
> To buy my love a sword of steel.
> May you go safely, my darling.

I'll dye my petticoats, I'll dye them red,
Around the world I will beg for bread,
Until my parents will wish me dead.
May you go safely, my darling.

I wish, I wish, I wish in vain,
I wish I had my heart again,
And vainly think I'd not complain.
May you go safely, my darling.

King James was routed in the fray.
The wild geese went with him away.
My boy went too, that dreary day.
May you go safely, my darling.
Is go dte tu mavourneen slan.

Her parents and grandmother had sung in the evening on Saturdays and sometimes they had all gone to the alehouse on the corner of Baggott Street and the canal to hear songs from old and young, locals and travellers. She loved the old Irish songs and entertained herself by singing them. She thought she sang softly. The officers in the great cabin were making a racket and would never hear her.

Later that night, the captain came in and said, "I am told that you like to sing."

His tone gave her alarm. "Yes, sir. I hope I do not disturb the ladies or the officers with my warbling."

"A couple of the officers have been most entertained." His smile was not a warm one; powerful folk like him or the master used cold smiles to make you feel guilty and fearful – and not good enough. He went on after a pause. "The ladies, alas, were displeased. That would be no matter except that your songs weren't in English. My informants had no notion what language you were singing in." His mouth twisted into a sneer but she wasn't comforted. "It was your Irish tongue, I presume?"

"Yes, sir." She kept her tone soft.

"It is not a good idea to sing in Irish, certainly not on this ship. Can you understand that?" He didn't look at her. "Probably not. You must endeavour to understand that members of the English gentry and those aspiring to be among that class do not wish to know that an Irishwoman is next door to them day and night. They don't wish to be reminded that the Irish have another language in which to plot their rebellions." He turned to her, his eyes cold and threatening. "They are disturbed and revolted by gibberish. Sing in English."

"Yes, sir."

He stood, walked into the great cabin and poured himself a brandy. The silence lengthened while he drank it and stared out at the sky.

"Was your father against the English? Your brothers? Did you have brothers? No. Cousins, no doubt. Any of them in the riots? Apart from Margaret Rafferty."

It felt like she was in the dock again. When would the English let girls like her out of the dock? She decided to mention her Uncle Peter, how she had asked him to help but he hadn't. The captain merely grunted.

The steward's search through her things and through every inch of the sleeping cabin and the great cabin the next day was no surprise. Probably the captain was sorry he had brought her above deck. Perhaps he wished he had brought some English girl on the voyage.

Two nights later, when he joined her after his dinner with the officers, he seemed more liquored up, she thought, from his colour and movements. He sat her on his knee and rested his head on her bosom.

"I don't dislike your singing, Bess. One day in port, I'll hear many songs from you. Sing me a song in English now. You Irish women have pleasant voices."

She thought for a moment, then sang:

> On the banks of the Roses,
> My love and I sat down,
> And I took out my violin
> To play my love a tune;
> In the middle of the tune,
> Oh she sighed and she said,
> O-ro, Johnny, lovely Johnny,
> Would you leave me?
>
> Oh, but I am no runaway
> And soon I'll let them know,
> I can take a good glass
> Or I can leave it alone;
> And the man that does not like me
> He can keep his daughter at home

And young Johnny will go roving
With another.

If ever I get married
Twill be in the month of May,
When the leaves they are green
And the meadows they are gay;
And I and my true love
Can sit and sport and play
On the lovely sweet banks
Of the Roses.

While she sang, he smiled and gazed at her as if she were someone else. Did he miss his wife? Did she play the harpsichord and sing for him, and for company? Elizabeth felt less resentment of him. He wasn't like the master whose family had lived in Ireland for generations but who treated Irish folk like a burden he had to suffer.

"Your voice is pretty, my dear."

She smiled. He hadn't called her that before. It was less distasteful to lie with him after that.

*

Walking on deck the next morning, she passed a lady and a young child of six or so. She had not seen them before and thought at first that they must be the family of a sailor. The lady gave her a look that was not unfriendly.

She asked Simmons when he appeared with her lunch and discovered that this was Mrs Silver, a free passenger who was married to a transportee. Somehow, she had been permitted to sail in the same ship as her husband. Simmons hinted that money had been paid, that the felon was not of the lowest class.

She mentioned Mrs Silver and her son to the captain.

"Ah yes, you may speak to her. She is a respectable enough woman, I am told. I understand that she chose to accompany her husband since if she had stayed, her family and his would not accept her."

"How harsh of them," Elizabeth said, without thinking. "But perhaps she followed her husband because she loves him."

The captain smiled. "I believe they have some means and will have an allowance from their families, or from his at least. So, perhaps they will make a comfortable life in New South Wales."

"Sir, may I ask what Mr Silver was charged with?"

"Aha, yes. A fraud in business, I believe. Not sedition or robbery or theft like most of you. A different kettle of fish. Not a responsible, reliable or honest man, apparently, but not vicious."

She hardly noticed the word; it could not cut her. It was only what she expected him to say.

Elizabeth found an opportunity to speak to Mrs Silver a few days later. She approached the lady with a little trepidation. Mrs Silver might think that all female felons were whores or fallen women. Elizabeth shuddered for that was not far from the truth, even though many convict women had not chosen such a label or fate.

Mrs Silver was reserved but willing to converse for a short time. Elizabeth wondered how much this was because the lady suspected or hoped that the captain's ship wife might be able to offer something to her or her son. Indeed, Elizabeth had brought some cake and cheese for them. She did not dare ask them to join her in the captain's cabin – she hadn't asked the captain if he would allow that.

She noticed by the shape of her that Mrs Silver was carrying a babe.

Elizabeth had hardly thought of it – how childish she was, how unable to think ahead, her situation being so full of hurdles already – but how would the captain react if she were to conceive? Would he provide for her? Or throw her back below? The surgeon appeared and passed without looking at her. He would be no help. He was with the young convict whom he was training as an assistant. Was the surgeon one of *those,* as Sue had hinted? Elizabeth had learned about them at Evanton – the butler and one of the footmen and the page. It horrified her at first; she had no idea what they did, till the scullery maid blurted it out. The surgeon had some ways of moving that reminded her of that footman. No wonder he hadn't cared for the chosen whores or sampled them. She looked at the convict boy. He had a guarded, closed, beaten look. Didn't most of the convicts, and she too, perhaps, when she wasn't careful? The surgeon seemed a cold fish and a boring, miserable old stick. Poor boy, cooped up with such a one, doing things he had never thought he would have to do, perhaps had not even known of. But at least he was fed well, and he would do better in the colony, surely, after his training in the surgery.

She waited for the best possible moment with the captain. On a night when the vigour of his action and the steadiness of his eye suggested that he had not swallowed much liquor, she said softly, "Sir, I wanted to ask you something about possible future eventualities." It was a phrase she recalled of Mrs Ryan's.

He looked sharply at her. No doubt he expected a grasping inquiry about money or a gift.

"I mean, sir, if I should happen to conceive and carry your child, sir."

To her astonishment, a look of sadness swept across his face. He turned away. "Do not fret on that account."

She waited. Nothing. What should she say? Would he be offended if she asked whether he had any children?

His tone was angry now. "You Irish breeders. Huge families, one popping out after the other, hardly time for the mother's breasts to dry." His face looked bitter and fierce. "You bore a child in Kilmainham. A warder's, I suppose, or was it a rebel's?"

"It was the young warder's child. He forced me, sir."

"How do you know it was the warder's infant? Didn't you have relations with the rebels? Didn't they take advantage?"

"No, sir. No rebel – I mean, convict – touched me. A few tried at first but…one of the older men stopped them."

"Protected you, did he? Who? Was it Brannan?"

She was sure she didn't blush. She widened her eyes, feigned astonishment.

He sneered. "I know all about you. Surely you realise that? Was it Brannan or Connelly or Boyle? The report mentions Brannan's name first, and he was a senior man in the Defenders. He was ruling the cell, wasn't he?"

She felt a tremor of fear for James and herself and Margaret. The hardness of his stare, she had never seen the like. She said softly, "I don't know, sir. I never understood the men's talk."

He perused her face. "Why didn't Brannan have you? He could have had his pick. With whom did he have relations?"

"No one, sir." She gulped. She had replied too quickly. She modified her tone. "He was so loyal or so choosy, I don't know which, sir." It would do no good to call James a good husband and father. "It was much remarked upon among the women how he didn't sleep with anyone."

"Then he's even more of a fool than most Irish rebels. He'll never be in that position again. Don't look surprised. Men like him do not prosper in New South Wales. Their reputation is known. The military keep them under surveillance. He and the rest of his gang will probably be behind bars immediately or shipped off to some far island."

She looked down at her hands in her lap. Her spirits were almost as low as in Kilmainham.

"What about when you were in service? Did you bear a child there? Your master's? Any others?"

"Oh, no, sir. I bore no babies at the Big House. I had relations only with the master. No others."

"Hmm. They wouldn't dare, I suppose. Except for your stable lad?"

"No, no, sir, we didn't."

"So, you didn't lose a babe of the master's?"

"No, sir, I didn't conceive. I was lucky. It was not so often or so long."

He stared at her. She couldn't read his expression.

He said, "It is unlikely you will have a child on the voyage."

"But sir, I lost the one in the gaol because I was skin and bone, so hungry. We ate only gruel for weeks, months. My family couldn't afford to bring me much, and when other prisoners stopped sharing food, I was practically starving, sir, so my babe was small and withered and came early. Because of the hunger." She couldn't stop her eyes filling with tears. She gazed at him. Would he not have a second's pity for her and for the babe?

His face lost the sharp look, but it couldn't have been said to show pity. "It was better that the babe died. How long do you think infants last below deck?"

She gasped. "Have some died, sir? Whose? How many?"

"Not for you to know or care," he said.

"But sadness comes upon me to hear of an infant's death. Does it not come upon you, sir?" She couldn't mask her surprise. At once, she was afraid he would scoff or shout.

His expression was grave, yet less harsh now. "If I let myself feel distress at the death of every peasant's babe, or even for the death of every sailor on my ships…" He shook his head. "You will need to become less soft-hearted, Bess. I'm sure this voyage will accomplish that."

"Can I ask you something, sir?"

"What?" He looked partly amused and partly wary; she could not tell how much of each. She paused.

His tone was guarded, testy. "You had better say it now."

"Sir, would you tell a child of yours to be hard-hearted?"

He looked surprised and offended. "You're cleverer than many of your sex, I see. I suspected that. Who have you heard talking of my personal circumstances? The lieutenant's girl? The mate's?"

"No, sir, no one. I am wondering, that is all. I am telling myself that you have a softness for someone, and who else but for your child, even more than for your wife, sir." She dropped her voice, afraid of his ire.

His face was no longer angry. "I'm sure you would be right if I had a child."

"Did you have one that died too, sir? Oh, I am sorry."

He kept his eyes locked with hers. It was perhaps the longest they had looked at each other.

"No. I always wonder if that would have been better or worse. I have had no children. My wife and I have stopped wishing for a child."

She was astonished and thought it best to say nought. She looked at him with sympathy and then lowered her eyes.

"So, there is nothing to worry about. You will not mention this again. You will not tell this to anyone. On your safety, Elizabeth."

She nodded, dared to glance at him, his face so severe and pained. "Yes, sir, I will never speak of it to any living soul."

He dressed and went up on deck, striding in the direction of the steersman.

She sat up and hugged her knees. Who would have thought? Never a child, and him so large and thrusting so deep and long. Not even with a black woman or whoever he had bedded on his many voyages? Did he have a disease? Would she get it? Folk said that's what happened. Some boys who sampled the brothels or streetwalkers in Dublin Town got sores down below and never had a family. Please God, she wouldn't get sores or run mad. Still, the captain hadn't, so that was all right.

She stretched out. No worry of a baby, no hobbling about the deck with a big heavy belly, no getting the sickness of a morning on this pitching ship. But she was sorry too. He might have done more for her if she had given him a child. Now she was just his whore for the voyage, nothing more at all.

7 Life and Death Onboard

The captain and the officers made a great to-do about Christmas Day. Their dinner and drinking afterwards lasted a good deal longer than usual. The cook sent up some better meat with a tasty, thick gravy. She was given hers early as usual; she half expected to be invited by the captain to his table in the great cabin, but it was not to be. As ever, she sat silently in the sleeping cabin. She could hear the merry-making next door and was pleased to hear mention of double rations that day for the convicts.

She thought next morning that the rich gravy had made her queasy. But the next two mornings she felt the same. Her bleeding still hadn't come. She tried to count up the weeks. Oh, she couldn't be, surely, after what he said – but yet? It had an odd familiar ache, this sickness. It was gone once she ate some bread. It didn't depend on whether the sea was rough or the wind strong. She hugged herself in the early mornings after he left her bed. What if the baby survived? Surely, he would be pleased?

It pleased her, no doubt at all. To have some one of her own in the colony, and half high-born. She smiled. Who would have thought she would have a gentleman's child? For surely, she would be allowed to keep it? He wouldn't be taking it back to his barren wife, not when its mother was a convict, and worst of all an Irish one. She must keep well and eat a lot and walk. And not tell him till she was sure, and the babe was growing strong.

On the first day of the New Year at daybreak, the watch called, "Ship ahoy." Outside their room, a sailor was shouting, "Strange sail, sir."

She watched his face, but he showed no alarm. "Portuguese, or a British trader," he muttered, getting up, instantly alert.

The ship was English, he told her later. On the deck next day, she heard talk from the sailors that alarmed her. They suggested that French ships might shoot at them. Should she ask the captain? She touched her stomach. Nothing must happen to the little creature this time, please God. Even though she could not feel that God was listening, she begged him not to punish her through the death of this child.

The next week, a sister ship was within sight and sent a signal with flags. She knew not what it signified but saw the surgeon set off at first light in the jollyboat. Later that morning, she heard from Simmons that on the ship, the *Thomas of Liverpool*, the surgeon was to attend to five sick men, but he would come back on board that same evening.

*

The sunshine felt stronger and the weather warmer in the second month at sea. When she remarked upon this to the captain one night in the cabin, he looked sharply at her.

"We're heading south, that's why, nearer to the equator." He half-laughed at her. "You're as ignorant as the ship's cats or cows, aren't you." It wasn't a question.

It was far from the first time that her lack of knowledge had been pointed out to her but the first time she had been compared to such beasts. She tried to keep all annoyance from her face; it was better to smile and simper. "Oh, sir, I wish you could tell me what you mean – what is equator? Don't you think, sir, that I sometimes wish I knew where we are going?" How did he imagine the convicts felt on their wooden planks in the dark, travelling into the unknown? But of course, he never gave them a thought.

He laughed openly this time, though his look was warmer. "I am glad you have some curiosity, Bess. It's more than I can say for some sailors on this vessel. You must say *the* equator. Come, I will show you."

He opened his desk in the great cabin and took out a scroll. When he unrolled it on the table, it looked like a large piece of parchment. Only when he placed the candle beside it could she see that it was thick, heavily backed paper. It was a large picture with lots of writing. She had never seen a map except under glass on the master's wall. The captain leant over it and beckoned her forward.

"We started in Ireland." He darted an amused glance at her. "You haven't the slightest idea where it is on this map?"

She shook her head.

"I suppose you cannot read."

"Not much at all, sir, no." Only her name. It had never occurred to her before that it might be a benefit to be able to read, like a lady. For the first time, she understood why the priests persisted with their secret schools; reading the notices posted around and the court papers and the journals gave you an advantage. "Our family and all the folk around did not go to a school, sir."

He nodded, and showed her Ireland, Dublin and Cork. It took her a minute to see that the picture was the way a bird might see, looking down on the land surrounded by ocean. He pointed to London and Paris.

"You have heard of Paris?"

"Yes, sir, it is where the uprisings happened some years back that brought the fear to everyone in Dublin Town."

"And in England." He took a quill from the desk and moved it along the route their ship had taken.

"Can you tell me the names of the countries we have passed, sir, and who lives there and if they speak English?"

He smiled. It cheered her to see his approval of her question. When he named the Portuguese, she asked, "Are they savages or pagans, sir, or Christian folk?"

"They are great sailors and learned men; they wrote maps like these before anyone. They are Christian. Their language is rather like Spanish, Italian and Latin, but of course you know nothing of those. We will stay at one of their ports, the great Rio de Janeiro."

She spoke in curiosity before she thought to worry about showing more ignorance. "I thought the English had discovered the world, sir."

He laughed. "Only some of it. Great men from Portugal, Spain and Holland took long voyages into unknown parts centuries before the English, Bess."

She stared. The English were not the greatest nation? Not the cleverest? Not the first everywhere? How this would have cheered her father and his friends, though now she recalled some mention by her father of the Spanish and their great sailors.

He showed her the equator and said a lot about it that she barely understood. On the desk, she spied a small globe on a stand. Her master had bought a larger, more ornate one, which he gave to his son. The captain saw her gaze.

"Yes, you may understand more readily looking at the globe of the world." He picked it up and put it on the table near the light.

The equator was like a thin belt around the world.

"Where is New South Wales, sir?" She was thrilled that now she would learn where it was, this strange place where she must live out her days.

His finger swept down the globe.

She gasped in dismay. "But it is so far. So far away from other lands. At the bottom of the world."

He laughed. "Exactly. That is why it makes a good gaol."

"What is it like, sir?"

"*I* haven't been there; surely you realise that? I would have no reason to go to such a place if not for this opportunity to take convict cargo and return through the East and take back cargo to London."

Cargo. Her, James, Meg and the rest. Less valuable than tea, cotton or silk.

"Don't look so downcast. I have read about the colony and seen sketches. It is not a bad place by all accounts – if you are near fresh water and can tolerate the hot summers. But look, this is where we go next – down to Rio and then down and across."

It looked so far. "How long till we are at Rio, sir, and till New South Wales?"

"Two weeks till Rio and probably we will stay for three weeks or more for the repairs to the ship and the re-stocking of supplies. Then it will be up to three months more to Sydney, New South Wales."

So long? Folk in the Dublin prison had said the voyage took six months at least but she hadn't believed them. Mrs Silver's baby would be born, perhaps before Rio. Hers would not be born on this ship, thank God. She would have it on firm land, in the colony. But she would be big before they reached there. She would have to tell him in two months when her belly grew rounder. She and the captain would know each other well by then, and very well by the end of the journey. She must ensure that his feelings towards her remained strong. She must make his affection grow.

*

When they reached the equator, even the captain seemed to become light-hearted. Early in the morning, those officers and sailors who had not crossed the equator before were paraded on the top deck, stripped and daubed with a soapy substance. The guffaws and shouts of the men kept her a distance away, but their enjoyment and good cheer brought a lightness of mood to her too. So often the sounds on the ship were of misery or tension; this was so different. She wondered if trading ships were more like this all the time. The chains and the floggings cast such mournfulness over this ship.

At dinner that night, she heard singing, clapping and laughter from the great cabin, women's laughter too. When the captain came to his sleeping cabin, his face was flushed, and he was the merriest she had seen him. It struck her that he could have allowed her to join the party; on such a boisterous occasion, the others would hardly have noticed. She could not mention it. He treated her with more affection than usual, so she decided to enjoy being caressed and complimented. Would he behave like this again? In the coming week, she waited. His manner was a little warmer to her, that was all, so she had to be satisfied and to hope that somehow, he would change. Would he care more about her when he learned that she was carrying his child?

"Do you know enough about childbirth to assist Mrs Silver?" The captain gave her his stern look.

"I do, sir."

"You will be more acceptable than a girl from below."

When she entered Mrs Silver's cabin, she found Mrs Martin already there.

For the first time, the lady spoke to her. "Have you assisted at births of your family, Elizabeth?"

"For my aunt, madam."

"When the birth is nigh, I will ask you to come forward. Wait outside until then."

"Yes, madam. We will need water and cloths."

"I have ordered the stewards to bring them. The doctor will come if there are difficulties, but we would prefer not to have him here."

She saw the reservation and distaste on Mrs Martin's face. It was gratifying to see that the surgeon was disliked by the real lady of the ship.

She waited anxiously. *Please God, it would be a live infant, and Mrs Silver would survive with no impairment.*

When she received the signal, she found that the lady's pains were intense but that she bore them well. Mrs Silver sat up on the small cabin bed and opened her knees. Elizabeth pressed on the stomach and asked permission to peer at where the baby's head would soon be seen, she hoped. Mrs Silver gripped her hand so hard it hurt. Time rolled on, and she did not relax her grip. From time to time, she asked for the brandy and another flask on the small table. The flask seemed to give more comfort, so Elizabeth kept it close at hand.

Thank God, the ship was merely rocking. To go through a birth in a gale would be dangerous. Mrs Silver groaned, writhed and sucked at the flask. Elizabeth wondered whether it was strong drink or Laudanum, the potion that ladies were wont to use for pain. It did not smell like liquor. It certainly relaxed Mrs Silver's features and softened her groans.

"I see the babe's head, madam. Not so long now."

The sounds the lady made were louder now.

"I have the head, ma'am." A tender feeling toward the tiny babe surged within her. If only the one she had borne had been so fully formed and vigorous – and so welcome. She steadied the little head and eased the shoulders out. The body slid out fast. It was rounded and perfect. Mrs Silver collapsed back on the pillows and Elizabeth held the infant close and reached for its swaddling blanket.

Mrs Silver murmured, "You must wash it off, girl. Is it a boy?"

"Yes, madam. It is a good-sized boy with strong pink colour on him."

Now she must cut the cord, the task she had been dreading. The knife was sharp, so it only took an instant. The baby began squalling when she knotted the end of the cord the way she recalled seeing her mother do. She worried that the water in the bowl would chill or burn the child. She felt it with her elbow. It was lukewarm only, so she washed the tiny body with a cloth. She dried him, wrapped him tight and when she held him close, he stopped his wailing.

"Shall I give him to you, Mrs Silver?"

"In a moment. Fetch me some brandy and call for some tea."

Elizabeth did both, still holding the child.

When she passed it to its mother, she felt again the pain of handing her dead child to James. She rejoiced even more at the warmth of her tiny one growing.

A week later, the winds blew stronger day and night. Sailors rushed to furl the sails. It was astonishing to see how they could stand on the footropes, up in the air, against that wind and pull up the heavy, billowing, straining sail. The ship pitched and tossed. The cabin window showed the sea high one second and invisible the next. It was like she was falling and rising. The ladies and the officers' convict girls were sick. No one could walk on the decks for they were awash half the time. She missed her walks. She wondered how Mrs Silver was bearing all the motion.

The winds kept up for days. She heard screaming from the ladies. She wondered how painfully the convicts were being hurled about in their hard, low cell.

The captain came to the cabin late and for sleep only. He hardly spoke. One morning before he moved to the door, she asked if they were in danger at all.

He looked amused. "Not in the slightest. The ship is standing up well. Only small leaks. We will be out of this weather in about three days."

"It is only that the ladies scream so, sir, I thought perhaps there was some risk of a shipwreck or of us sinking?"

He laughed. "There is no danger. I have known much worse weather. We will see worse when we go far south. This is nothing to worry about."

She felt such gratitude that she leapt out of the bed and put her arms around him.

"You were not frightened like the others, were you?"

"No, sir. I saw that you were not anxious."

"Good." He stroked her hair and went swiftly onto the deck. She watched him bend and walk against the wind quickly and steadily, as if he were on a Dublin Town street.

*

Were there always deaths on voyages? Two sailors and a soldier died. She had never thought about it, but of course the captain had to bury them. Burial at sea seemed so savage, like from an earlier time. She wondered how the captain could read the death service and bury people so calmly. On those occasions, he seemed like a clergyman. The ceremony happened at first light, to get it over with. She watched from afar one morning while a young cabin boy was "committed to the sea". No matter how much the captain and officers tried to make it sound dignified, it was like throwing away waste.

And then Mrs Silver's baby died.

"Sir, do you think I could attend the burial?" She asked him the night before the service.

"Yes. Since you helped bring him into the world, it will be seemly for you to farewell him."

As the captain read a prayer and intoned, "We commit his body to the deep," Mrs Silver collapsed in tears onto Mrs Martin. The little one, so small and light, was wrapped and thrown over the rails into the cold, dark sea. Elizabeth could not keep back her tears but wept silently for two dead sons. Wept for fear of losing the one in her womb. The two ladies acknowledged her with a glance and a nod when they returned to their cabins.

8 Rio de Janeiro

February, 1797

"In two days, we will be in port, Bess." He slapped her on the rump as she came back to bed.

"What is it like, sir? Have you seen it?"

"Yes. It's picturesque. You'll be astonished."

There was a glimmer of fondness in his smile, she thought. For her or the port of Rio?

"You can explore the place with Lieutenant Fordham and his girl – the one you know."

She kept her face from showing anything but acquiescence and contentedness. "Thank you, sir." Of course, he would not show himself with her. He couldn't, she supposed. What would the officials at the port think, and the ship's officers? But disappointment shrouded her and she struggled to maintain her cheer.

Two mornings later, she did not hear the shout of the watchman, but the captain did, though he had been asleep. He leapt up, dressed and said, "Get up in an hour, Bess, and you will see the most beautiful sights. Come up on deck and go to the rail when the sun is up."

She was to have no choice in the matter, of course. She snuggled into the down quilt and closed her eyes. When the shaft of sunlight gleamed through the porthole sometime later, it woke her in a flash, so bright that she blinked and rubbed her eyes. As the captain said, the light in the middle and south of the world was sharper and brighter. She looked out but could not see land.

How she loved watching young sailors scramble up the ratlines to the tops to man the lookouts. If she had been born a boy, going to sea might have been the best choice, to sail and see the world, and to rise up the ranks of the sailors to a mate or even an officer.

Up on deck was a different world from before. Coming into view were high fingers of land and curves of bays. She ran to the rail. Mountains – but the odd, abrupt, sharp shape of them! Who would have thought such things could be?

She stared for some moments and then looked up at the bridge deck. Was he at the helm? He looked down, nodded at her and almost smiled. The next moment he turned back to the wheel and the long view ahead. She looked out at the strange sharp green mountains sticking up so suddenly from the blue green sea and was so engrossed at the long sweep of coast slowly coming closer that she was startled when a voice addressed her.

The third officer said, "Come this way, if you please, Miss Rafferty."

She smiled at his civility. *Come where?* she wondered. To her astonishment and joy, she found herself helped up to the poop deck, and the captain right there.

"Bess, isn't it a grand sight? Not one to sleep through. This is one of the most spectacular coasts and harbours in the world." He handed her a long tube. "Look through this, my girl."

She must have seemed a fool. Not having looked through such a thing before, she almost jumped with shock to see the mountains and the beaches suddenly looming so close.

"What is this magic, sir?"

He laughed. "It's a telescope, Bess. A wonderful instrument for seeing distant things close up. A boon for steering."

"Indeed, sir. Oh, it's pretty there, but it looks wild."

"You will see there is a town further on where we shall go."

He moved the tube this way and that for her and she gasped and cried out in delight at the sights. She had not known such places existed.

He took back the telescope and motioned the third officer to take her back to the main deck.

"Thank you so much, sir. I will never forget such beauty."

"Stay watching, or come back out when we get closer."

"I will stay, sir. I love to see it."

She saw him nearly smile again, and, in the corner of her eye, she noticed the mate grinning at them both, not impertinently but in a sort of friendly way. She knew that the obedience of them all was ever the first thing in her captain's mind. She would do nothing to destroy it or make it falter. She avoided catching the mate's eye. She went back to the rail.

The third officer said, "Would you like the boy to bring you a cup of ale or tea, Miss?"

This was the life. She stood sipping tea from her beaker like an officer. They began moving close to one of the high mountains, then swung around it and began threading through sharp mounts and hills. She glanced up and saw the captain and mate at the helm. What a task. It relieved her to recall that he had done this before. All the officers were on deck, and the surgeon. The ladies emerged from their rooms. Mrs Silver smiled at her. Mrs Martin nodded. Polly came over and Elizabeth enjoyed her surprise and delight at the hills and coves.

They followed the coastline into the harbour: such wide yellow strands, such waves with white tops and yet, so near, green hills and mountains.

Once they were in the wide harbour and could see a ring of buildings, Elizabeth was even more excited. To leave this small deck and walk – she longed to run, except she couldn't now, with the baby inside her – to see new places and new people, talk with Polly, and eat something other than old, salted meat.

In the harbour at the dock were dark people, brown, like the chocolate her mistress and the children used to drink. The women had bright bundles on their heads, not like laundry but like food or goods. They walked in such a different way. Barefoot, of course, but it wasn't only that. They swung more from side to side than strumpet Sue. They moved fast. The men were tall and thin, but their muscles bulged out more than she had seen on any man except on the black sailor who had chosen Sue.

The captain went ashore, and the ship stayed close at the dock. She saw well-dressed people she took for English till she saw their light-brown faces – were they Portuguese? They walked with pride and dignity or rode in ornate carriages, the ladies finely attired. There were large imposing houses a little away from the dock.

Later, at noon, the captain sent the boat back for some officers, their ladies – and her. She wondered what to bring and hastily swept her best garments into a bag Simmons provided.

As she was helped down into the boat, she felt happier than she had for so long. A proper room and bed. A meal ashore.

The sailors escorted them to a large house. Only she and Simmons were led to the door. The others were heading elsewhere. She barely had time to farewell Polly before her bag was handed to a dark servant and she was ushered upstairs. Even to be kept out of sight in a place like this would be delightful. There was an entrancing shady garden below that she could surely explore tomorrow.

Along a wide corridor, the servant led her to a large door. The servant knocked. She heard the captain answer. The servant opened the door.

"Oh, sir." She could not help but gaze about the room; it was elegant and vast, like Milady's.

"You like our new house?"

"Is it all for the two of us then, sir?"

His laughter echoed in the large stone room. He drew her to him.

Later, he told her to put on her best day dress and bonnet and led her out the front door. He slipped her arm through his and walked with her onto the main street of the town. She felt a surge of affection for him − and she had been thinking he was ashamed of her. Her figure was still fine, her waist hadn't thickened yet, though she was drawing her corset less tight now. He didn't notice. Men never did, did they? How long would they have put up with the pain of hard tight bones and lacing? Not for a second probably, for all their talk of war and hunting.

The buildings were a little like the grand ones she had seen once in the middle of Dublin Town. There were shops where the captain let her look about. He bought her some trinkets as if they were nothing, when they were the prettiest things she had ever been given. He told her to come another time with one or two of the officers' women and to order a few good dresses.

"They will charge it to me," he said, and she gasped.

They walked to where the town thinned out and the beach curved before them.

"Such yellow sand and such waves I never imagined," she said.

He told her that he and the officers and sailors would swim there. She felt a strange envy. She supposed the women never swam. She was sweating in her gown, even though it was of light muslin, and her curls were sticking to her forehead.

He glanced at her. "There is an even bigger and lovelier beach further around the bay. We can take a carriage, and you can walk into the water if you wish. The local native women do. You must not stay in the sun for long and you should wear a wide bonnet − we must buy you one of the wide-brimmed straw ones that the Portuguese girls wear." He laughed at her eager face. "Why, Bess, have you sometimes wanted to swim in the sea?"

"Only since this last week of heat. Before then, such an idea never came into my head. At home, no girls or women bathe in the river, and I am sure not in the sea either."

"There are many compensations of travel from home."

His face looked younger and less proper.

She smiled, "Yes, sir, I see."

Did he imagine that she found the black people disturbing but exciting too? She had seen black women giving him stares full of invitation. He hadn't responded, but perhaps he had succumbed the last time he was here. Perhaps he would leave her some nights for these local temptresses?

They walked on past the houses and into forest each side. He seemed to read her mind. He pulled her into a thick grove of trees and leaned her up against one. To her surprise, she felt the pleasure strong and long and had to stop herself from shouting as he did. He held her in an embrace afterwards longer than she expected. She stroked his face and kissed it. She truly felt more fondness for him and of course she was keen to draw him to her.

They ate in the huge dining room in their house – wonderful beef and poultry and strange vegetables that she liked. He told her their names and those of the Portuguese spices. He spoke of China and the different spices, meats and fruits there. It seemed that all parts of the world ate with different tastes – who would have thought it?

He commented on her manners, mostly in a complimentary fashion but with some criticisms she vowed to memorise. His surprise at her skill with the cutlery annoyed her.

"We are not savages in Dublin Town, sir, after all," she said, and he laughed. Really, of course, she had learned more of such manners at Evanton.

She wondered if she would see Meg, but the convicts were sent to an island nearby with some of the sailors and a roster of officers. No wonder the captain became a new man. So relaxed, even charming.

The next day, he took her in an open carriage to the beach he had mentioned. There were some Portuguese men and ladies there. The ladies wore loose cotton gowns and walked to the water where they held their skirts up past their ankles and waded along the lacy edge of the waves. Further along the beach were some black women swimming and diving, wearing tiny skirts that stuck to them and nothing above the waist.

The captain laughed. "The savages know how to keep cool in this heat."

He took off his jacket, boots and stockings and led her to the water. She drew up her skirts with one hand. They would dry in a short while afterwards in any case. She let them go and leant down to sweep some water over her face and neck. It was deliciously cool.

"Paradise, isn't it?" he murmured. "No wonder Portuguese captains retire here."

She had a fleeting fantasy of living with him here with their child. Better surely than New South Wales. But he had a wife in Ireland.

She looked up at him with water dripping down her face. "I won't want to leave here."

His face softened. "Ah, well. New South Wales has warm summers, and some beaches, no doubt. I hear the winters are mild. Better than Ireland, my dear."

How could he say or think that? Of course, Ireland was not his land. She missed it every day. Was it only that she missed the people? No, it was the green country and the streets of Dublin Town. But there was comfort for her in this strong southern sun and in the very air which embraced you rather than half-skinning you with wind and cold, leaving you ever shivering in damp clothing.

Could her life be better in the colony than it had been in Ireland? Sure, she was a convict, yet couldn't he make her future more comfortable than it ever could have been back home? But perhaps he would do little for her and she would always be a servant, fending off the hands of masters.

He took a small boat out to sail around the bay and the near bays with just her and a basket of food and wine. She trailed her hand in the water and leaned back like a lady. When they reached a deserted small cove with a wide lip of sand, he threw the anchor and carried her ashore. When he undressed and made to walk into the sea, he gave her a look – young, mischievous and reckless.

"Undress and come in with me. We're alone here. No one will ever know."

She held her breath. Should she? Would he remember it with excitement or condemn her as a strumpet? His look was warm, fonder than she recalled. She threw off her things and took his hand.

She had rarely had a bath and only at Evanton Manor had she bathed by herself. This was so much more luxurious and delightful.

"Your first time in the sea, Bess. Ah, there's nothing like it. Good for the skin and the constitution."

She felt a sting of panic. Would it hurt her babe? Then she thought of the native women swimming at all sizes and months of carrying.

She unwound her hair and let it fall. To wet all of it and feel it losing its tangles was exhilarating. She waved it around under the water. Shook it back as she stood up.

"You are a true beauty, Bess." He held her close. He pulled her down into the water, but it wasn't frightening; it was the best feeling. Perhaps he felt more for her than she had dared to hope.

*

Almost as exciting as their trips to deserted, secluded coves were the banquets the captain held at their house, at first with a few junior officers but later with them all. Even Mrs Martin came and talked pleasantly to Elizabeth. Another evening, the captain invited some Portuguese gentlemen and their ladies – their wives, she assumed, because the ladies had many sparkling rings and jewels. One evening, the captain took her to a mansion on a hill. The men who governed Rio were there. She didn't understand their titles or their rank, but the evening was thrilling and the food splendid. She had come to love the local fruits and the ways of cooking too. One or two of the gentlemen spoke English and addressed her once or twice. Several complimented her beauty; she didn't need to know their language to catch their import. The captain's demeanour to her was respectful and considerate; she felt almost like a lady. Mrs Martin was there that night and was given little more attention than Elizabeth. Indeed, Mrs Martin waved Elizabeth to sit near her after dinner and began conversing, at first concerning the town and then about the future.

"What do you think you might do in New South Wales, Mrs Rafferty?"

Elizabeth felt dumbfounded for a second at the polite yet embarrassing 'Mrs' and at the difficult question. "I hope I might find a good position, ma'am."

"You should start a household of your own. Could you manage a farm or a dairy? Or a shop in the town? The captain should help you. While you are here, you should buy cloth, lace and jewellery to sell in New South Wales. Some of the perfumes and soaps in the Portuguese shops are quite good too."

"Thank you, ma'am, I appreciate your advice. That is a very helpful notion. Perhaps I should ask the captain if he would like me to do so?"

"Yes. Indeed, you should tell him it is your own idea; then he may be more confident that you will make a success of it."

"Thank you, ma'am. You are most kind."

Elizabeth felt truly grateful to the lady. Her hint about tactics with the captain was clever. A shop would be easier to run than a farm. She would never have dared to think of it.

"You should hire convict girls of good record to work for you in the shop, and then you can retain the position of the manager and owner. It would be good for you to begin in the colony as a person of some standing."

Elizabeth nodded. She hoped that Mrs Martin would still be helpful when she found out that there was a baby to come, a gentleman's child.

When the captain came in next evening with a face like thunder, she feared some disaster had befallen the ship. But it was the convicts – a small group had escaped. She put her hand to her heart and wondered – James? Meg? She dared not ask. Listening that night at dinner, she learned from an officer that it was neither her friend nor her kinswoman but a few of the younger men. Within days, the officers had re-captured all but one of the men, a convict she did not know.

Escape. It had never occurred to her. Where would he go? Would he pair up with a native woman, work for local men or sail to another colony? What courage – or foolishness; she couldn't decide which. How would he know where to go? But to be free! She couldn't blame him. She had to admire such nerve.

The captain's mood had changed. It stayed severe and tense. She heard from Polly that two of the convict women had been put in stocks on the island for drunkenness and fighting. It seemed that a lot of liquor had reached the convicts. She half-laughed at that news.

Rio was still beautiful, but the captain was no longer that joyful lover on the deserted beach or that gentleman steering her around the coast.

The only time he became relaxed and friendly again was the day he summoned guides and mules to climb the large sharp mountain across from the town. He had proposed a party of officers. She asked to join them. At first, he laughed and then gave a pleased smile.

"Why shouldn't you see one of the wonders of the world? I will tell the men to ask their ladies, but I doubt that any will be as adventurous as you, Bess."

Simmons, who had been accustomed to conversing with her now and then on the ship, had become her constant confidant in the house, where he evidently admired her new status and, even more, enjoyed his own small room and the company of local lasses. He was looking forward to the mountain climb. With much amusement, he told her how the other officers' women had shrieked or rolled their eyes at the thought of ascending the mountain on a mule. She didn't care, though she did worry that she might fall. But once she saw how short the mule was and how carefully the native led her, she sat easy and felt a surge of excitement. The native holding the head of the mule was a slim dark man who never looked her in the eye. She felt like an Englishwoman in Ireland; for a second, she took pride in that but then she thought it was perhaps a pity that one soul must always be the slave of another. The path was steep but winding and safe. The bumps were not sudden. Her baby would not be jolted or hurt.

The view down to the dark blue sea was like a painting she could never have imagined. You could see the coves, hills and bays like an eagle on high.

The captain had taken this ride before but his eye sparkled when he pointed out the ship in the harbour, their house in town and the convicts on their island. They sat and ate and walked about the peak for a time. Though the sun was piercing and strong, they were up so high that the wind cooled them, and it felt no hotter than an Irish summer's day.

Coming down was a little more daunting. The steepness sometimes frightened her into holding tight to the pommel but the man holding her mule kept a very slow pace and she could feel his calm and that of the beast. The captain instructed her to lean back a little against the incline. She breathed easy and took joy in the sights, the fragrances and the warmth.

When they stopped below, she wished she had some money to give to her guide. It pleased her when the captain gave all the men some coins.

*

Sailing out of Rio was almost as stunning as arriving. She stood on deck till all the land was out of sight. Was it possible she might see it again? She guessed not, but who knew?

There were several more days of warmth, and then the ship was in a cold world of biting wild winds and high green seas.

9 Mutiny

One afternoon, the captain entered his cabin suddenly. He looked almost unrecognisable. She didn't know why he shook with anger, or was it with fear too? The winds could not be the cause, for he was confident about all weathers. Was it a fault or weakness in the ship?

Only when the muster was so violent did she begin to understand. When most of the convicts were sent below again, with a whip to their backs, and twenty or so were kept in chains on deck, she began to fear. James was in the front row with Connelly and Boyle. The captain was shouting at them. Each of their answers displeased him for he kept bellowing at their chained, slumped bodies. She heard him roar, "Three hundred lashes for Brannan, do you hear?"

She gripped the window ledge. For all, or for James alone? For him. Him alone.

The captain leant forward, looming over James, whose neck was yoked and chained, so that he stooped. "Five hundred after that if you do not confess." He stood straight and glared at the prisoners. "I will not hang you. It is too gentle a death, but I will cut you to pieces."

James and the others were dragged down to the whipping station. The lashes started. She put her hands over her ears. Was James the one getting this scourging? She heard some cries, half-screams. She couldn't recognise his voice. Was it him? Would he die? Oh God, they would all die.

Still the lashes cracked the air, each with its answering scream and groan. Then a pause. Then again. Another victim, or was the same one washed down and revived to bear yet more?

She knew she should not go to see. James would hate her to watch. The captain would too. But to sit by and hear it – she shook and felt a sickness in her belly rising up her gorge. She rushed to the cabin, slammed the door shut, fell upon the bed. But still she could hear. She pulled the pillow over her head and wept.

And this was his bed, theirs. How would she bear his touch? She had to bear it and she had to appear pleased every second in his company.

Even if James died. And he surely would.

A light knock. Maybe not Simmons'. A woman's knock.

She wiped her eyes, smoothed her hair and skirts and opened the door to Polly who had the wit to refuse to enter, so they sat in the great cabin. "It's a mutiny. They say the ones being flogged are the ringleaders."

Elizabeth shook her head. "How did they find out?"

"Informers – William Tanner was flogged and gave many names. The officers found weapons hidden in the convicts' cots."

If the captain had seemed angry about the escape and the misbehaviour at Rio, he seemed like a mad devil now. She barely recognised him out there shouting and screaming. Then he came in with the first officer and shooed her and Polly out with no glance or word of greeting. She felt like a servant, a whore whose services were currently not needed.

On deck, the crack of the lash, the screeching of the men and the grunts of the floggers were unbearable. They went to Polly's officer's cabin and hugged each other for comfort.

She ate in isolation in his cabin and waited in his bed. He came in with a heavy tread, a dark face still. Not dark with liquor or weariness but with rancour and resentment. He gave her a look that made her quail.

"Did you know aught of this?"

"No, sir. I hardly know what has transpired except what I heard from Polly and she from the third officer."

He glared, his eyes suspicious, hostile.

"Is it really a mutiny, sir? How could they think they had a chance against the muskets and guns?"

"They had gathered weapons – knives, nails, glass."

She could not bear his eyes. "Do you want me to sleep elsewhere, sir?"

"Should I protect myself from you, too, Elizabeth?"

"Oh no, sir, I just meant—"

"Who was leading the mutiny?"

"I don't know, sir."

"Who would you expect?"

"I have no idea, sir."

"Really? I doubt that completely. James Brannan has been named by the men."

She paused, fearing to do James more harm. "How can you trust those informers?"

He threw his waistcoat across the cabin. "Precisely. How can I trust any of them? How can one trust a convict?"

She flushed.

"Yes, you, too. I have no idea what you think all the time inside that pretty head."

He threw off his breeches and pushed her roughly across the small bed into the wall. "But if you or any convict on this ship think you can get the better of me, you are wrong. Not one of you will survive if you threaten my ship."

She couldn't stop watching him. Men in battle, men slicing each other, men firing holes into each other must look like this. "I know, sir. You will win. You have won. You are punishing them, and no one will dare to start a mutiny."

He was silent, lying tensely against her, breathing hard.

"Sir, the informers may be telling you the names of those they have a grudge against."

He said harshly, "I know that, of course. I will find out if there are more culprits. I have men on guard listening all night on the convict deck."

She hardly dared to breathe.

"You are keen to move the blame off Brannan," he said.

She took a breath. "No, sir, but he is clever and would not try to start an impossible uprising."

He turned and glared. "Clever! He does not need to be clever. He has over a hundred men he could set against me."

She shook her head. "I do not think he would do that, sir."

"Why not? What does he have to lose? He is going to his death in a prison. If he and his ruffians killed me and the officers, they could sail to an island. Of course, they would no doubt perish trying to find their way, but I dare say they think they know how to sail; they think it no harder than slaughtering Englishmen."

She knew not what to say. James had killed or caused the death of Englishmen. He would not deny it; he took pride in it.

"So many lashes, sir. Hasn't he died already? Or he will. All the men you have flogged will surely die."

"You want to know if he lives, do you?" Suddenly, he thrust himself inside her, rammed in a fast rhythm, whacking her bone with his till he collapsed with groans less of pleasure than anger.

He threw himself onto his back beside her. "He will die, but not yet. He is a fighter. I will relish seeing the fight die in him day after day."

He pushed her over him out of the bed. She managed not to fall or bump into the chair. She retreated to the great cabin. A soldier was standing there on guard. He leered at her partly open gown. She wrapped it closer around her. She did not dare to go back for her shawl or for a blanket. There was a heavy dust cloth on the desk; she dragged it off slowly and pulled it over herself. If she pulled up her knees to her round belly, it covered her enough as she curled up in one of the big chairs. Sadness was heavy on her, but the rolling of the ship was strong and regular tonight, like a baby's cradle – like the one she had pushed with her feet to settle her little sisters – and while she hugged herself and the baby within her, the ship rocked both of them to sleep.

*

The next day, the captain did not speak when he passed her. She sat up and saw him stride away.

She withdrew to the sleeping cabin and later heard Simmons talking to the guard. The mutineers were below in the cells. The guard had seen the flogged ones with pieces of flesh hanging off them.

"I wouldn't go in there," Simmons said. "They must reek."

The guard had not gone in. He had been in the gunroom and along from it was a spyhole down into the cells.

She could not stop hearing James, his cries, his screams. She could not stop thinking of his shredded flesh, his pain – he must be in despair. How long could he last? He might die today. When Simmons had brought her breakfast, taken her dishes, tidied the great cabin and gone, she put on a light dress that made no noise and walked along the deck and down the stair. She saw no one along the passage to the gunroom. Almost shaking, she walked quickly to the spy hole. She looked down.

Several men in chains, in unnatural poses on their sides on the floor, blood all around them. James with the most blood. He was facing her. His eyes were open. But he would not see her in the small aperture. Her tears blinded her for a moment. There were no bottles of ale or pitchers of water down there for the men. Nothing at all. She walked quickly back the way she came.

The convicts below were all kept chained that day. No muster, no airing. Officers went down to check the chains.

Late in the morning, the flogging recommenced. She walked along the deck above, but it was only the floggers' chairs and bottles of liquor she could see, not the triangle nor the man on it. One flogger stood and went out of her sight. The sound of his intake of breath as he heaved and swung brought her tears; she clutched her head at the screams of the man. Dear God!

When she saw the captain and the mate leave the bridge, she turned to go inside.

She almost collided with the surgeon. He had been at the triangle. His colour was pale, but his eyes had an odd, feverish, excited glint.

"Girl, you must be gone."

"Yes, sir. Is the man dead? Who is it, sir?"

"Brannan. He is alive. He barely flinches. His back is falling apart – in chunks. The blood."

She watched his face, horrified and amazed. He was smiling.

He put his face near hers. "You convicts should remember this – Dennett will flay any one of you to death. Even you, bitch. He's not one of your English enlightened gentlemen or your disciplined naval officers. He's a captain of the old school, the traders who know that half the world's vermin are not worth keeping alive."

"Sir, should not the prisoners have water and rest? Otherwise, the number of lashes will never be reached."

"Don't worry, Irish whore. Your old master Brannan will get his number of lashes. Dennett and I will see to that."

His laugh startled her. He pushed past her roughly and she smelt liquor on his breath and another smell, rather like Laudanum. He disappeared in the direction of the triangle. She cowered in the shadow and saw the captain and the mate go there too. Surely the mate could not be so harsh? He was an ordinary sailor, not one of these officers who hated everyone except rich Englishmen. She recalled the friendliness in his countenance when he looked at her, a decent man. But he was part of this crew that was tearing the flesh off their fellow creatures – the crew that stood by and let it happen.

As she did, too, for she was like one of them. She was not with the convicts, but against them, and against James, even though she had not said a word to implicate him – indeed, she had tried to steer the blame away from him. She was with the captain against her poor, beaten countrymen who were living their last hours being torn apart.

She heard the captain shout. "Here's a new whip. Put these tails on 'er. Now Brannan, damn your eyes, this will open your carcass."

She ran back to the great cabin. On her way, she saw the surgeon at the rail, spewing over the side, collapsing to his haunches and shaking, retreating below. The lashes went on. The captain stayed. Watching or contributing some blows? Giving an example, he would say. To vent his fury at James, rather, a rage made hotter because of her.

She sat and bore witness. She heard the high animal sounds James probably didn't hear himself make – she hoped not. Yelps and cries the like of which she had never thought possible from a beast, let alone a man. She prayed with him, parts of Irish prayers, Granny's old words, the ones Ma used when they were sick, not the Latin prayers said in church. She thought of how James could conjure up in his mind the vision of the places he loved. *Dear man, may you be able to do that, afterwards at least.*

Later that afternoon while the flogging dragged on, Polly came to her door and knocked softly. Elizabeth opened the door and Polly made no attempt to come in but stood and stared at Elizabeth for a few moments – sorrow, gloom and shame in her face, guilt even – and then she disappeared back to her cabin. Still the lashes cut the air. Each ended in a thud. She heard the grunt of the flogger a second before the answering scream.

The captain did not come to his cabin till late that night. She was lying awake under a blanket in the great cabin. He passed her without a look.

Just before dawn, she woke and saw that the guard by the door was asleep.

She picked up her folded shawl where she had hidden one flask of brandy and another of water. She slipped out quietly.

On bare silent feet, she climbed down to the dungeon. A sailor was slumped near the entrance, asleep or drunk. She moved silently towards him, took his key and opened the door a crack, put the key back and went inside. If they locked her in with James, so be it. She might feel better in her heart if they did.

James was at the wall on his stomach, his back open to the air. She had to stop herself from screeching at the sight. The black blood was what she expected, but pale lines like his very bones shone in the dim light.

She whispered softly to him. "Oh, James, how can you bear this? Oh, the captain is a fiend."

His eyes seemed to focus. "He will kill you, girl."

"No one saw me. James, drink this. I know they give you nought."

"Ah." He lifted his head up a little with a groan and drank.

She had to hold him and the water bottle.

His voice was weak. "You should go back."

She gave him a draught of the brandy. Her Ma and Granny had used it as medicine. "I'll leave this water and brandy. Drink it before day."

"Betsy, I will die tomorrow. Tell them I died for something. Get word to Ireland that I died for freedom."

"I will, James." She could not stop her tears. "I tried to tell him it was not you."

"Don't bait him. Live, Betsy, live for me."

She pressed her lips to his sunken cheek and helped him down onto his side with the flasks near his hand. She put the brandy to his lips again, afraid the others there would take it, though they all seemed more dead than alive.

When she got back to her room, the guard had not woken.

She turned to climb onto the bench.

"You took him drink?"

The captain loomed over her in his nightshirt, his eyes boring into her very skin.

She sat and leaned back against the wall. "No, sir. How could I get past the armed soldiers, sir?"

He spat out his words in fury. "Convict whore. I know the men are half-drunk and unable to keep the watch. You risked your life to go to your old protector, your friend, your man."

"He was not my friend only, sir. He was everyone's friend."

"Liar. I have heard from many who were in the Dublin gaol. You were his favourite, his little friend, by him every night."

"Not just me, sir. My cousin and other girls and men, too."

"Stop your lying." He raised his hand.

She did not cringe, but her hand went over her belly.

He stared. "Why do you shield your belly and not your face?"

She held out her hand toward him. "Sir, I am carrying your child. Hit me on my face or my legs, sir, but not on my belly, I beg you."

He stilled, lowered his hand.

She said softly, "I was waiting to tell you this joyous news. I hoped you would be pleased. I want this child. Your child. Our child."

His eyes were almost wet, but his mouth still held its grim anger.

"Sir, the thing I must hold dear and protect with my life is this child."

He made a low cry. "You're lying, wretched whore, to save your hide."

"Why would I say such a thing when you will see soon enough if it is true or not?"

"To buy yourself time."

They stared at each other, hardly breathing. She could feel his wish to believe her, his longing for a child.

"Sir, if you feel my waist, you'll find it softer and larger, my belly and bosom have become harder, you can feel." She guided his hand. He felt the hardness of the breasts. She saw his face change.

"Are you sure?" He searched her face. "It is mine?"

"Sir, there is no other has been near me, you know that."

"But before me? In Cork or Dublin?"

"Sir, I had my bleeding when I was first on this ship. You saw my blood." He had shown a little distaste, she recalled. "I must have conceived very soon after that. It is yours, sir, near three months. In a month, I will be stout and rounded."

He sighed, his shoulders sank, a look almost of pride on his face.

"So, sir, I am on your side. More than anyone else could be."

"You want me to provide for the child."

She said carefully, "Sir, I understand how you feel about your ship. I see that for you the main thing in life is your ship, keeping it safe."

His jaw relaxed a little. His eyes were still cold, watching her.

She added, "Just like for me the only thing in this life is to keep my baby alive."

"You took a flask of my brandy to Brannan."

"Yes, sir, and water. Those men should all have water. I would do it for any creature, sir."

"Do it again and I will flog you, babe or no babe."

"I will not do it again, not for any of them. He will die tomorrow."

He pushed her onto his bed but did not look at her face. He kept her by him but fell asleep and did not bother her. She willed herself to become calm, to stop her silent weeping, to breathe deep for the child and to cling to the rhythm of the ship's rolling. It was hard to stay still and not to creep away from his body.

*

James did not die the next day. His last lashes were delayed. She hoped he was unconscious.

Two other men died that day.

She passed the surgeon on the deck. He looked ill and wild. He ignored her. She was still standing at the rail when the first officer came up to him.

"Sir, you are to tend to the flogged men."

The doctor raised tormented eyes. "They are hours or days from death. Nothing I nor any man can do for them."

"Then you must oversee the conditions of the sick convicts in the hold."

"I won't touch them. They have a contagion."

"Then, sir, I will have them brought up on the deck and tended, in order to keep them from the other convicts."

The doctor shrugged and continued his walk.

More convicts died. She knew not how many, but perhaps no more than four. They were tossed overboard with little ceremony shortly after the dawn.

*

The captain resumed relations with her. Though he was not brutal, he showed no warmth or refinement anymore. He never took pains to give her pleasure. He rammed into her. He barely looked at her. She kept her face blank or sometimes tried to smile at the painting of his house on the wall. She did not try to respond. It was as if she were old now, past pleasure. Or a real whore, nothing but his receptacle, with little feeling, not even pain.

The weather grew rougher. Winds blew constantly and burst into gales some days. The ship rocked up so far and then down so deep that everything had to be battened down. Simmons brought food in covered dishes and flasks. He still had moments where he spoke with her, but his manner was cold. She was but an Irish felon. The convicts were not seen on deck. She guessed they were chained below to their berths. Storms tossed the ship most nights and ripped the sails. The men strove in sleet and pelting rain to raise new sail. She could not walk on deck most days so she moved around all the inner areas she could. Except near the dungeon.

James was still alive. She wished she knew if he was awake or in a stupor. What did he suffer? On a rare walk, she overheard sailors talking of how he took no food yet would not die. They spoke with contempt as if he were a dog or a rat.

Three weeks later, in less violent weather, he was dragged up on deck and flogged again. He was unconscious before half the hundred blows were dealt. The doctor was summoned to check if the man was alive or dead. Polly told Elizabeth that, when he said, "Alive," he was then asked if the man could bear more lashes. He shrugged. "He will die sooner or later. What is the difference?" The captain had ordered the flogger to continue.

"He refuses to die, they say," Polly told her.

Another week went by. She did not dare to visit. Polly told her that he did not speak or move; he took no food or drink.

Her belly had popped out and she almost laughed at the easing of the captain's features when he saw it the first night. He said nothing.

His mood was sombre but steady. He had lost the frenzy of the flogging days. Yet he handed out punishments more than before to his men and the felons alike, though the felons fared worse.

One morning she heard a commotion on the deck and went to where she could survey the scene. A convict girl she barely knew was in the stocks, being shorn of her hair. Later in chains and neck yoke, she was marched up to the poop deck, where the captain stood eye-to-eye with her. Elizabeth saw him striding back to the great cabin with a nasty look of satisfaction on his face.

When he took her now, she kept waiting for him to hurt her. Mostly he did not. A sudden push or pinch occasionally. Once, he held her face hard within his hand. She looked past him. She made no sound.

One night, a convict girl who had been whored and beaten jumped overboard. The watch saw her go, so there was no doubt.

"Good riddance," the captain said when he heard.

Polly heard this from Mrs Silver, who was shocked. Elizabeth noticed that the captain seemed to dine only with the first officer and the mate now. Chains were checked and repaired more often. Guards at night were doubled. He had less time to monitor her and less concern about her conversing with Polly.

Once, when the captain was overseeing a change in the rigging, she told Simmons to bring Meg to the sleeping cabin. He raised his eyebrows. She felt a stab of fear but told herself to think clearly – the captain would not beat or kill her now. But would Simmons suffer?

"Will you inform on me to the captain, Simmons? Will someone else? Will you be punished?"

"I don't believe there will be any need to report a conversation between relatives about your condition, Miss. No one will see your cousin here coming or going. I'll make sure of that."

"Thank you, Simmons. I would not manage here without you, don't you know?"

Meg stared at her belly. "Will he let you keep it?" she asked.

"Yes. He is pleased – in a way. Do you know how James is?"

"What do you care?"

"Please, Meg. I cannot bear what has been done to him. I did visit him."

Meg stared. "You? You took him the brandy? We thought it was Connor, who works for the doctor. He hasn't denied it to us."

Elizabeth sighed. She could hardly blame the poor lad, who was despised by both the convicts and the sailors as the plaything of the macabre surgeon. "Can I send something to James, through you or one of the men?"

"He is near death – he cannot eat or speak. Shanahan, who got one hundred only, has come back down to the hold and he's not the same. He screams at night and can hardly walk. His back is wrecked, they say. James is better off dead."

"Can you tell me who can take something to James?"

"Won't the captain kill you?"

"Not now that I have his child – and we cannot let one of the officers or crew know."

"Listen to you. How dare you pretend to speak like my countrywoman. You're practically an Englishwoman now."

"Oh, Meg."

"You spend your days talking to the ladies and the officers. What would you know? I'll wager that when we reach the colony, if we ever do, you will get some big house with servants and all, and I will break my hands scrubbing for some English brutes. I want to go back below now."

"I will do all I can for you – you know that, Meg." Elizabeth pressed more food on her to take below.

Meg said, "If the captain does not dash us on the rocks or sink us below these waves. Does he know where he is going? Is he a demon leading us to our graves?"

Elizabeth stared and shook her head. "He knows well what he is doing. He has sailed over the known world, and the one thing he will never do is lose a ship. Never fear, Meg. Tell the others to rest easy now and to stop spreading tales of woe."

Yet, in the next weeks, they passed through such steep seas that it took all Elizabeth's courage and sense to stop herself from complaining along with the ladies, whose shrieks she could hear. It was so wet on deck that Polly could not visit. Each morning, Elizabeth rubbed the window clear and gazed at the sea. When the sun came out, the water glistened and sparkled in colours of mauve, blue and silver-grey. It was beautiful in an eerie way. She pictured fairy people and seals living below in ice castles. What was the story she had heard once about the seal and the maiden? She wished someone on the ship would sing the old Irish songs or tell some tales. Perhaps someone did, below among the felons.

One evening, when the captain came in to change his clothes, she was staring into the waves and singing softly.

"What do you think of this world of water, Elizabeth?"

"It is beautiful. It calls to mind stories I heard as a child, sir."

"You are not fearful?"

"No, sir, I know you will steer us out of this with your maps that have those lines up and across them. How do you know which line you are on? Is it by the stars?"

"By the instruments and the stars. The stars here are different, though some are recorded. I have not time to tell you and you would not understand."

"No, sir. I am glad there are the metal things you hold that tell you so much."

He grunted, a little amused. "We are not lost, whatever the silly women in the salon may think."

"I know, sir. It is an adventure to see these sights that hardly any folk have seen."

He nodded. "Take care on the deck. Take the arm of the steward or a sailor, or at least ask them to walk beside you if you cross the deck."

One night, when he came in late, he had been drinking more than usual. He pushed her aside to take up most of the bed.

"Shall I go next door, sir?"

"No. Any woman is better than none even if she is an Irish convict whore as stupid as a pig in the peat."

Elizabeth held her tongue, though suddenly there was a heavy feeling in her stomach and a soreness at her throat.

He put his hands on her belly, feeling the swelling. She wished he were friendlier; she might have told him to wait for the movement that came so often now.

He said roughly, "What a joke life is. The one child I have is from an Irish convict whore."

Her spirit flared. "Well, sir, at least I am white. I dare say you sampled plenty of black and yellow heathens. Your child has a white Christian mother, and not so stupid, neither."

He laughed and put his head near her belly. She thought he had fallen asleep, but after a time the baby kicked and he lifted his head, his hand feeling the movement.

"Ha. It is strong."

"Yes, sir. More and more vigorous it is."

"Probably a boy."

Her eyes shone. "Yes." She dared to ask, "Sir, what sort of life can he have in New South Wales?"

"If it's a boy, I will pay to bring him home to England to attend the Naval College, to become an officer."

She knew she had no say in it, but she hoped the boy would not be taken too soon. "That would be a great life and a good position, sir."

"I'll not leave him fatherless. Or you destitute. Did you not know that?"

She barely realised that she was weeping with relief. He held her more gently than in the past weeks.

A little later, he said, "I saw Brannan. He takes his time still. I told him you are carrying my child. He cursed me with his black eyes, damn him. He can no longer speak; he barely raised his head. I could almost admire his tenacity."

It took much effort to keep her face impassive. She lowered her eyes. She felt a rush of pride in James – *he has given you the evil eye, sir, and you did not even know. It may not be soon, but you can be sure that some evil will befall you. He has a stronger will, a freer spirit and the power of the dying, and you have done the killing of the devil.* She would mourn again for James once the captain had fallen asleep or sent her away.

Three weeks more the poor man had suffered. How long could he last? She wished for death to take him – that was evil and godless of her, but why should he keep half-living in such pain? Apart from pleasing Captain Dennett, there was no purpose in his ghastly half-life. She thought again of the Defenders' call, *Death or Liberty*; it always seemed to her a frightening, desperate motto. James believed it and was dying for it. She admired his flicker of defiance, of strength, of pride, but she prayed he could let it go. He had made his name now, his legend, among the heroes back home. Only the captain wanted him to linger as a senseless creature.

The captain examined her face and then looked away. "The surgeon is no use to the sick convicts. What do you hear about him?"

"Sir?"

"What do the women say about the lad he keeps in the gun room? Has it been the same lad for the whole voyage? They say he makes the poor boy carry his doings – won't use the heads, filthy creature."

She said, "I believe the womenfolk are sorry for the lad spending all his time with the doctor."

"Why are they sorry?"

"The doctor being such an unnatural man, sir, and so morose, and I fear cruel, too."

"Hmm. Unnatural he is. Never showed interest in the females, did he?"

"I believe not, sir."

"When he saw you first, he showed no attraction?"

"I couldn't tell, sir."

"He showed no interest in the respectable Portuguese girls at Rio. I despise such men. Ships can be poisoned by them."

"Poisoned, sir?"

"Morally poisoned. I don't mean he gives out bad potions. I suppose he knows his medicine – though he shies away from surgery more than any doctor I've seen. He has taken a set against me. He found the floggings disturbing."

"He didn't disapprove at the time, sir."

"No, he didn't, and he took little care to supervise. I had to seek him out to tell me if the men could survive more lashes. He always said yes whether he looked at them carefully or not. But now he holds a grudge against me for the deaths; he thinks he may get the blame, that it will dirty his record. But if he thinks he will get the better of me, he is even more of a fool than I thought."

"Yes, sir. You will be believed and not him, sir."

He nodded. "If he fights me, he'll be finished in government ships – in any ships."

*

The winds whipped around them day and night and blew the ship fast through high mountainous seas. When she managed to walk slowly to see Polly, she found her agog with stories.

"An officer is confined by the captain. Another man has been promoted in his place. He was in…oh, whatever they say for disobedient."

"Insubordinate," Elizabeth said.

"Yes. I hope my Mr Fordham will not be demoted. I could get thrown below after all these months."

"If anything happens, I will ask to have you with me."

"I would be pleased to be your servant, Bessie."

Elizabeth was taken aback. "No, my companion, Polly. I'm sure Mr Fordham will keep his position. He is obedient and dutiful, is he not?"

Next morning, the surgeon's boy knocked on the cabin door. He said she was wanted in the medical room.

Could the surgeon have heard of the captain's doubts about him, or of what she had said? She wondered for a second why Meg was walking on the lower deck and loitering near the rail. Then her heart tensed. She was not surprised to find the medical room empty and the surgeon nowhere to be seen. In moments, Meg was at the door. The boy ushered her in and stood outside the door on guard.

Elizabeth said softly, "He's gone? When? Were you there?"

"Last night," Meg said. "No. How could I be? I was chained below. We heard nothing till the word went around at muster that his body was thrown overboard this morning before dawn."

Elizabeth felt her pulse race. "With no prayers?"

"No. Nothing."

Their tears were falling. Elizabeth vowed to pray for him; she would say all the prayers she could recall. He must surely go to the angels. He had suffered enough. Thirty days since his first three hundred lashes. It was like a story from the gospels. She reached for Meg's hand. "He has no more suffering, Meg."

"But no prayers, not even the English ones. That's your devil of a captain. How can you stay with him? Bear his child? Is it his?"

"You know it is. And you know I have no choice."

"You made a choice. You tried your hardest to get him."

Elizabeth shook with sobs, still mostly for James, though a little for herself, Meg's eyes were so fierce and full of contempt. "Meg, this life is too hard to have hatred between us. Who was there when James was thrown overboard?"

"I don't know. Not all the officers."

"Did you hear more of how he died?"

"He finally stopped breathing. He had not spoken for weeks, had not eaten or moved."

Was the captain not there at the burial? He would have been. "Meg, I will do all I can for you in the colony. Don't speak against the captain to anyone. The officers and sailors are listening everywhere, day and night."

The captain ordered Simmons to keep the young cat they had brought on board in Rio up in their quarters once the rats bred another generation in the warmer weather. Elizabeth was glad not only to deter the rats but to play with the lively cat, throwing a ball of twine for it and having it sit warm in her lap. The captain half-smiled to see how fond of it she became.

The sun was hotter now. The days were brighter and, though the wind still blew, she could walk on deck. She felt the child kicking and swimming inside. A child of the sea.

The captain said they were near to the colony.

When she heard the shout, "Land ahoy", she rushed up to the deck, but the coast was far off, and they did not approach it. Still, it was comforting to her that they followed the coastline.

The captain had shown her their route on the map some time back at Rio, and one morning, she went into the great cabin when no one was there and looked at the globe again. On the globe, the coast looked different from what she could see in the distance.

That night she asked gently, "Sir, will we reach our port in a few days?"

He turned to her. "It will be some days yet. We have but reached a landmark we must pass on our way to Port Jackson. This coast is a help to our steering. We will not stop. You are not tired of the ship, or feeling unwell?"

"No, sir." How could she not be sick near to death of this ship, this cabin, this master? Yet the creaking and rhythms of the vessel, the rolling and roaring of the sea, the space, winds and birds of the sky were friends now, and she knew that she would miss them.

A week later he told her that they would reach their port in two days.

10 Sydney Town

Port Jackson, Sydney, May, 1797

She watched the land come into view. He was up on the bridge and saw her standing and looking at the coast. When they came closer to shore later in the day, she saw pretty coves and beaches and vast forests of strange, wild trees.

As they sailed into Port Jackson, she was delighted by the hills, woods and beaches. But then they came closer, and she saw the settlement. Most of it looked rough and poor, with none of the grace of Rio. She told herself it was but a young town, barely settled yet. One or two large buildings reassured her. It was a relief too that the few natives she sighted were wearing some clothes and seemed tame.

The captain had told her that liquor was used in place of money, for there was neither coin nor note yet. But, despite his warning, when she went ashore she felt revolted by the drunkards lurching about, women too, and she could not help but feel a little afraid, recalling the fights among drunken tinkers and such near the canal in Dublin Town. She knew she was to stay on the ship for the first nights but in the day, she could walk ashore with Polly and a sailor to guard them. To stand on hard ground felt so strange, yet welcome, even more than at Rio. So much had come to pass. A transformation of herself, a gamble with her soul. A lifetime with the captain – an outbreak of passion, and then a cooling and a promise. And James killed.

*

A few days after she had been settled in the house he purchased, the captain said that he had important news to tell her. "I will need to sail on, while you will live here. The governor understands our liaison. Several of his officers have set up with convict women. He will see the need to expedite a pardon for you."

She said quickly. "Is it a pardon he would grant for the likes of me, sir?"

He half-smiled. "If not for you, then for whom, Bess? You are the mother of the captain's child. If all goes well with the babe, I expect the governor will see fit to pardon you quite soon. Indeed, I will request that he do so."

"Thank you, sir."

"Why, girl, surely you understood that I would remove the stain from my son or even my daughter?"

"I hoped so, sir, but I know nought of such things. Sir, will you await the birth of our son?"

His face turned sombre. "I almost – nay, I wish I could, Bess."

She stared at him. There was no artifice in her look of sorrow. "Sir, I wanted you to be here. You would have liked to see the infant."

He nodded and kept her gaze. In such moments, what she felt was more than gratitude. If they had met in some other way, if she were not a convict, what would she have felt for him?

She guessed the answer, but she had to know. "Sir, will you return to New South Wales?"

"I very much doubt it."

She felt her body slump. She had no heart to sit up straight. He would have no reason to return so far for so little profit.

He sat beside her and took her hand. "Sometimes I wish things could be different in the future but there is little chance of that. You have played your part well, Bess."

She glanced quickly at him. "Thank you, sir. I will always be grateful to you for noticing me, sir."

He laughed gently. "Only a blind fool would not have noticed you. In this place, Bess, you could do very well. After a time, you could marry. Try to marry well. My son will remain mine and must not be mistreated or poorly trained by your husband. Promise me that."

"Oh, yes, sir. I could not abide seeing a child mistreated."

He nodded. "I know. It is not your heart that I doubt, but your inexperience. Be careful of men who court you. I will provide some money for you and the child, and that will make you a woman whom men will pursue; many would pursue you for your beauty, but more will seek you for your property. Be wary. Do not be fooled by fine words or manners. Inquire about the past of each suitor and about his prospects."

"Yes, sir."

He stroked her face. She wondered for an instant if he might send for her, want her back in Ireland, but then of course there was his wife.

He stood up and his face lost the gentler look. "There is to be an inquiry here into the deaths on the voyage. And the surgeon has made a complaint about the floggings, as I feared he would."

She looked up. So, the English government cared about the deaths. She felt surprised and then relieved. "Who will inquire? Who will decide?"

"The governor and the senior judge in the colony will preside over the inquiry and other officials will take part."

"Is this done for all the convict voyages, sir?"

He looked sharply at her. "Sometimes your tone and your questions…" he stopped and looked away. He walked to the window, and she could not see his face. "No, it is not done after all voyages. Some earlier convict fleets had many deaths. Most of the deaths on the *Britannia* happened after the administration of punishment. It seems that the English parliament and the colonial secretary have ideas about how to treat convicts – but I wager they have no idea of how hard it is to control felons, hordes of them, for months. There will be many questions. It is tiring even to think of it, after such a voyage, I would wish for some rest and some tranquillity." He bowed his head.

Sorry for himself – but not sorry for the dead like James.

She said quietly, "Is it like a court, sir, will you have a lawyer to speak for you?"

"I will speak for myself. I need no lawyer."

She kept her head inclined respectfully. So, he was the accused. He had to answer for those floggings, and the deaths. She felt a wave of jubilation. He was the bad one now. He would be recorded as a killer, or a cruel master at the least. He would be known always as the killer of James and the rest.

There was some justice in God's world, even in this forgotten, desperate corner. The English were not prepared to ignore these deaths of Irish convicts.

Yet, what would Dennett's disgrace mean for her? Would she lose any respect that might have been offered to her as the captain's woman and the mother of his child? She might be despised all the more, by the English as well as her countrymen. Would he lose his ship? Would he suffer some punishment?

"Sir, what could the governor and court do against you if they do not accept your words?"

He turned back to her, his face dark. "I could lose my command. And it would be completely unjust. I delivered almost all my consignment of convicts safely to their prison. The court will not decide to imprison me, neither here nor in England, if that's what you are worrying about. That would only encourage convicts to mutiny. Governor Hunter will write a report to the colonial secretary and will probably recommend more officers to maintain order on the convict ships. Then the colonial secretary will issue instructions."

Might he establish some rules about flogging, she wondered. She said nothing. It struck her that the surgeon's complaint was merely a spur to this inquiry or an additional piece of information for the governor and his judge.

He spoke on. "Hunter, at least, has had experience of convict ships. He will appreciate the need for severity."

She looked down. He expected some assent or a nod but she could not give it. She wanted to thank Governor Hunter for caring about the convicts. She wished she could tell him what she knew. But she would be the last one asked.

The captain stood up straighter. "I have the support of the officers and crew, of course. And some of the convicts. Your cousin Margaret I will call as a witness if you think she has the sense to say the right thing. I will do my best for her afterwards. What is the other name she goes by, or her man's name? We will call her that, not your name, to avoid confusion or the suspicion that she is too close to me. I alone will question her, and only on things she knows. I will make it clear to the hearing that she spent her voyage in the hold, not with you or the officers. What is her temperament, her sense?"

"Sir, she is wilful and not always moderate. She does not feel kindly toward me, but she is not a fool, and she will grasp this opportunity to do some good for herself. She will follow your lead if it is clear to her."

"Good. I shall prepare her the day before. She can have a good assignment or a land grant with her fellow."

Elizabeth wondered what he hoped Meg would say. That he had not punished the women unduly? That the girl who leapt into the sea had been mad from the start?

He said, "I will ask her to verify that I fed the convicts and gave them proper care. I won't ask her about the punishments. No doubt she was angered by that, perhaps especially by the punishment of the women."

"Yes, sir, I would think she was."

When he returned from the enquiry the first night, the captain seemed less sure than when he had set out. It almost amused her to see the change in him, the worry lining his face and the fury stiffening his figure. He had never been the one accused before. From his angry answers to her queries, she pieced together how the surgeon had described the floggings. How he pretended that he had always been against such punishment, but Captain Dennett had insisted, Captain Dennett had gone too far. Anger rose in her against the doctor; she recalled the glint of pleasure in his eye that day on the deck after he had watched the flogging. His own guilt, his own negligence and his own cruelty were worse than the captain's – he had been excited and glad, whereas the captain had been angry and determined, not cold-hearted like the surgeon. The captain ordered such punishment for the sake of the ship, cruel though those long floggings were.

In their parlour, the captain paced furiously and threw rum down his throat. She knew he would tell her; he couldn't help himself, thank goodness. It was not long till pity for him was stronger in her than she expected.

You killed James and the others, she thought, yet she could picture him in the court room, threatened, facing a man whose power over him could ruin him, stop him sailing, take his ship, imprison him. How could pity not flood her heart? She remembered standing in the dock in Dublin County Court as if it were an hour ago. She would never forget it. That man sitting high above you had the power to kill or gaol you. A man so far away, who did not know you, who did not care about you, whose loyalty was to the Crown and to the laws and to the wealth they protected. Her Da had been right: the world ran on money; without it, you were nothing. The captain had some money and he worked for men with vast amounts; would that save him? She listened while he ranted of how he had demolished the surgeon's claims and countered the blackguard's evidence with statements of support from the mate and the officers, how tomorrow he would question the felons and even they would support him.

"You will prevail, sir." She poured him some tea.

He gave her a surprised look. Whether because it was not in doubt, or because she dared to offer comfort, she could not tell.

He sat down. "My God, if they don't rule in my favour, I'll wring that so-called surgeon's neck."

She looked down and said nothing. Were all men the same then? Ready to stamp out anyone who got in their way? He sounded like the savage men she had heard raving in the Dublin gaol.

"Bess, I'm too old to start again and too old for pirating. I must win. I will, of course." He stood and paced once more. "Hunter is a sensible man. He knows that the authority of the captain must be maintained, and that the convicts must be punished and stopped from mutiny. Whenever I utter the word 'mutiny', he practically nods at me. Indeed, he remarked that a ship full of Irishmen is every captain's nightmare." She glanced at him under her lashes, but he did not look at her. "I will convince them all tomorrow, even the chaplain." He gulped his tea and looked at her. "Hunter does not want to damage the reputation of a fleet ship captain, or to suggest that convicts should not be punished when they disobey or threaten rebellion. There is fear of rebellion here too – the numbers of convicts, the small force of soldiers. He will decide in my favour. He will reprimand the surgeon."

"You are right, sir."

The next evening, she gleaned that Margaret had done well. The morning afterwards, Meg came to see her, dying to talk about it. She drew quite a picture of the court – less formal than the Dublin one – and of the grand way the captain spoke, like a lord, for hours.

But that night and the two after, while awaiting the judgement, the captain slept badly. He had nightmares that Elizabeth couldn't fathom, shouting and flailing his arms and then whimpering. Was he back in his boyhood? She held him, and he settled. In the morning, he awoke in her arms and buried his head in her breast, his hand on the babe in her belly.

"At least we have a child, Bess. This hellish voyage was worth it for him – and for you."

She felt a smile break over her face. "It was, sir. I never thought I would think so, but I am glad to have the child and to have been with you." *Even if I wish you had left James alone*, she thought.

"Are you glad, Bess? I think you are. You have a good heart." He held her close. "You have been a loyal and considerate ship wife. I cannot say I ever had a better."

She stared. It was a compliment, but such a one. She swallowed. "Thank you, sir, for taking care of me on the voyage, and now."

"You will receive a pardon a short time after the child is born. You will need to go to the Office of the Superintendent of Convicts to collect the Certificate of Pardon." He smiled.

"Sir, I am so grateful. A pardon will mean so much. I can send word home that I am pardoned. My poor mother and my sisters – it will mean the world to them. And to my father." Tears were running down her face.

After the judgement, the captain met the mate and the officers. It was not till the evening that she saw him. From his posture, she knew it was all right, though as he threw himself on the sofa, there was still strain in his face. He had won, but Hunter had criticised the number of floggings. So, she thought, the governor has some sense and some decency. The surgeon had been criticised much more; quite right, she agreed aloud.

The captain said he would depart, once the ship was repaired. She drew a breath.

He gave her a kind look. "I will hear the news when a ship comes up from Sydney to Madras. I stay there for a time. I hope, I feel sure, it is a boy. I will provide for you and him, Bess." He stroked her cheek and held her swollen belly. "I wish I could see the babe."

She smiled. It was of course the baby he wished to help.

He said, "I have asked the lieutenant to make sure that Mrs Silver or other ladies attend you when the child is to be born. And you have Margaret and the officer's girl."

*

When her time came in late August, earlier than she expected, the servant girl was with her. Mrs Silver, Meg and Polly arrived quickly. The pains came upon her so hard she was amazed, but she endured them. The moment the babe slid out, she called, "Is it a boy?" She would love any child, but the captain might ignore a daughter, whatever he'd promised.

Her healthy son had her smiling. He cried and then suckled as if he knew how to get on with life.

A few hours later, Polly came in with a flushed face.

"Elizabeth, the captain is here. He is asking to see you."

Elizabeth stirred and sat up. "I will show him his son."

She expected him to look first at the child and pay little attention to her. She was surprised when he looked only at her, with a soft expression she rarely saw in his eyes. He put a hand on her arm.

"You look well, my dear. Mrs Silver tells me that the birth was swift, without any problems."

She half-smiled. If a birth was ever without the problem of pain, she had never heard so. "Look at our beautiful son."

He reached for the child. "If only I could stay to see him grow." He sat in the chair beside her bed, gazing at the infant in his arms. "He shall have my first and last names. I shall remember this first sight of my only son all my days." He met her eyes. "I set sail tomorrow. I can stay no longer."

She nodded. Thank the Virgin that the baby had known when to arrive.

From her bed the next day, she could not see the *Britannia* sail out, though she heard the single firing of the gun announce its departure. She felt some sadness, some relief, and a twinge of fear: fear of the *Britannia* convicts, of the natives, of the soldiers, of being alone in the colony, and of being the only one to care for her child.

*

In her first weeks with little Thomas, she basked in contentment, watching him feed, sleep and look about him with startled blue eyes. To be a mother, to have a warm, strong baby, and the time to look after him – she was not only luckier than a servant, she was luckier than a lady. She had no duties, and no family or social obligations. In a month or so, she would need to make appointments with the managers Captain Dennett had engaged to oversee his properties, but that would not take much of her time and for now, she could play with her little son.

Her bed was soft and high, and the windows were surprisingly large with a view out to the sea. She loved to feed Thomas there in the bright sunny mornings. Almost every morning in this land seemed to be bright and blue-skied. If this was winter, she could not imagine how lovely spring and summer would be. When she had spent almost a week in bed, she felt a restless wish to be moving again, though many ladies spent at least two weeks lying in.

She told the servant girl, Molly, to bring the cradle down to the warm sunny living room. Elizabeth sat for her first breakfast downstairs as a mother, prepared by Sally, the cook she and the captain had chosen – a convict, of course, but one who had a good reputation and had worked for gentry in England and officers in the colony. Who would have believed it? She looked about at her yellow and white wallpaper and her comfortable, finely made wooden table and chairs.

Molly had put a vase of blue and yellow flowers on the table. Elizabeth did not know the name of the blue flowers, which were from her front garden. A convict man, Ben, came to tend it two mornings a week and to bring feed for the cow and chickens kept behind the house. There were shortages of food in Sydney Town, but she had enough at her house for breakfasts. She ate her eggs and bread and drank the tea the captain had left her. He had taught her to enjoy it.

She moved to her front window near Thomas's cradle and sat on the window seat, staring down the street to the sea. Small craft were about the trade and supply of the colony. No foreign ships, nor British visiting ones, at present. Down the street, some officers were strolling, their redcoats bright in the sun. Behind the nearby houses, she could see gardens being tended by convict men. Some other men were painting the window frames of the shop on the corner. A couple of convicts were carrying a load of boxes up the street. She waited to see if they were bound for the shop or a house, but they rounded the corner and out of sight. A servant woman with an empty basket headed down the hill towards the shop.

Thomas woke and murmured. She did not wait for him to cry but picked him up and fed him in the large armchair opposite the window. She gazed at his fair, even features and his dark blue eyes. It was lovely the way babies gazed at you when you fed them. She was amazed again at the rush of love that came with the sudden flood of milk. Had she ever loved a creature as she did this perfect boy? She thanked God for preserving her child despite her sins. There was no fear in her heart except that he might weaken and become sick – she could not bear to lose another. But he was a loud, vigorous, good-sized babe, who held her breast and drank her dry. Perhaps he would be a larger, taller man than his father. She trusted that he had inherited his father's mind and quick understanding. The captain had left them this house, another, and a farm and house in Parramatta. Soon, she would visit them and keep an owner's eye, for her son's sake.

The next week, Mrs Silver came to visit. Polly was now Mrs Silver's maid and accompanied her. Mrs Silver was expecting again. Her husband was working in an office for the government. His skills were rare in the colony. Mrs Silver made a great fuss of little Thomas and was gracious to Elizabeth. Although she would never invite Elizabeth to her evening parties, she respected her as a mother and a sensible woman who had improved herself. Elizabeth felt ever teetering between gratitude and resentment, but what good could the latter do? Better to smile and enjoy Mrs Silver's news and gossip, and to learn from her comments about the respectable folk in the town. More importantly, Elizabeth wanted to ask if Mr Silver would recommend someone to check the management and accounts of Captain Dennett's farm and of the shop she was soon to establish in town. She had a fear of being swindled, now that the captain had gone. She needed to convince her workers that she was more than a convict girl, that she would command them and expect good work. She needed to learn how things should be done at the farm and the shop.

Polly sat a little apart. Mrs Silver did not seem to expect Elizabeth to banish her old friend to the kitchen, but both convict girls knew better than to have a three-way conversation. Polly managed to whisper to Elizabeth before she left that she had met an officer. Elizabeth squeezed her hand and nodded.

Meg did not visit. Elizabeth was not surprised. Meg had never expressed any thanks to Elizabeth or to the captain for the land grant he had arranged for her and her convict man. Elizabeth could not blame her for that. How could Meg ever see the captain as anything but the murderer of James and the others? Yet, Elizabeth wished Meg could have kept a little family feeling for her.

When Meg had arrived to help with the birthing, Elizabeth asked her if Michael was in Sydney Town and if she had heard news of him, the question she had asked everyone from the moment she arrived, except the captain. Meg claimed ignorance. But on a farm out of the town, perhaps she might hear something?

Thomas was but six weeks old when Elizabeth went to see Meg to ask again. She took the nursemaid Sarah with her to hold Thomas for she wanted to work on Meg's man, Sam, who seemed less determined to disappoint her. She took a bottle of the captain's whisky.

As the level went down, Sam narrowed his eyes and said, "If ye have more o' this whisky, girl, I can find your man, to be sure."

He named a public house past Parramatta. "He drinks there all the time. Go on a Saturday in the evening."

"You will not give anyone a hint about my inquiry?" Elizabeth feared that Michael would never go there if he knew she might seek him out.

"No, girl. But I wouldn't hold my hopes up if I were you."

Meg sniffed. "That's right. How could you think he still wants you? He won't even look at you. Can't you understand that we all despise you? You will just make a bigger fool of yourself – and bring more shame to me. Stay in your fine house with your Englishman's bastard."

But, the next Saturday, Elizabeth left the baby with Sarah the nursemaid and set off in a cart, first to Meg's to give Sam another bottle of whisky and then straight on to the public house. She engaged a driver and took her gardener Ben with her for safety on the road and in the pub. She wished she knew an Irish convict who could accompany her, but the captain had set up an English household.

Ben was big and taciturn, a little fearsome, almost unhinged to look at, but she could see that he had suffered beatings and who knew what else. When he bent over to dig or to wash, she had to look away from the scars on his back and his legs. She never tried to talk to him or question him. In the way that her farm convict, John, got on best with cows, Ben got on best with plants. He was a dour man but when she outlined her plan to visit the public house and speak to an old friend, he showed no disdain. His eyes became sad, and she caught a moment of sympathy. Who had he lost?

She said to him, "It is possible that this man will not want to see me, after the captain and all."

Ben nodded. "Your countrymen are not a forgiving lot, ma'am."

His words rang in her head while they bumped along the rough road. What would Michael have heard about her? Would he still want her? Would he remember their times together the way she did? Had he re-thought it all, and changed?

The moment she entered the pub, she saw him, hardly changed in his frame, though a little thinner. She walked slowly to where he sat with three men and two women. His face was lined, redder and less gentle. She swallowed, took a breath and stood facing him with the table between them.

"Michael, it's grand to see that you are alive. You look well. How are you?"

He turned his face away.

She waited. The woman by his side gave her an angry look and grasped Michael's arm.

Silence swept over the whole room. Every eye was upon her, hostile, belittling glares, full of disgust. They knew who she was.

"Michael, can I speak to you?"

"Not now, not ever." He did not turn his face to her. His voice was deeper, his tone unrecognisable. "How could you become such a traitor, such a whore? I wish I'd never set eyes on you."

A large man grabbed her arm and wheeled her around. Her gardener, Ben, faced the man, and he backed away. Ben put his hand on her shoulder and walked her quickly out. She could not see, her eyes were streaming, her head was pounding.

An Irishman's voice shouted, "Get out, you rotten bitch. Show your face in here again, and we'll slash it till your child won't know you."

11 Captain Rhodes

1799

For more than a year after his departure, she heard nothing of Captain Dennett. Then a ship arrived with the news that he had arrived in London safely, avoiding French vessels. Soon after, she was shocked when another ship brought her the news of his death, and letters from his lawyers to the chief justice. It was all she could do not to cry out. His death brought relief mixed with sadness. His health had been weakened by the tropics, the lawyer's letter said. And also due to the *Britannia* voyage to New South Wales, she thought. Had he managed to see his wife? She would never know but she supposed so.

He had written the will in London after he returned from the long voyage back from Port Jackson. The judge's assistant read it out to her. She was impressed at the large sums of money left to the captain's wife, mother, sisters and brothers. She thought there would be a small something for young Thomas, but then she heard the words as if the captain were speaking to them all in his stern, careful voice: "To Elizabeth Rafferty upon whose body I begat a child, fifty pounds a year as long as she shall live."

She drew in breath. He had promised to help her, but she had never expected money for herself alone, or so much, or for life. She blessed him. Who would have thought he had such kindness in him?

The assistant continued. "My lands and houses in New South Wales to the child Thomas Dennett when he reaches his maturity… until then, to Elizabeth Rafferty."

He had bought it all for the child, and for her. He did not even know, when he wrote the will, if the child was still living. But he wanted the child to be rich, a gentleman more or less. And he had acknowledged his name for the child.

But her annuity was conditional: "to be paid as long as Elizabeth Rafferty resides in the colony of New South Wales."

She must be kept out of the way, never be seen by the wife. Her comfort and her child's inheritance would keep her out of the captain of the *Britannia*'s world. The child was to be excluded from her influence and probably also from his father's family. Her heart hardened. She would never tell young Thomas how things were. And then she wondered – had the captain hoped to set eyes on his son at the Naval College? Did he write the will before he knew he was soon to die?

*

Elizabeth put the strongbox in her cupboard and locked it. Profits were steady now; the new girl was getting the knack of closing a sale. But soon the shop would display the last quality goods she had, the remainder of Captain Dennett's gift from Rio. She had supplemented the Rio stock with goods from other visiting ships, but she hoped that she could presently buy more cloth, spice and perfume. Even a whaling ship with native cloth or woven mats would help fill her shelves.

She still felt a moment of excitement every time she locked up the shop. If her father and mother could have seen it – and mean Uncle Peter – why, her shop was bigger than his and soon it would be almost as genteel because ladies of the colony came to her for their cloth, perfume and soap. They knew she had the taste from the Old World, from the big country houses, and she had good cloth brought from Rio, cloth that had not been eaten by vermin but kept with cloves and soaps. She often gave thanks for Mrs Martin's suggestion, the captain's generosity and her own careful choices.

She thought at first that any fool could make a shop a success in Sydney Town. Yet there was much to discover. She realised quickly the importance of displaying her wares to advantage, of keeping superior things back till the others were sold, and of keeping the better goods aside rather than wasting them on a customer without much discernment. She knew she had more knowledge of the different classes of women than most of the other shopkeepers in Sydney; it had been her good fortune and she made use of it.

The captain had made it possible, of course, but she had helped to choose the location of her shop, near to the wharf and hence to supplies and custom from visiting ships – not that there were many, but everyone said that would change. Her shop was not too far from the bigger grain-stores and the government store, so the free settlers did not have to venture into the poorer part of town to buy from her, yet it was also near the small cottages being built near the wharf on the rocky cliffs. It was in one of the better streets of the trading area on the hill above the wharf. The whalers and sailors and, more so, their women found it useful for new supplies of linen and soap or for small gifts. Elizabeth used the upstairs front room as her office-parlour; it gave her a view over the front yard of the shop, of the whole street and down the steep hill to the wharf and the water. She had chosen to plant a garden in the front that added to the prettiness of the building and made it like a cottage that a lady might visit. For the sign above the gate, she had taken pains to consult an ex-convict who was an artist and he had made a very superior sign. She taught herself to read it. Alas, it was beyond her to read much else.

Staffing the shop was difficult. The first apparently suitable girl turned out to be so light-fingered that her pretty voice and smile were worthless. Elizabeth trained another girl, and then another, and sat upstairs listening to their efforts. Exasperated, she rushed downstairs one morning to take over herself when an officer's wife was on the point of walking out. After that, she instructed her girl to call her if the quality came in or if the girl couldn't tell what a person was saying.

Polly would have been so much better, with her quiet voice and her way of lowering her head, but when Mrs Silver snapped her up for her household, Elizabeth could not stand in the way of such a chance, and now Polly had married her officer and was expecting a child.

Meg would only have been good for stocking the shelves, but Meg wanted nothing to do with her. Elizabeth visited her after the dreadful night in the pub with Michael. Meg was not well. She was scrawnier than ever and a bad colour after she lost another baby. Elizabeth took her food and linen, but Meg would not speak to her. What hurt most was that Meg wasn't only closing ranks or copying her friends in attacking Elizabeth; she meant it. It wasn't just the Irish fighting the English or the story of the *Britannia* – Meg felt no love or kinship for Elizabeth.

The English convict women and emancipists in the streets around her shop were the only folk who talked to Elizabeth, apart from all manner of men who tried their luck with her. The closest tavern to her shop was the Sailors' Arms, run by English ex-convict Joan, a big-boned, loud-voiced but kind and clever woman. Elizabeth liked her from the first and found her a good source of news and of hints about handling customers.

It surprised Elizabeth to find that she enjoyed the shop more than the rough house at Vaucluse and the farm at Parramatta. It was picturesque at Vaucluse but windy and secluded. After some visits there, she decided to rent it to a gentleman who was pleased to take a long lease. The farm at Parramatta seemed lonely too. The silence – or rather, the unfamiliar noises – of the country around the farm frightened her. She did not sleep as well there, and she missed the sea and the breezes of Port Jackson. The nearest neighbouring farms were not close enough: what if Thomas had a fever or what if natives appeared? She had purchased a gun just in case, though it had not been needed except to scare some escaping convicts. Now that Thomas was a sturdy two-year-old, what if he wandered and was trampled, or fell, or became lost? She had Sarah the nursemaid but could barely trust her; she was less capable than Meg or the average Irish girl, and less affectionate to Thomas than Elizabeth had expected. It seemed that the girl had never been cuddled or rocked to sleep or played with or told any stories. Elizabeth was shocked to find that, apart from a dour London nursery rhyme, the girl knew only two or three ditties from the public houses.

Labour was a problem in the whole colony. And without the presence of the captain, Elizabeth was not of the class who had the first pick. She had been lucky with her Parramatta farm manager, John. A lad from a farm in England, good with cows, happy in the countryside and not hankering for the town. Gentle enough to get the best from the dairymaid and labourer. Once he found a wife, the farm would be set for a generation.

Elizabeth visited once in a while and enjoyed the carriage ride if the weather was not too hot. On the way, a visit to Mrs Silver enlivened the journey; that lady and her husband had taken up land somewhat closer to Sydney. For Elizabeth, it was a rare visit to a respectable household, and the lady's kind attentions to Thomas were welcome.

In springtime, Elizabeth enjoyed the flowering trees and wildflowers on her own land. She gathered some and dried them to make bundles of decorative bouquets or to fill out lavender bags for the shop. But after the first long stay at the captain's farm in Parramatta, she was happy to leave the draughty house and make her home back in the town. The house the captain had chosen was in a good position and a short walk from her shop.

She thought of Captain Dennett often – how could she not? – she hated him yet she missed his conversation, even his sharp comments, and the way he stared at her, and caressed and praised her. The sound of the whip and the sight of James in the ship's dungeon would never leave her. When she recalled them, she cursed the captain. There was much in that voyage to loathe but she told herself that she had behaved wisely.

She thought so again when she walked to the superintendent's office near the Barracks Prison to receive her pardon. Her decisions on the ship had been right, for her and her baby and any other children she might have, because she had won her freedom.

Little Thomas could barely stay quiet for the short time it took for the superintendent to glance at her and the others and for his man to read their names. She stared at the precious piece of paper; she would need to show it at times in the future, to prove that she was no longer a prisoner. Free – free to return to Ireland. As if she ever could. Captain Dennett's will forbade her, and her son's properties were here. But it was a joy to be free, even in Sydney Town.

*

One sunny morning, Elizabeth stood at her office window to watch a whaling ship sail up the harbour, a big vessel, and prosperous looking. When it drew up at the wharf, she saw the ship's captain, it must be, next to the helmsman. Her aunts would have called him a fine figure of a man. He towered over the sailors. As he called out orders, his moustache gleamed black in the sun.

She often took her morning tea in her garden, but this day she left Thomas with his sulky nursemaid and walked down to the little house opposite the wharf that doubled as the Sailors' Arms tavern. She enjoyed a gossip with Joan, who sold the drinks. Joan was a person of some judgement and the first to know the name and history of arriving ships.

He was Captain Rhodes, an explorer, whaler and trader.

Elizabeth did not linger lest she was accosted by the sailors when they rushed into the pub. She twirled her parasol to avoid catching their eye and walked up the wharf till she was alongside the ship. She stood to look at it, well aware that the captain and officers were on board, supervising the unloading of cargo.

The captain looked straight at her, flourished his hat and bowed. She turned, paused, let him admire her side on and then walked to the sailor overseeing the cargo. She handed him her card, told him to give it to the master, since she was interested in purchasing some goods.

She wasn't surprised when the captain himself came to her shop that afternoon. While the silly girl stammered, Elizabeth swept down the stairs and held out her hand. He bowed, and she saw that he was as handsome and healthy as he had looked in the distance.

He arrived ready to trade but immediately decided to court her. Not for marriage, doubtless, but with more elegance and courtesy than she had ever received from a gentleman. She had been given some attention in the colony by officers and by pardoned convict farmers but Captain Rhodes had style and charm, even when he was only half trying to please. With envy, she wondered what he would be like with young ladies in England who were of his class. His manner acknowledged at once that she was not riff-raff, and she tried to put ladylike touches to her behaviour so that he would think well of her and want to talk with her, not just bed her. Yet she knew that, like any whaler and most sailors, he would not tarry with a common woman he couldn't bed, so she did not hide how much he took her fancy.

He took her straightaway to his ship to show her some merchandise. They stood in his salon, and she smiled, thinking of the *Britannia*. If he had pulled her into his sleeping cabin, she would have laughed and let him have her. But, of course, she kept her poise, and he did not put a finger on her except to hold her hand as she stepped down the stair and onto the wharf. She suggested a drink at Joan's inn to seal the agreement. When he leant close across the narrow table, she let herself pant, felt herself flushing, and let desire fill her eyes.

When they walked back to her house, she took his arm and gave him that look again. There were few people about, just one or two urchins. It struck her that she'd be better off making him wait the way uppity young ladies did, so that he'd not be off with the whores of the docks once he'd had her. On the other hand, it was a worry that he might find a whore he liked. When they reached her door, she allowed him to clasp her tight and kiss her cheek, but then she drew back and said she must go in, and would he come to tea in her garden the next day.

A look of surprise and then amusement swept over his features, and he accepted instantly.

She said softly, "You will hear soon that I have a little son. The son of a ship's captain, but we can talk of that tomorrow."

"You are a widow?"

"He sailed to England with his ship and cargo." She felt like saying yes, a widow in fact if not in law.

"Of course." He smiled. "You live alone with your son?"

"And my servants and the nursemaid."

"Ah, yes." He was still working out her station and her wealth, she could see.

When she walked inside, little Thomas cried out with pleasure. He had eaten his supper and Sarah had washed him and put him in his night clothes. He tottered towards his mother, holding out his arms. She caught him up on her hip and danced about the room with him, singing a lively tune. He liked to bounce on her hip. Songs were what he loved most. She adored his ecstatic face and his little calls as she twirled and stepped. She kept up her pace until the sun set, and then she collapsed in laughter onto the sofa with her little boy.

The next day, Captain Rhodes came to tea and behaved like a gentleman. He played sweetly for a short time with Thomas, and then she sent the child away with Sarah. When she invited the captain to have supper with her that evening, his look turned triumphant and challenging. He was certain she was inviting him to her bed.

As they walked out to the water's edge that night after dinner, he told her of his travels in the Southern Ocean and of the islands he had seen. He never uttered the word "convict". He asked how she had liked the sights of her voyage, and the port of Rio in particular. They recalled the mountains and beaches there. She talked of the water, its beauty.

She turned and looked up at him. "I was convicted of sedition for standing with a crowd outside a burning manor house."

He nodded, his face showing nothing but sympathy.

She raised her head. "I was given a pardon."

He smiled and held her hand in his.

They walked around the cove under the shelter of the hill. The water of the harbour was lapping the shore and the breeze was sweet. There was a sliver of moon. He stopped on the slope where they could look out across the gentle waves. It was entrancing and refreshing to be so close to its surface. She admired him for choosing to stand below the trees on the hill, just where they were hidden from view of the houses.

When he kissed her mouth, she thought he did that better than anyone had, and she knew she'd better not make him wait. It was a decision she never regretted. The first night they were together, she knew she would never want him to go.

1800

A girl – Elizabeth was glad. Thomas was her boy and as the Dennett heir would always be the superior child, whatever children she had after him. So it filled her with joy to imagine playing with her little girl, treasuring her company and finding her a good, rich husband.

Rhodes was not disappointed, she was relieved to see. He visited her that very day and held the babe with enjoyment – excitement even.

"We must get her christened, Lizzie," he said, depositing the infant back in her arms.

She beamed. Did that mean…? She could not ask.

He was always quick to know what others thought. "She will have my name."

Rachel Rhodes. Elizabeth said it over and over in her head. She loved it more than she could love poor Thomas's name. Rachel Rafferty would have sounded pretty, but Rachel Rhodes did not sound Irish. A girl with such a name could pass for a lady.

She had not dared to ask if there were children of his in London or any other country. He talked as if there were not, but she knew better than to question a man, especially one who seemed to be a gentleman. He never said much about his home or his parents except that he was from the south, in Cornwall and, from the odd word, she gathered that he had grown up in the countryside in a house with stairs and servants.

He was young for a captain. He wasn't a Royal Navy officer or an East India man like Dennett, but he had charted lands and presented his findings to the Royal Geographical Society in London. He was learned, perhaps more than Captain Dennett. Elizabeth nodded, thrilled, when he showed her some of his maps of islands and sea routes. She had been told by an officer that Captain Dennett, too, had published an account of some voyages and routes, though he had made no discoveries of new lands.

Rhodes was an explorer and let everyone know it; he was his own best spruiker. Unlike Captain Dennett, he spoke easily and won the confidence and admiration of all who heard him. He had made money, though she noted that he ploughed the money back into business constantly and did not amass property or a backlog of funds. What if he had bad luck, she wondered.

*

"We'll take her to London, the lad too, and show her the world," Robert said, a month later as they walked to the shore in front of Elizabeth's house.

And what will I be? Mrs Rhodes or Mrs Rafferty? She didn't dare ask, of course. It was no surprise that he never mentioned marriage. She presumed he was unmarried since he never spoke of a wife, and, at first, she was relieved that there was no whisper of a fiancée.

She came to see how much he was a law unto himself. Convention seemed to be for others, never for Robert Rhodes. Whalers were like that, even those with book learning. One of his crew, an older man with a strange face and the foreign name of Jorgensen, was a man of learning and wrote books about the places he visited. He was wilder than Robert. She tried to like him, but there was something hidden about him that brought to mind some masters and convicts she had known, so she kept her distance. Robert had no shadow of harshness or shiftiness; he was tough and assured, but true to his word.

She never expected an offer of marriage from him – no doubt he had many English ladies to choose from – but, had he asked, she would have joyfully accepted. Not that a whaler made a good husband, so folks said, for a whaler was too much away, too likely to die or become a cripple, and too fond of liquor and native women. But Robert would be worth the worry and the loneliness. He was such a good man while he was around; he surpassed anyone she had seen, by miles – his looks, his way of treating a woman, his talk, his cheer, his humour. He could drink and talk and laugh all night and still be more exciting than anyone had ever been in her bed. She felt like saying to him one night, "Do you know you're the best man in the colony?" but he might think she had slept with them all when she'd only had an officer and a trader. She liked the idea of being by herself some of the time, so a whaler was not such a bad bet. She had become used to being her own boss. A husband would take all that away, even Robert, though he would be more charming about it than most.

Yet, in the church on the hill above the wharf, when she stood beside him at the christening of their daughter, she ached with the knowledge that they would never marry. Before she met him, she had decided that marriage was not something to wish for, not something that she would ever have. Oh, she could have managed it with any number of local men of different stations in life. She might have made an officer marry her, a young one, or an emancipated convict with a bit of charm. But her money from the captain would then become her husband's. She hated the thought of that. She had earned that money with the pain and labour of her body; she had paid for it with her name, her reputation, and her loneliness. And yet, she would have given it up to marry Robert.

The minister was polite, and pleased with the donation Robert made, but Elizabeth saw the looks he and his assistant gave her. She had left young Thomas at home with the nursemaid, but they remembered his existence, even though Captain Dennett had asked the governor to arrange a baptism quietly without her presence. Now three years later, here she was with another child, another man, and still no wedding. And this time, showing herself off at the church brazenly, not having the sense or politeness to stay away. She met the eyes of the minister. He was happy to baptise her child because Rhodes was the father. He had probably baptised the children that Governor King sired with the convict woman on Norfolk Island. One thing Elizabeth knew for sure was that the convict mother hadn't stood here beside the governor for any christening but had been forced to give her children away to the governor and his wife.

Elizabeth stood up straighter. The churchmen could do their worst to shame her, but she refused to blush. Captain Rhodes had brought her here, and he stood beside her, unashamed.

*

Meg was becoming sicker. Elizabeth visited with food and gifts, but Meg shouted at her to go away. Two weeks later, she visited again, and Sam beckoned her in. Meg was ill in bed, wasted, pale and half-conscious. She did not respond when Elizabeth greeted her but stared coldly and then looked away.

Some days later, Elizabeth went there again. Sam was by Meg's bed. Meg was past speaking. Her dull eyes barely noticed her cousin standing there. Elizabeth offered to stay, to help, but Sam and some other Irish friends said that Meg would not like that.

When Meg died, Elizabeth went to the house with food, but Sam's friends told her not to come to the funeral or the wake. Meg left her meagre possessions to Sam. She did not mention Elizabeth in her will.

Now there was no one who knew how she had felt about James.

*

When the Irish convicts rioted at Parramatta in 1804, she heard talk in Joan's inn and on the streets. What a panic. She hurried home, glad that Rhodes was in Sydney and not sailing in search of whales.

"I will be questioned, I think, Robert," she said, feeling the important one for once. "I half expected some officers to visit my shop." It was a relief that they hadn't and that if they turned up at her home, Rhodes would be with her.

"Why? Do you know some of the escapees?" He spoke urgently but with no disapproval or judgement. "Or did you know their families in Ireland?"

"No, not at all."

"Does the major or the chief justice think you are a sympathiser, that you will help the men – or that you have helped them?"

"No, no." She stared in surprise. "Why, Robert, are you worried for me from the soldiers? I have nought to fear from them. It is my farm and the workers there that I am afeared for; the escapers may steal everything or even burn the place."

"But would they do that to an Irishwoman's farm, to one of their own people?"

She gave a wry smile. "No Irish in the colony think of me as one of their own."

He paused and looked at her with his kind eyes. "I haven't noticed it. Have I been obtuse? Do they refuse to speak to you?"

"Not face to face in a crowd mostly, though some will spit at me, whoever is watching."

"Oh, my dear Lizzie."

"The older ones especially will always call me the captain's whore, and since Irish parents are so good at teaching their children to hate, the young will always condemn me for picking the side of the English."

"Did you really choose to be the possession of the captain? Of course, you didn't, Lizzie."

"Well, not the captain, but I tried to be chosen by an officer or a sailor. I set out to escape the hold."

He nodded. "Anyone might do so. You were hardly choosing to side with the English. Why should other Irish convicts blame you? That is harsh."

"Captain Dennett has the worst name among the Irish."

"Yes, but you were not to blame for his cruelties. I am sure you gave him no help, no information."

She lifted her chin proudly. Thank the Lord she hadn't. "No. He questioned me over and over and I told him nothing. I named no one." She wanted to tell Robert now; it was so long since she had spoken of it, and then only to Meg. "I took water and spirits to James Brannan one night after he had been flogged." She felt a sob rise in her throat; she saw him still. "I slipped past the watch. The captain guessed it was me, but I never told him a word about James."

Rhodes embraced her. "Well, then," he said, "don't some of the Irish here know that you tried to help Brannan?"

"Few would believe it, I fear. There is no one that can attest to it."

"But even so, your farm workers will not be killed. The escapees will merely ask for provisions."

"There are some hard creatures among the escaping convicts. I would like soldiers to guard my place."

"Lizzie, my dear," his black eyes bored into her, still warm with fondness but filled with dismay and disappointment. "How can you contemplate using the guns of British soldiers against your countrymen? I don't think you would do it when it came to the point. You're a kind lass, but to say you are ready to do it... oh, Lizzie!"

"But it is Thomas's birthright and all he has, apart from the house in Sydney."

"He will not prosper if he is known to be a killer of Irishmen."

She faltered, half-convinced.

He took her hand and spoke gently but with a fervour that almost set her shaking. "How could you live with your head held high if these escapees are shot, hanged or sent to Norfolk Island on your word? What threat are they to you? Are not many of them from the battle in Ireland in '98? The Battle of Vinegar Hill is famed, Lizzie; I have heard how brave those Irishmen were. Many of the men in chains in Parramatta fought for their own land and to feed their families."

She collapsed on him in tears. Yet confusion sat in her heart. Wasn't she now a trader, a shop owner and a landowner, so shouldn't she stand with the authorities, even if she was not received anywhere except by ex-convicts made good? Didn't she have to support the soldiers so that the colony would be safe for her and little Rachel?

From the first, her countrymen had not given her the time of day in this colony; she was shunned as the cursed whore of the damned demon Dennett, bearing his devil child. She knew well what they said. How chilled she had felt the first time she went to the Irish pub in Cumberland Street and the whole crowd hushed, and then people turned their heads away. It grew worse after the men from '98 arrived, and the women too. Joan never repeated any of the unpleasant talk, but she told Elizabeth news of Ireland that came from drinkers and traders.

When Elizabeth received a letter from her mother, she rushed in joy to hear it read. But her mother spoke only of so many dead from the fighting, and so many in the gaol. Her own cousins had fought and surrendered. It was much worse than the trouble of Elizabeth's time, her mother said. She heard folk talk in the Sailors' Arms and in the street about heroes executed in Dublin, though she had not recognised the names. She didn't dare enter the other pubs run by her countrymen and women. There she was nought but the traitor of the *Britannia*, the Irishwoman who had betrayed James Brannan, one of the great rebel heroes. She was the whore who had let him be tortured and killed, even after all his kindness to her and his months of protection of her.

She suspected that what Rhodes said was true. The rioters were not likely to come for her or even her property, despite the betrayals they pinned against her chest. They despised her but she was not important enough to be an enemy, a target.

She felt ashamed. If not for Rhodes, she would have become a traitor again.

For Rhodes was proved right. The Parramatta escapees did not harm her workers or burn her property. When they tried to surrender and parley, the soldiers shot them down. When she heard that, horror and sadness flooded through her, and she remembered James, the broken shape of him, the hollowed face, the unseeing eyes. And she was even more grateful to Rhodes.

Soon, he was off to New Zealand, and she didn't see him for two months. Then, after a brief stay with her in Sydney, he was to sail north, and to England. When he said farewell, he lifted her high in the air. "I will be back, Lizzie." He smiled up at her.

Of course, she believed him, or at least she hoped as hard as any woman could.

12 A Voyage with Captain Rhodes

He was true to his word, even if it took him five years. He burst in, grasped her, kissed Rachel and shook Thomas's hand. Later, when the children were in bed, she sat with him in her front garden, looking down the hill at the water.

He said, "A little more whaling up the coast and then next year, will you come to London with me, Lizzie? We'll show the children London Town, and show them off too, eh? Why, Rachel is a beautiful angel and Thomas is a fine young lad."

"But I'm forbidden to step out of the colony," she said, adding with less certainty, "Aren't I? In Captain Dennett's will?"

Robert looked at her. "You have a copy or a summary, have you not? Let me see the paper you have."

They went into her drawing room, and she gave him the pages from her escritoire.

He perused one of them. "No, Lizzie, my darling. You must live in New South Wales, but there is nothing to say you may not go for a visit to other lands. Dead old Dennett can't imprison you here for life."

She wanted to hug him, but she was so relieved she had to sit down. To see London, and with him as her companion and guide. To go there a free woman and almost a lady – wealthy enough to look respectable, even if that was just her clothes and all. And to take young Thomas to his rightful future as a British naval officer.

Robert was laughing. "Lizzie, you didn't tell me the reason for your pardon. How amusing, and what a compliment."

"What reason?" She felt a flash of fear. "Do you mean that Captain Dennett recommended the pardon?"

"Indeed, the pardon states his support. But my dear girl, have you never heard the reason for your pardon?"

She shook her head. " All that official language. I never understand it."

"You will understand these words: 'Elizabeth Rafferty, pardoned for her good behaviour.'"

She burst out laughing. He caught her up and swung her around the room.

*

She stood on the deck of their London-bound ship after the children were asleep. Robert came to stand with her and clasped her waist. She thought again how glad she was not to be pregnant on this voyage. She hoped not to have another child with him until – unless – he returned with her and settled in Sydney. She had no idea if that would ever happen, and there was not much hope of it. He would surely settle on his own land one day. She had never told him her hope or asked about his plans, but ever since Rachel's weaning, he had kept on using the French things that felt so odd inside her, though they seemed to work.

She smiled again at the motion of the ship and the cool breeze off the waves. A voyage with no convicts, no crack of the lash, no clanking of the manacles, and, most of all, no fears for a friend. And no nervous waiting in bed for a man she hardly knew, but who owned her.

She breathed deep. The air was cool, moist, and salty on her face. Her body felt different from on land; she stood with her legs apart, braced against the rolling. The roar and swish of the waves comforted her like a friend. She relished the rare feelings of peace and contentment. Later, she thought of this voyage as the happiest time of her life. Robert was charmed at her steady sea legs, her strong stomach and her love of the ship's motion, the sea, the birds, and the stars. He was surprised by her comprehension of the maps and smiled at her eagerness to look through the telescope. He took time to show young Thomas much about navigation and the running of the ship.

They were to see India. She had no idea of it, though she now knew where it was on the map. When they sailed into Madras, the colours of the sea and sky and mountains, the teeming streets, the grand mansions, the markets of cloth and jewels and spices, she loved it all. Such new smells and sounds, such different people. The women wore wondrously coloured garments and had glittering jewels resting on, or pierced into, their faces.

Robert had friends there, English, and Indian. He took her to a palace where a rajah lived. The women were in a separate wing where she was welcomed and given strange but not unpleasant food and drink. She presumed her skin colour gave her instant status and afforded her courteous treatment even as the unwed companion of Captain Rhodes. The women here seemed not to be like the English or the colonials – so many wives for the one man. It revolted her at first, and then she wondered at it. Did each woman have some power and pleasure, did some have power over the others, did the rajah have favourites and did he change his preference from time to time? Could it be less tiring and restricting than being the one wife of an all-powerful man? Did the first wife welcome the others, rather like some of the Irish gentry with the master's mistresses and servant girls? These wives had comfort and perhaps luxury, but did they have much more status than Irish mistresses and maids? She would never know. Robert might tell her, interested as he was in foreign ways, but she felt ashamed to ask, and she felt constrained to keep him treating her like a lady. She wanted his approval and his affection, not his derision. She must not slip into talking commonly like his fellow whalers, or salaciously as his gentlemen friends probably did.

The gifts the Indian women gave her of cloth and jewellery nearly took her breath away, but she kept her poise and gave thanks in what she hoped was a lady's manner. She guessed that the Indian women knew little of the Irish and thought she was English. What did it matter in the end; she still felt Irish, though her countrymen disowned her.

The next night Robert took her and young Thomas to the house of an important man in the East India Company. Robert introduced the boy as the son of Captain Thomas Dennett. Elizabeth took a breath and hoped that Robert was not being too unconventional. She could not bear to see young Tom slighted.

The gentleman looked at her and said, "Thomas Dennett was a good man and I'm sure he did the right thing by you and the boy, yes?" At her assurances, he smiled at Thomas. "I knew your father. A very good captain and a very good company man. Are you to be a sailor, sir?"

Thomas's face brightened. "Oh yes, sir. I am to go to the Royal Naval College."

Elizabeth gazed at his happy face. She was glad again to see his contentment and his hopeful ambition, yet she could not feel any of his joy or confidence. She hoped his career on the sea would be nothing like his father's and not much like Rhodes'.

Robert's crew was all colours and creeds. There were two from New Zealand, with painted skin, and three from Tahiti. There were Lascars, Indians, Chinamen, and Malays. Elizabeth was not really surprised to see that he treated them all the same, except for promoting and rewarding those most able. He had a great curiosity about other peoples and their beliefs and ways. He sometimes wore native teeth or animal tusks around his neck. This wasn't so unusual for whalers. She presumed he would dress properly in London; she hoped so.

She hardly dared ask him if they would sail near to Ireland.

As they sailed close to England, she wanted to pinch herself. She had tried to imagine it but had little idea of what it would be like. Though summer was near, the air was fresh and the clouds grey. The land looked rich, but not with the soft, deep green of Ireland.

The port was huge. She couldn't stop staring. She was as excited as young Thomas. The size of the ships, the number of them, the grand prows, the crowds of sailors, officers and traders, and travellers too. She could not look for long at the women hanging around the wharf and the pubs or the corners, some of them addled by grog, some of them crippled or disfigured, and some of them so very young.

"You would like to sail round to Dublin Town, Lizzie, would you not?" Robert said casually, a day later. "I have a friend sailing there next week who could take us."

She rushed over to hug him.

So, once his cargo was unloaded, off they sailed. They moored first at Wexford Harbour and had drinks at an inn. She nearly wept to stand on her homeland, to hear the voices, see the green meadows and feel the soft air. The harbour port was like a painting, the town so pretty, the gardens full of flowers, and the hills nearby so like the ones she always remembered. The next day, they sailed on up to Dublin Town. She marvelled at the beauty of the coast.

Though Thomas considered himself thoroughly English and was unimpressed by anything Irish, even he looked at the coast with sparkling eyes. They disembarked at the North Wall, and she shuddered, remembering the day she had arrived there from the Kilmainham gaol. Robert took them to a part of Dublin Town she did not recognise, to an inn she could never have entered in her youth.

The innkeeper called her Mrs Rhodes. She and Robert had decided this was best for appearances and to avoid any problem from the past.

The next day, she walked with Robert and her children to her old house. Would her Ma and Da be there? Any of her sisters? When she stood at the door, she found herself trembling. She knocked. The street was full of people and a few looked familiar but she did not greet them. They stepped around her and her party as if encountering strange gentry.

Her mother opened the small door. She stared in amazement and then smiled with joy. "How can it be? Oh, my love, my Elizabeth, you are so beautiful, so fine. Just like a lady."

Like enough, Ma, she thought, and stopped herself shuddering. They fell into each other's arms, crying and smiling. Then her mother gazed at the children, and she ushered them inside.

How Rachel took to her granny! Thomas was a little less ready to kiss and be sweet, but he was pleased nonetheless at the stream of compliments he received. Her mother did not comment on his pale hair and eyes, so unlike Rachel's or Elizabeth's or Rhodes'. Elizabeth avoided using the child's surname.

Her mother asked about Meg. Elizabeth told of her death from sickness in her chest and of her earlier, happier life on her little patch of land.

She had put a thin gold ring from India on her wedding finger for the journey. She had no idea if such rings were a custom in Ireland now.

Ma whispered softly as Elizabeth helped her put out cups for the tea, "Is it married to him, you are? With his name?"

Elizabeth smiled and gave a nod. She was prepared to lie but could find no voice. Robert would not deny it, and she was past blushing, so her deceit would succeed. Her mother's face lit up.

Her father came in and gave her a grim, sad look. For a moment, she was afraid that he might turn on his heel. He was wizened and grey now. He stood stiffly but relaxed a little once he heard Robert's name and his manner of speech. She wondered if he had feared that Robert was Captain Dennett. Robert held out his hand, the way he did to most men. He introduced himself as a whaler, and her father's face became less hostile. Rhodes complimented him on his beautiful daughter, and Elizabeth drank in her father's relief and her mother's delight.

After the greetings, her father asked about her property and nodded in flushed satisfaction when she explained. She learned that her parents had only heard one letter read, not the many that she had paid for in Sydney. They would have had to pay for a reader, for they would not have asked the priest to read the words of their convicted daughter. Did they not want to hear her news, she thought with resentment and sadness – then she felt relieved. It meant that her family knew even less about her relations with Captain Dennett than she had been prepared to admit in her letters.

But her relief was short-lived for she quickly gathered that her father had been told something of her voyage with Dennett. He hinted that he had not passed it on to her mother or sisters. *Thank God,* she thought, and tried not to tremble. She could not take her eyes off his face. His eyes did not smile at her in the way that she remembered. He made it plain that the talk at the pub had been grisly and angry; the deaths on the *Britannia* were mourned and the floggings loathed, over and over.

Rhodes commiserated with her father and condemned Dennett. "You and I are agreed, I am sure, that the floggers of those early transports were a scourge on the poor of England and Ireland. There are more checks now on the captains and the surgeons. Regarding your battles here, Mr Rafferty, I met some survivors of '98 and their stories of prison time are another terrible scandal. Great men, heroes. Elizabeth told me of a letter from you, ma'am, telling of the members of your family who were lost or injured or imprisoned. My sympathies to you, and to you, sir."

Elizabeth was grateful for Robert's talk, but she could not stop wondering how much Da knew of her life with Dennett. Had he heard her called a whore and a traitor? Even if some folk tempered their words in his presence, he might know. It took all her strength not to weep, fall to her knees and beg him for forgiveness. She could not do such a thing; she could not shame Thomas or frighten Rachel or break her mother's heart. Or her father's, if he did not know her story. Could he ever understand what had led her to be a ship wife, what she had feared and suffered?

Her sister Susan had died giving birth to her first child, who now lived with her sister, Ellen. Elizabeth wept with her mother, and Robert clasped her father's hand. Da leapt up and called a boy in the street to go to Ellen who lived a few houses down. She came with the little ones. To see Ellen's eyes widen at her sister's finery, her sister's husband and children, Elizabeth almost felt a faint upon her.

Robert charmed them all, of course, and produced his gifts of whisky, salt, and soaps to the joy of all the family. He entertained them with his tales of whaling and the high seas. Rachel sat with her granny, full of smiles and whispered chatter.

Elizabeth left gifts of money, port wine and Indian shawls, including a delicate, pretty one for Ellen. She could not tell her family how afraid she had been that they would turn her away. She would not waste time wondering what her mother might have said if she had admitted that she was not a wife, and never likely to be. When she said that the children were christened in the Church of England, her mother smiled wistfully, and her father nodded.

Elizabeth promised more letters, hoping her family might find a reliable reader. She would not embarrass them with promises of money, but she vowed to send it always. Compared to them, she was wealthy, so she would send as much as she could spare for their survival and, she hoped, for small comforts, not merely for the reading of her letters.

"I will commission portraits and send them to you," Robert announced.

His grand gesture set her laughing and everyone was prevented from too much sadness at the parting. Da held her close and she felt him sob, but when he drew back, he smiled at her.

Robert remarked that evening as they strolled down the hill in the shadow of Dublin Castle that he would rather stay in Ireland than return to London. She had no idea why. She knew that he was due in London, and she was not sorry. To stay past the joyous, surprised welcome of her family would have made the parting unbearable.

Little Rachel was happy to have met her Irish relatives, but Thomas was far more excited to be going next to see his Uncle Dennett and family in Suffolk. Robert had written to arrange it. Elizabeth would not go; they did not want to set eyes on her, and it would be unthinkable for Thomas to see her slighted by them. Robert, with his background and aplomb, would be welcome as the stepfather. She hardly dared to hope that they would be kind to the boy; at least they intended to be civil.

When they asked Thomas and Robert to stay, she was both pleased and sad. Mr John Dennett would take the boy to the college with Robert. That would be a fine thing for Thomas.

When Robert brought the lad back to collect his things and to farewell her, she steeled herself. Boys hated blubbering women. How long till she would see him again?

"I'll come to New South Wales, Mother, to see you and my land, when I obtain a commission."

*

Robert's face was serious when he returned from his business meeting some days later. It did not surprise her when he wanted only a small dinner and little ale. But later in their room, he told her what was on his mind. He warned her gently not to be frightened.

"Don't the owners pay you what is needed?" She felt her neck hot with resentment on his behalf.

"Indeed, but so much less, you see, because of the falling oil price; it has cut their profit." He showed no resentment, just a resignation. Had this happened to him before?

"So, will you need to go back to sea straightaway to make more money?"

"If only." He took her hand. "I will not be able to leave London for some time."

She shrugged. What did it matter? She loved exploring the streets and watching the ladies and children in the parks and by the river.

His dark eyes stared into hers. "I will not be able to pay all my debts for the equipment of this past voyage. I am bankrupt."

She sat frozen. What did gentlemen or whalers do when they went bankrupt?

When he said it, she was not completely surprised but it hurt. "I will be detained in debtors' prison, Lizzie." He laughed for a second. "I am a prisoner, too, my girl, though I can't pretend my prison will be fearsome like yours."

"Oh, Robert, it shouldn't happen to *you*. Can't someone speak for you at the trial or make an appeal on your behalf to the lords or whoever?"

He smiled. "There is no trial. Debtors are merely rounded up and marched to confinement."

No trial. She could not comprehend.

"It is a different prison from Newgate. Not really like a prison, more like bad digs."

"Are you guarded by screws – I mean, warders?"

"Well, there is a turnkey, but no beatings and so on."

A gentleman's gaol. She hadn't heard of such a place, but it made sense. Gentlemen looked after their own kind. She was silent for a moment, and then she said so softly that he leaned his head to hear, "No chains?"

He looked shocked. "Of course not. But you weren't chained, Lizzie, surely? Dennett could not have allowed that?"

"Only at the start of the voyage. It is a terrible thing to have chains on, Robert. I will never forget the feeling. I am so glad it will not be done to you." She stroked his hand and then his cheek. "But the sailors? Will they be thrown in a worse prison?"

His face lifted for the first time that evening. "No, no, they will remain free. At least I can ensure that. It is not their debt, not their management, not their loss. They will be paid and free to find another whaleboat."

She stared. "Who will pay their wages?"

"I will, of course, I am their captain."

"But how can you afford to?"

"I have enough to do that."

"You will need to pay them less, Robert, or pay them later when you have recovered your losses."

He sat up straighter. "No. Certainly not."

"But wouldn't it decrease your debt?"

"Some of it, but they risked their skins and their very peace of mind for me. I'll not leave them unrewarded. I'll not go back on my word to them. They will get what they deserve and what they expected. At least I will keep my reputation with my men and those who might sail with me in the future."

Relief swept over her to hear him talk so casually of captaining a ship again. Yet her anger at the sailors rose. "But, Robert, many of the sailors will just drink the money away in the pubs near the docks. Why shouldn't you cut their wages? They will understand. It's more important to look after yourself, to survive."

His face became sterner, and he shook his head. He looked steadily above her, out the window at the cloudy sky. Was he too angry to answer? She had never seen him angry with her.

She said quickly, "How long will you be in prison? How will you get the money to repay?"

He looked across the room at where Rachel was sleeping in her small bed. "It is hard to say how long. I have some other investments. I hope the ones from North America may come in within the next six months. I will raise some funds by selling some of my private effects. I will ask a few friends for help, though I do not expect that they will be able to offer much capital."

Her mind kept turning on his words, six months. What was she to do? How long should she and Rachel stay? Did he plan to remain in England, perhaps never to return to New South Wales?

"Robert, what can I do to help you?" Her stash of saved money, she imagined, would be almost nothing compared to his debts, but she owed him for his kindness to Rachel and for this voyage. She could not sell any land in New South Wales; it belonged to young Thomas.

He drew her into his arms. "You're a good woman, Lizzie. You can visit me with Rachel a few times. But I must arrange a passage for you back to Sydney."

Sadness flooded over her. Was he not so sad to send her off?

Then fear gripped her. "Robert, you will let me take Rachel with me?"

His eyes flashed with a twinkle. "Lizzie, I will not take your greatest joy from you. I would never take away your reason to live."

They embraced. How she would miss the strength of his arms, the weight of his legs, the heat of his skin. The way he spoke of her, as no one else did. "You are a loving, solicitous mother, Lizzie, the only mother for my daughter. And she loves you. I could give Rachel the upbringing of a lady, but that would not be worth her losing you. She can do very well without me, but not without you."

Elizabeth squeezed him till she thought her arms would dissolve.

"In a few years," he went on, "perhaps I will marry a young lady I have visited for some time now in my part of the country. I will always love Rachel, but of course, I will have more children with my wife." He stroked Elizabeth's face and gazed at her with the tenderness and fire that always left her breathless. "I would marry you, Lizzie, if you could live here at least part of your life, if a marriage to me would not leave you and perhaps young Thomas without your legacies from Captain Dennett. That would wreck young Thomas's life. You and I always knew we could not live together except in New South Wales, and that I could not live there all my days." He kissed her. "I will sail to Sydney again, surely."

He did not let her follow him when the men took him. She tried not to wail. His back was so straight as he was marched between the two guards; he was a foot taller than them. She called her farewell calmly and strongly but when his figure turned the corner, she nearly collapsed on the hard stones of the street as Rachel clung to her.

The next day, she felt queasy when she reached the King's Bench Prison, and sicker once she was admitted inside the gate. She walked with Rachel to the door of the rooms where he was. Rachel held her hand tightly while they waited for the thick, heavy door to open. Elizabeth wondered if she should have prepared the little girl more for the horrors within. How to put into words the stench, or the gloom? Rachel knew that her mother had been transported, but Elizabeth had never told the child a word about the gaols in Ireland.

Inside, there was no stench like in the Dublin or Cork gaols. There was furniture. There was a window at eye level. Light and the sun's rays did not merely stripe the room but filled it.

Rachel ran to Robert as he rose from an armchair. He had been reading, and there was a table and chair for his writing. There was a pitcher of something that looked like ale. A lamp on the table awaited the evening. She saw candlesticks on the mantelpiece, for there was even a fire. She had been so hungry to look at Robert that she hadn't noticed at first. A fire! And built ready again for the evening. The room was not chilly. There was a slight feeling of damp, but not of mould. The walls at some recent time had been washed.

She dropped her basket, stepped over to Robert and was engulfed in his embrace. He kept one hand on Rachel, who snuggled into them both.

"You are thinking this is a poor pretence of a prison, Lizzie," he laughed. "I cannot think how you withstood the dark, diseased holes they threw you into, my strong girl. I had not appreciated my Amazon till now."

She felt tears all down her cheeks. She did not know the strange word, Amazon, but she caught his meaning. She could not speak to tell him he was the first who had said any such thing to her. It should not matter now, so long after that year and a half in the gaols she should not need comfort, but it meant so much that he felt that and said that. How did he know?

"I will miss you so much, Robert." She spoke softly so Rachel would not hear.

He sat down and began to eat the meat and wine she set out for him. He had some news for her.

"Lizzie, I have asked Robert Bostock, a ship owner and merchant, to assist you in your business in London while I am in here and to arrange your passage home. You will find him a pleasant fellow, but I must inform you that the source of his profits includes slaves, and I cannot forgive him for that. He is one of those contradictory characters: a man who does evil and yet seems not evil in himself. He has somehow not transformed into a monster even though he has inherited the role of slave dealer from his father. It is probably mainly his business acumen rather than his good nature that leads him to treat the slaves well; if they are healthy, he gets good prices for them. Yet he robs so many suffering souls of their freedom, their country, their family and often their sanity and their lives. He does not see them in the lowest state, when they are sick and broken down from labour on the sugar cane plantations; perhaps this is partly why he does not feel revulsion at his work. He has never been beaten or locked up, and, like most men, cannot imagine how such things feel. I hold out a dim hope that one day he might recognise the horror and pain in those African towns and West Indian plantations and that he will shun the ghastly trade. But I am an optimist, as we all know, and probably, a fool."

Elizabeth smiled. "Probably, but if Mr Bostock is as pleasant as you say, perhaps he will see how cruel his slaving is when he becomes older and has children."

"I fear that few men extend the love they feel for their children to others, let alone to black slaves. And, of course, all the rich in England – the monarch, the bankers, the investors, the factory owners, and shop keepers – are happily sharing the profits of slave traders like Bostock."

Later that evening, Mr Bostock came to visit Rhodes. He was younger than she expected, several years younger than her, she judged. His countenance was pleasant and full of assurance. His look held shrewdness and cleverness rather than open friendliness, but his reserve did not disguise his regard for Rhodes. His suit and boots were of the finest quality, and his bearing, though not military, showed dignity and privilege. He was not as well born as Rhodes, but Elizabeth was not confident that she could place English gentlemen in their correct rank.

Rhodes said, "Bostock, you will not presume that I have been silent to Mrs Rhodes about the nature of your business, that you engage in the evil trade of slaves. I cannot presume to know Mrs Rhodes' mind on these matters, but I suspect that she harbours some pity for creatures in chains, and a lot more understanding of their suffering than most of us."

Elizabeth felt herself flush. She thought of James talking in Kilmainham about the Irish slaves shipped to the Caribbean. This handsome man before her sent slaves there still. It sent a shiver through her. She rarely thought of the devil now, but surely slaves were his business. Young Bostock's eyes glanced at her, still with respect, and without surprise. He knew her background, of course – Rhodes never dissembled and indeed, did not consider her history a disgrace but rather a misfortune. She waited for Mr Bostock to show contempt, but he did not.

Rhodes was saying, "Nonetheless, Mrs Rhodes is not sentimental about business and money. Like you, Robert, she thinks that I am a soft-hearted fool, that I should have kept my money and left my men high and dry. Mrs Rhodes is a businesswoman and runs a flourishing shop and farm in Sydney. You might find that your interests overlap. Lizzie, it may be that Robert can direct you to some goods to buy wholesale and take back with you – good prices, mind you, Bostock." Rhodes flashed the challenging grin he kept for other men when he aimed to influence them, to let them know that he would be watching what they did.

Once again, Elizabeth saw it do its work admirably.

The next day, Mr Bostock assisted her in obtaining some of her allowance from the London office that administered Dennett's bequest. He introduced and addressed her as Mrs Rafferty. She noticed that he continued to use that name for her. It was sensible but losing Rhodes's name left her desolate; it was hard to keep a calm and cheerful manner. She was thankful for the distraction when Mr Bostock took her to some cloth merchants' and milliners' establishments. He introduced her to the managers, and she not only made some purchases but also arranged to receive instruction the following day in the latest fashion of trimming hats. Her customers in Sydney Town would benefit, and so would she. Then Mr Bostock led her on a tour of some warehouses at the East India dock. He mentioned Captain Dennett once when they passed an East India office.

"You know, Mrs Rafferty, Captain Dennett's cargoes were exceptionally fine. His profits on the return voyage from New South Wales were large. His name will be a most useful recommendation for your son, ma'am, when the lad seeks a commission in the navy or a position on a merchant ship."

Since his family was in Liverpool, Mr Bostock could not stay long in London. He discussed the purchase of her passage, explaining the advantages of the ship he recommended. She tried to pay the full cost, but he insisted on adding more to give her a superior cabin. He asked if her business in Sydney was in the name of Rafferty and, upon her answer, bought her passage in that name.

The day before Bostock was to depart for Liverpool, he visited Rhodes with Elizabeth and asked if he might introduce to her Mr Robert Stewart Walker, a young man of his acquaintance who would be the second officer on the ship on which Elizabeth and Rachel were to travel. Walker could assist Mrs Rafferty during the voyage and at embarkation and disembarkation. His support would add to the safety and comfort of the lady and her child.

Rhodes nodded and gave his thanks, though there was a hesitation both his hearers noticed.

Bostock said, "He is a gentleman, Rhodes. A Scot, a quiet Presbyterian, very proper."

Rhodes grinned for a second. "My poor Lizzie, he sounds tedious."

Bostock smiled. "I doubt that. Actually, his manners are genteel and pleasing. He is a good negotiator and has concluded some business for me very effectively."

Rhodes shot his friend a dark look. "He is not too effective and pleasing, I hope."

"He is quite young," Bostock said evenly. "More than a few years younger than me."

Ah, also younger than me, Elizabeth thought wryly, and unlikely to be attracted to an older lady with a child. But it amused and touched her that Rhodes did not look relieved.

The last time she saw Rhodes, she stayed till the evening. They put Rachel to sleep on the sofa and later withdrew into the small room where Rhodes slept. Though the bed was narrow and hard and the pillow flat and scratchy, Elizabeth knew she would remember that hour again and again all her life. They closed the threadbare curtain and, with no candle, undressed completely. In the dimness, they gazed at each other and stood beside the bed, embracing and then locked together. He lifted her, and she wrapped her legs around him. It was all she could do not to cry out, so she had to pant and whisper. When they moved down onto the bed, still entwined, she wanted to tell him she loved him. She did not expect him to have any such impulse.

"How I will miss you, Robert. I have never known a man like you before, and I think I never shall again."

"I doubt I shall see your like either, my dear Lizzie." He kissed her again and again.

"Dearest Robert."

"Lizzie, I will never forget you. Think of our good times. I will often."

His warm smile cheered her. He was the happiest man she had ever seen, happy even in a prison. And he called *her* strong. She must remember his spirit, always.

He said tenderly, "I know you will take care of yourself and Rachel, but I wish you luck, too. And every good fortune."

As she walked back to her rooms with Rachel at dawn, a plain, inexpensive shawl covering her head and upper body, she dodged and brushed aside any cadgers and loiterers, with her face downcast and with the occasional rough word. Her dress was cheap, and Rachel's too; she took care in this part of London to look unworthy of a thief's notice.

When she reached their rooms and settled Rachel to sleep again, she sat next to her, soothed by the child's even breathing. She quelled her tears for Robert and remembered stifling hot days in Sydney when he had taken her and the children bathing in the harbour coves. He could swim a long way out and then breast the wave back to the shore, a skill he had learned from natives or islanders. He tried to teach young Thomas, and though the boy was a little fearful, he learned to swim. At first, he was inclined to dismiss Robert's whaler experience and hence his advice – thinking it of no account for one who was to become an officer in the Royal Navy – so Elizabeth was intrigued to watch Rhodes persuading the boy.

"A sailor must be able to stay afloat and swim back to his boat if the need arises, Tom," Robert told him. "I have seen many a man swept overboard and under the sea in a minute, but the men who can swim and float have a chance of survival. Think of battles, not just ordinary voyages. The chances of being thrown overboard as an officer are not insignificant."

To Elizabeth's surprise, he taught Rachel, too, and she became a darting, fishlike little figure that Elizabeth watched with joy and fright. But Rhodes never let the child swim without him, so her mother's fear was but a fancy.

On the hottest nights, he pulled Elizabeth away from the sleeping children and the nursery maid and took her walking to the deserted cove around from their hill. When he stripped off his clothes, she gasped and laughed.

"Come on, Lizzie. No one will see you – well, except a native or two, but they will not disapprove."

She looked about in alarm. On several occasions, Rhodes had laughed at her fear and wariness of the natives. It was all very well for him; he could not know the fear of a woman. Besides, he was a whaler who had seen all kinds of strange Indians in different corners of the world. He loved to note how different and weird they were. Even their ceremonies and how they ate fascinated him. Elizabeth marvelled at how he did not seem to shrink from the natives or to fear them.

She plunged into the cool water. He taught her how to swim too, and she would always thank him, even if she would swim but rarely. It was like being another creature. She laughed with delight.

He said, "Did you swim in Ireland, or go into the water at least?"

"Oh no. I was never near the sea, and it is so cold."

"No colder than Cornwall, I would guess," he laughed.

"Did you swim there when you were a child?"

"Yes, Lizzie, with the children of the fishermen, and in more recent times too."

"But ladies do not swim there, do they?"

"No. Only the young daughters of the fishermen."

"I went into the water at Rio de Janeiro," she said, with a quick glance at him. What would he think?

"With the natives or the other women?"

She flushed.

"With Dennett!"

"I had a little clothing on," she protested. "Well, at first."

He laughed again. "Ah, the beaches of Rio. Unforgettable, aren't they? So, you and old dog Dennett frolicked in the sea!"

He clasped her by the waist and whirled her around on the sand.

They embraced and more in the water. She should have felt ashamed, but she was exhilarated. The salty water billowed and rocked about them, so cool and clean. She squeezed the water out of her long hair and let it blow in the night breeze while they walked home.

"You will be able to take Rachel into the water if I am away," he said.

But she knew she would be too afraid without him, of the creatures of the sea, of the elusive natives and of the gossip of the town.

The next morning, Mr Bostock introduced her to Mr Robert Stewart Walker. He did look young, and remarkably refined. He was more of a gentleman than Mr Bostock, she fancied, despite his less expensive and less fashionable clothes. He was well-spoken, and, though his Scottish accent was strong, she liked the soft sound of his voice and the lilting of his tone. There was something of home about it, something of Ireland, though it was not like the sound of Dublin Town, of course.

He stared at her when they met, seeming embarrassed that he could not disguise his sensation. She could not help but smile at him the more, though she took pains to be proper and reserved. He seemed to think she was a lady. She sighed afterwards. Had Mr Bostock not told him of her history? Perhaps he thought it an unnecessary detail, or perhaps he meant to be kind. She wondered if Mr Walker would be so charming once he found out the truth.

13 Captain Walker in Sydney Town

1810

Sailing back to Sydney, she would have been miserable but for Robert Stewart Walker. Without him, she would have missed Rhodes even more. Mr Walker sought her company whenever he could. He could not hide how much he wished to be more than a friend. He treated her like a lady. Indeed, he treated most people with great courtesy. He had the sort of sweetness and youth that made it easy for her to grow fond of him. She saw how captivated he was, and at first, she felt hard-hearted, for she saw how useful he would be as a partner. He didn't sweep her into a fever the way Rhodes had done. She could be the one in charge. It felt pleasant but dangerous – she could hurt him, and she could harm herself if he became possessive. But when his ardour became more obvious, she decided that to reject him would be foolish; she wanted to attach him, and he intrigued her. When he wanted to sit with her in her cabin while Rachel was asleep, his warmth and excitement drew her in. She would not make him wait too long.

In his soft brogue, his every word was like a song to her. How pleasing it was to her ears to hear the old tongue – perhaps someone had told her once that the Scots spoke a Gaelic like the Irish, but if so, she had forgotten. At the sound the first time, she found the tears welling.

She saw that he was the sort of man to become attached, to be fond, to enjoy being with women and children. His gentle play with Rachel was a joy to watch. Where Rhodes had tossed the child upside down and taught her about seals and dolphins, Robbie sang her Gaelic and Scots songs and told her stories of the woods, the moors, and the sea. Elizabeth loved to hear them. There was a poem about a changeling and the fairy folk that moved her to tears the first time he sang it: a maiden took the changeling youth as her lover and fought for him as the father of her child, winning him from the fairy queen, enduring many trials. She asked Robbie to sing it often, though it was so long.

It began rather like some other songs, only it was more commanding:

O I forbid ye maidens all
That wear gold in your hair
To come or go by Carterhaugh
For young Tam Lin is there.

There's none that goes to Carterhaugh
But they leave him a wad,
Either their rings or green mantles
Or else their maidenhead.

But its ending thrilled her.

They'll turn me in your arms, lady,
A forest deer so wild,
But hold me fast, don't let me go,
The father of your child.

They'll turn me in your arms again
A hot iron at the fire,
But hold me fast, don't let me go,
To be your heart's desire.

They'll turn me in your arms at last
A mother naked man.
Throw your green mantle over me
And so shall I be won.

She wondered if she would have bedded him so soon if not for that song. Their first night together she would never forget. Not wild and exciting like with Robert Rhodes, but sweeter. Robbie was the gentlest and most endearing of men, his passion deep and strong but never veering into roughness. He was as likely to laugh as to kiss, or to break into song or verse.

He knew *The Great Silkie*, the song about the seal and the maiden, where the maiden lived on land, and her seal (silkie) lover lived in the sea. It was the song she had tried to recall on the *Britannia*. She listened, thrilled, and asked for it again and again. It was only when singing it herself later that she realised it brought Robert Rhodes back to her – he who was forever away, he who seemed more than a man, he who was like a creature of the sea. When she sang it, she could see and feel him.

> *In Norway land there lived a maid.*
> *Hush ba loo lillie, this maid did sing,*
> *I know not where my babe's father is,*
> *Whether land or sea he travels in.*
>
> *It happened on a certain day*
> *When this fair lady fell asleep*
> *That in there came a good grey silkie*
> *And sat him down at her bed's feet.*
>
> *I am a man upon the land*
> *And I am a silkie in the sea*
> *And when I'm far from every strand*
> *My home it is on shoal Skerry.*
>
> *And it shall pass on a summer's day*
> *When the sun shines hot on every stone*
> *That I will take my wee young son*
> *And teach him for to swim the foam.*

When they passed the southern tip of New South Wales and began their way up to Sydney, she thought of Rhodes stomping about in the Sailors' Arms back in 1803, shouting, "Matt Flinders is the greatest sailor of us all – do you hear he has sailed round the whole of this land?"

She smiled at the memory of Rhodes standing drinks for the whole tavern and toasting Flinders for his wondrous voyages. Then, when news arrived months later that Flinders was a prisoner of the French in Mauritius, how impossible that had seemed, and how sad. Rhodes had marched off to the governor to talk about what could be done, while she stared at the harbour and marvelled that such a captain, such a giant of the sea, was in gaol.

Though a life with Rhodes would have more than satisfied her, she thought at the start that Robbie was more her match. His soul, his spirit, his family, his land, his memories and those of his kin were all so like hers, despite any differences in comfort, learning and fortune. While Rhodes and she had fitted well together in their bodies, and in their love of life and adventure, she and Robbie shared a contentment that was stronger for the memories and words and songs they shared. She admired his fidelity to the sufferings of his kinsfolk in their clan wars and battles with the English. She understood how his people regretted the failure of Bonnie Prince Charlie – to have come so close to independence, to unity, to a Stuart king. Her father and her granny would have nodded at every word he uttered. When he spoke of his countrymen's longing for land and work and their desperate poverty, he might have been talking of her people at home.

When he spoke about his dislike of the English, she felt pangs of anger and sadness that she had almost forgotten. Though she would have never given it a thought had she been still with Rhodes, she felt the resentment and the pain that Robbie sang about. She understood his anger when he spoke of the land seized by wealthy Englishmen, land that had been in his clan for as long as anyone could remember.

"Ireland and Scotland are but playgrounds to the English lords. Your poor countrymen have lost their fight, Bess, but we Scots will be a thorn in the side of the English till we drop, even though they think they have defeated us."

How her Da would have hated such a claim about Ireland but she did not dare argue. She didn't take in all he said about the past battles but she understood that so much blood had been shed, and that the menfolk of his clan had seen their fathers, uncles, brothers, and cousins fall. More exciting to her were the miniatures he carried of his father and mother, his grandparents and his sisters, and the sketches of his house, his village, and his church – kirk, she should say. The house was lovely, a genteel place with latticed windows and flowers along the path from the gate. He had been to school; he brought books with him that were not just maps but poems and stories. He told her that Scotland had great poets, some living, some dead. So had Ireland, he added, and she nodded, pleased.

The night before they reached Sydney Town, they stood on deck staring at the distant land. Robbie lifted her chin in his hand and said, "We should call you Elizabeth Walker in New South Wales, Bess, shouldna' we?"

He said he would like Rachel to have his name. Elizabeth agreed at once, though in her head she kept saying, Rachel Rhodes. It was a name that none could sneer at, and it had such a ring to it. But if Robbie would be a father to Rachel, what did the name matter?

Several times on the ship, she invited Robbie Walker to live with her in Sydney Town and assured him that she had a pleasant house and a farm. He accepted her offer after a while but declared that he was keen to look for a house of his own – "For us three," he said, patting Rachel's head as she slept on the small upper bed in Elizabeth's cabin.

*

When they arrived in Sydney Town, she felt proud to be walking up from the wharf with Robbie Walker by her side. Joan was standing at the door of the Sailors' Arms, and she rolled her eyes at Elizabeth as if to say, "you've bagged another good 'un there."

Robbie set up happily with her, but she saw him surveying the houses of the rich settlers up on the hill whenever she walked with him. Once he had gained his first ship as captain, he bought some land there and had some drawings made. She was relieved when she showed them to her. Her fear was that he might be planning a separation – not that he was less affectionate, but she saw his ambition grow.

He was hungry for money but also for acceptance. It was with bitter sadness that she saw his disappointment at her position in Sydney society. He was keen to see Governor Macquarie and arranged for an invitation for them both to a large afternoon garden reception with the governor and Mrs Macquarie. Robbie expected more invitations. She was not sure; the Macquaries were benevolent to emancipists, but she was not the average ex-convict. Another invitation arrived for Captain Walker alone. He attended, of course. With great excitement, he told her all about it and, only after relating the fine details of conversations and dress, did he pause to say that he hoped he didn't make her regret even more that she had not been present. She could not admit that her evening with the friendly crowd at the Sailors' Arms had given her far more pleasure than she would have found in the company of the governor and those other stuffy look-down-their-noses.

But the governor's stuffiness had one good point. He was encouraging marriage, for convicts, too. It crossed her mind that Robbie might like to win his approval by marrying her, and that he might be more persuaded because Governor Macquarie was a Scot and very proper. But Robbie said nothing.

Letters came for him, some of business and some from Scotland. One day, a large packet arrived from his mother, a leather-bound book, a letter – and a picture that fell out. His face the moment he bent to retrieve it – the flush, the sadness, the guilt. Her heart felt cold inside her.

"Who is that?" she said lightly.

"Ach, just a friend of my sister's."

And your mother sends a portrait of her across the world to you, Elizabeth wanted to say, but she knew better than to protest. Was this girl a betrothed, the one favoured by his mother, the one he had promised to marry? The woman waiting for him? Had he requested this picture, or did his mother wish to jog his memory or his conscience or his better judgement?

Had he told anyone of his current bedfellow – the woman providing his home, food, love, companionship, child, trading connections and contracts for goods? Of course, she had never dared to hope that a man like Robbie would marry her. But she could not stop herself from dreaming that he might follow his heart and his body and ask her.

Again, she wished bitterly that she could read. When he was out the next day, she found the letter and the picture and pored over them. The girl was young, not much over twenty. Sure, Robbie was not out of his twenties himself – twenty-eight this year. He must have grown up with this girl. She was pretty, slender, and well made, though not so shapely as Elizabeth. Who knew what her hair was really like – those sketchers and portrait makers were not always truth tellers, and it was not clear whether the hair was fair or red since the whole picture was in tones of pale brown. Elizabeth could see the big 'S' at the start of her name and at the start of her family name – was she another Stewart?

She rushed to Robbie's books and looked at his name inside the flyleaf of one. Yes, the girl's name was Stewart. She studied the first name. Sarah? Yes, it was. She took up the mother's letter. She found the line about Sarah but could not make it out. She could not see words that looked like "wife" or "marry". If she took the letter to a reader – no, she would not shame herself or Robbie or Rachel. Best just to leave the future to luck. Robbie might not want to return. Or he might not want this Sarah, not now that he had a real woman who knew what men wanted and was willing to give it.

One evening soon after she had seen that girl's portrait, they sat in her garden cooled by the summer breeze, and she dared to say, "Robbie, do you think you might go back to your village to live, or to visit, at all?"

"I dinna' want to waste the money or the time, Bess. I will visit my family some years hence."

"I often think," she said with a smile, "that, even though I miss the old place and the soft air and all, I would not want to go back. It would cause me more pain than I could bear to see and farewell my family again. And I would cause them more pain. They are content to hear that I am well and that I prosper."

The look he threw her was shrewder than his usual glance. It was not just that he seemed to agree, to understand the pain of visiting home. She felt she was receiving his trading manner, not the face of her darling.

He said, "I cannot imagine that I will live in my village again. But I hold hopes of visiting and seeing my mother and father before they die. I want to take them some wealth."

And children, grandchildren, she longed to add. He said no more for some time.

"They always thought to see me marry in the kirk" – she held her breath – "but when I eventually visit them, I will have been married for some time, I expect."

He lit his pipe and stared ahead at the harbour. She turned her face away.

After a pause, he spoke in a low voice. "Do you hope that I will marry you? You must know, I wish that I could, but I could never tell my father and mother that I married a convict."

Not a tear did she cry. Not a word did she speak.

When their child was born, he would want to stay with her.

1811

He was thrilled with his daughter. He chose the name Helen. Elizabeth was pleased by the choice – a Scottish name, so he was indeed owning the child. He was a devoted father. If he had been patient and loving with Rachel, he was doting and pandering with Helen. Elizabeth half wanted to avoid another child, at least for a time, but she feared that he hankered after a son. Didn't all men? So, she didn't try any ruses or bring out the pig's bladder she had bought from the girls in the room above the Sailors' Arms. She was afraid of losing her bloom from the strain of carrying her fourth baby, but she ate as well as she could – mutton, fish, eggs, and greens – and when their son was still at her breast, she saw that her skin had remained fresh, fine and high-coloured.

When Elizabeth gave birth to a son, Robbie seemed overjoyed. He chose his father's name for the boy, David. He had both children christened by a Scottish churchman recently arrived in the colony, but he did not invite her to attend. She took a breath as he said that, but later when she sat feeding little David, she told herself that it would have brought her humiliation and distress. A Scottish clergyman would be disapproving, just like the English minister, probably with a dour coldness too. Churches were not for the likes of her, and she had no time for them. She recalled her Da's bitter scorn; how she understood it now. Living their comfortable lives, did churchmen give a thought to women and children in the gaols and the convict ships, let alone to women like her who tried to get along with life, doing no harm to anyone? But, of course, they would think she was doing harm, keeping one of their churchgoers in a life of sin, stopping him from marrying a decent woman, one of theirs.

Just before the christening, Robbie told her that his big house on the hill was built and that he would entertain traders and gentleman friends there and stay in it some nights. She wondered if he was avoiding the crying of little David, though the baby only woke twice at night. Robbie couldn't be planning a life without her by his side, she told herself. Surely, he wanted to be with the children. He sought friends among those free settlers known as the exclusives, men – and women – who would not want to meet an ex-convict whore, and perhaps not even an Irishwoman.

Often when he sat with her in the evening, he seemed distant and there passed across his face a look, whether of concern or determination, she could not tell. He sailed more often on his trading trips up and down to Hobart Town. She had made a friend of his mate; she would have heard if there had been another woman. For several years, there wasn't. She told herself to be satisfied that he spent most nights with her at her house. Her little one, James, was weaned when she saw in Mrs Silver's parlour one afternoon that Robbie's eye rested too long on Miss Mary Ann Bellaire – young, beautiful, of Scottish-French descent and, so it was said, with genteel, respectable parents. She needed no one to tell her.

14 An Old Acquaintance

1815

Rachel was now fifteen, almost the age that Elizabeth had been when the captain of the *Britannia* cast eyes upon her. Elizabeth had been searching the colony among those she knew, and even those she didn't, for a possible suitor. Robbie was not helpful. It horrified her to see that, although he loved his adopted daughter, he considered her contaminated by her mother's stain. He might give her away in a church wedding, but he would not bring young officers or rich traders or ships' captains home to meet her.

One rich trader he did not need to introduce turned up one day in Sydney. Elizabeth had not read the newspapers – still could not – but the word spread around. Robert Bostock, the wealthy slave trader from England was in the colony.

As a convict.

"Dear God, for what?" Elizabeth asked Joan, who was always full of the news.

"Slaving, of course. Only what he always did. But the parliament in England has outlawed it in some parts. They say he makes an appeal to the courts in London and won't be here long."

"He was a friend of Robert Rhodes," Elizabeth said quickly. "I want to see him."

"Better hurry to the barracks. He won't be there long. Someone will hire him quick as a wink, won't they?"

Elizabeth walked up Macquarie Street, her mind made up. When she reached the office, she announced that she would like to hire the convict Bostock, that he would be advantageous to her business and to her husband's trade. He had been in line to work at the government stores, but the commandant of the barracks was amenable to coming to an agreement with Mrs Walker. She stood in the mournful courtyard awaiting the prisoner.

He looked older and a touch stooped but the chains could do that – temporarily, she trusted, in this case.

He raised his head and a look of surprise, relief and gratitude swept over his face, followed by a moment of amused wonderment. "Mrs…Walker?"

"Yes. You recall Robert Stewart Walker, now Captain Walker?"

"Of course. How very good of you, Mrs Walker, to come to see me."

"Mr Bostock, I am offering to hire you to help us with our ledgers and such. If you would be content with being assigned to my business rather than working here for the government stores."

"Thank you, Mrs Walker. That would be most kind."

"You will leave here and live in the lodgings I provide. I understand that you may be pardoned soon, and I do hope so, but until then I can make you more comfortable."

"I have not yet received word of when my appeal is to be heard but I have been told that it may commence in London in a few months. It may be that I cannot be of service to you for long, but perhaps I can make improvements to your books or instruct your man."

She said gently, "Thank you, Mr Bostock. It would be very much to our benefit, I am sure. Now, sir, how far and how comfortably can you walk? It is a short walk to my house, but I can call a carriage or a cart if your feet or legs are indisposed. I know the voyage can be harsh."

"A walk would do me good."

"I shall attend to your chains at once, Mr Bostock. Guard." She winced at the clang of the chains as they fell; she looked away from the marks they had made on his skin.

She led Bostock out of the Barracks, refusing the offer of a guard to accompany her.

Bostock said, "I should walk behind, not with you."

Elizabeth hesitated.

He said, "It is well not to cause talk. You need not show me such consideration. To be your servant is improvement enough in my station for today." He could not stop a smile, but he quickly banished it. "We must keep the proprieties, and I wish to show my respect for your position, Mrs Walker."

She looked around a few times to see that he was walking comfortably. It gave her pain to see the convict garb on him. Such a dignified, proud countenance and figure – and still so much more assured than most of the men about him, despite his clothes, unkempt hair and unwashed, unshaven face. It delighted her that he had kept his spirit undiminished. How she admired that. She would order well-fitting suits and shirts of good cloth for him that very day.

At her house, she led him to the kitchen, bade Molly to serve him ale, cold mutton, bread and greens. Then she brewed some tea, shooed Molly out to the market and sat with him.

She smiled to see that he did not eat like a convict, but like a gentleman. "Mr Bostock, it does not at all surprise me to see that you have borne the voyage very well."

"The captain knew of my business and my reputation, of course, and my wealth. And the fact that I have lodged an appeal for a pardon. He and the crew knew to treat me well – I may be offering them positions or business in the future. Although my appeal may be costly, when I am pardoned, my fortune may be restored."

She was greatly pleased to hear that he had not suffered badly. She did not need to add that she of all people would never blame him for making the best of his voyage. Yet she could not help thinking for a moment of the slaves in his ships, worse off than those convicts, and all for his profit. Did it not give him some disquiet to think of those suffering creatures once he saw the cramped quarters at close hand? She could not ask him any such question. When he spoke with revulsion of the depravity and stink of the felons on board, she looked down and said nothing.

He glanced at her. "I do not mean to be condemnatory of your past companions, Mrs Walker, or of people you know here. There are of course exceptional people like you and me who find themselves unfairly sentenced. And indeed, several like you, ma'am, do very well here afterwards, and it is as though they had never been convicts for they attain a secure and comfortable position."

"Indeed." She nodded, she hoped, graciously.

Yet could he not find a stab of pity for the poor felons on the ships even now? Of course not; no slave trader would have, any more than a captain of a convict transport. Only Rhodes would have understood how she felt. Rhodes, who cared about every man he ever sailed with. Only Rhodes could have broached such a subject. How he had set her head spinning with his notions of equality and brotherhood. She could not expect Robert Bostock to be soft-hearted and fair-minded like Rhodes.

She said, "I am pleased to hear, Mr Bostock, that you expect to be free presently and to return to your business."

"Thank you. Who would have thought, eh?" he laughed. "You must have been surprised to find that I was in the convict list?"

"I was astonished and very sorry to find that fate had dealt you such a blow."

"How the world can turn upside down, as Rhodes would say."

"How is Rhodes?" She smiled. He did not write; he knew letters were not alive for her.

"Prosperous, not rich of course, still paying his sailors the highest rates around. Doing well in London. The writing he completed in the King's Bench prison made his name with the men of science and navigation. He frequents the Royal Society; he is a toff, now more than ever."

She laughed. "He always was a bit of a toff, I suppose, but such a pleasant one, wasn't he, never looking down on anyone."

"Indeed, and always a good friend, Mrs Walker. He visited me and did his best to convey messages and letters for me. I have hopes of support from the highest levels, you see, and Robert was of assistance in speaking for me."

"I am pleased to hear that. Captain Rhodes has sent gifts and a miniature portrait of himself for Rachel. I suppose he has no plans to come to these seas."

"I fear not. He is much engaged in London and sometimes in America."

What she would have liked to know about was Rhodes's private life. He had told her of his marriage and his two sons, but nothing of his heart. Perhaps he was now as happy at home as he had been on his ships or in her house.

She learned that Mr Bostock was still unmarried. Rhodes had said that Bostock was wed to work.

Some days later, Robbie was back in Sydney and met Robert Bostock, now clad in a respectable suit of clothes from her tailor. The two met in friendliness, yet she noted Mr Bostock's surprised discomfort at the tone Robbie now used to him. It embarrassed her. Mr Bostock was an established, rich man, well known in England and America; she wished Robbie would not forget it, nor the fact that Mr Bostock had been his employer. She was disappointed to see Robbie gloat; she hadn't seen cruelty in him before. Men were so eager to surpass other men. So were women, of course, especially when in a race for a better man, or the same man. But she had thought Robbie was more generous.

That evening, after Bostock had gone to the pleasant rooms nearby that Elizabeth was renting for him, Robbie took a drachm of whisky and laughed. "Who would have thought that we'd have the wealthy Robert Bostock working for us!"

For me, she thought, but did not correct him. She had been surprised when he declined to use Mr Bostock in his trading.

"I might end up as successful as he was, Bess. Imagine that!"

She stared. She couldn't imagine it at all. What would make him such a fortune? Not the goods and fish he was trading now. He was doing well, it was true, but he was not much richer than her with her shop and her farm. It worried her that he was such a dreamer.

Robbie said, "He talks of his appeal to the Privy Council, but who knows what the English lords and their court will do, or what they will cost him! He may succeed, but I cannot wish him well. You don't understand how important this is, Bess. The English parliament had taken a feeble first step to oppose their vile slave trade, but now the first major trader sentenced may be rescued by the lords on some problem of where exactly he was when arrested in 1813 – if he had been on one of the slave ships, there would be no question, but he was on land, not Crown land some say, and he argues it is not covered in the *Act of Parliament*. Slave traders will be encouraged if Bostock goes free."

She nodded and sighed. She could not seem to convince Robbie of her horror at slave trading, given her concern for Bostock's welfare. Lately, she could not bear to think of slavery. It brought back the floggings on the *Britannia* and James' death. And the slaves had such harder lives than the convicts, and no hope. Since seeing Mr Bostock again, it had struck her anew that those African slaves never gained pardons and were lucky if they kept their own children.

*

One afternoon, Mr Bostock was explaining some accounts to her when Rachel came into the shop. Mr Bostock gazed at her in admiration and, though he showed the deference his present position demanded, he also made the most of the introduction Elizabeth was obliged, and indeed pleased, to make. He engaged Rachel in a conversation about the delights of the harbour shore and put her at her ease so that she spoke with less reserve than usual and described the beaches, rockpools and sandhills she had explored since she was small. Elizabeth watched her lovely daughter with pride. The luxurious black hair, the clear glow of her white skin, the fineness of her straight features, and those dark eyes like her father's – she was a beauty already. It was a joy to see her confidence and poise when speaking to a gentleman, for that was what Mr Bostock was, in the colony at least, even with the disadvantage of his current misfortune.

Elizabeth felt pleased to see how impressed he was by her daughter. For a moment, she understood how some women became jealous of their daughters, but she wasn't; she revelled in Rachel's beauty. It brought her joy to see that her daughter had the power that looks gave, and to see how similar Rachel was to her mother though her colouring was different. It was only that Elizabeth could not help regretting the fading of her body, the changing of her person: she could not but regret how her own teeth were no longer white and whole, how her waist was thickening, and her legs were becoming ropey with veins after the last two baby boys, so large. No wonder Robbie was straying, even if only with his glances and words so far, she hoped.

When Rachel went home, Robert Bostock said, "Mrs Walker, may I compliment you on your daughter. She is so charming in her manner and her person. She must surely be one of the jewels of the colony. Has Rhodes seen her – since she was a child, I mean? He hasn't, has he? That is a pity indeed. Perhaps I might be so bold as to suggest that I might take a portrait of her back for him?"

Elizabeth smiled: a vision of Rhodes viewing a portrait of Rachel came to her, his black eyes softening into glistening pools, his mouth pursing with delight, dimpling one cheek. She agreed to arrange for one to be painted. As Robbie said, perhaps Mr Bostock was over-hopeful about his pardon and return, but a portrait was an excellent notion and somehow, she would send it to Rhodes.

*

It was only half a year later that Robert Bostock was granted a full pardon by the Prince Regent himself. The case was the talk of the colony, if not of London. The lords of the Privy Council had accepted Mr Bostock's appeal.

Robbie said indignantly, "England can split hairs when it comes to the rich industry of slaves. When will England give up her profits from the sale of souls, the suffering of wretches?"

*

In his first week as a pardoned man, Mr Bostock visited Elizabeth.

She received him in the parlour. "Mr Bostock, I am so very glad to see you and in your proper station, sir."

She could see that he was pleased to find in her address and posture an appreciation of the change in his position, and though he made light of it, he bowed. She did her version of a half-curtsy and invited him to dinner at her house.

It only surprised her for an instant how keen Robbie was to meet him now. But when they sat down to table, Robbie's words surprised her.

"Will you cease your slave trading or hand it over to another now, Robert? I suppose the trade will go on. The English and the French and the Americans are set on it. I have to say, and Bess knows it is my view, that I find slavery and slave trading abominable. It is inhumane and immoral. The English Church seems to stomach it, but we Scots cannot, especially those of us who are serious churchgoers. Perhaps your conviction and imprisonment have done you a favour."

Elizabeth sat uneasily, embarrassed more by the slight sneer on Robbie's face than by his words.

Mr Bostock listened without a change of expression. Elizabeth had noticed that he was always admirably self-possessed.

He spoke calmly. "My interests other than slaves are more than enough to keep my business prospering."

Robbie's attitude to Bostock improved a little after that, though he kept a hostile, superior tone towards him that Elizabeth disliked intensely.

Mr Bostock quickly arranged a passage to London to manage his affairs. Elizabeth farewelled him at her house and entrusted him with the large portrait of Rachel. She hated to see it go. She watched his ship pull out and pass the heads of the harbour. She presumed she would never see him again.

162

Rachel looked even more beautiful in her second portrait. She was nearly seventeen, and again Robert Bostock had suggested the painting.

Less than a year after he left Sydney, he returned and straightaway bought premises in Hunter Street. The volume of business he commanded grew rapidly.

Very soon after his arrival, he visited Elizabeth.

"Mrs Walker, it has always been a pleasure to see you, whatever my circumstances, and to receive your friendship. Your kindness and consideration in my previous time in Sydney I will never forget. Indeed, I must insist that you accept, as a token of my appreciation, some merchandise for your shop, to be chosen whenever you wish from my warehouses. But we can talk of that whenever it may suit you. Now, I have the great pleasure to give you a packet from our friend Rhodes."

Her heart leapt. Foolish it was, and she loved Robbie, but the thought of a message or gift from Rhodes was a joy. She opened the large packet and found first a portrait of him and of a ship. She laughed. Bostock joined in.

"Still obsessed by his ship! I told him it was a mistake to give a picture of a ship to a lady, even one who is a good sailor. Oh yes, he always sings your praises, of your sea legs, your keen eye. He wanted you to see his pride and joy, the mighty and grand ship he sails in now."

"Are not his children his pride and joy?"

"One died, alas, Robert, the older one, but the other son, Edward, is a joy. A very steady and strong boy, less wild than his father, which is not a bad thing, you understand."

Inside the package, she also found a sketch of the Rhodes house in Cornwall and the coast there. And there was an emerald. A large stone, it gleamed with the soft, deep lights of Ireland. She held it in her hands and could not but weep for a second.

She apologised but Robert Bostock shook his head and smiled. "I understand a little of what this may mean to you. Rhodes said you would think of the green of your countryside and of the seas. He hopes you may wear it. Mrs Walker, I would be proud to present you with a gold chain of your choosing on which you could wear the stone. Rhodes would like me to assist. It is a way for me to repay both of you."

She smiled. To have such a jewel – she had never dreamed of owning anything as beautiful or valuable. Like a real lady, as she and Polly would have said. It was painful to think of Polly, for she had this month died in childbirth on her farm near the river. Elizabeth would always keep a watch over Polly's first child, a daughter.

Elizabeth could buy a gold chain herself, she supposed, but it would be pleasant to have Mr Bostock assist her. And, after all, he was doing this as a favour to Rhodes, and to show his gratitude to her.

The packet held a further gem: a ruby, large and bright, for Rachel.

She invited Mr Bostock to dinner with her and Robbie.

Mr Bostock accepted with pleasure. Then he looked at her with an earnest, excited expression. "Mrs Walker, tell me, how is your elder daughter?"

*

"Perhaps, Robbie," Elizabeth said, "we should have Rachel with us to dine with Mr Bostock tomorrow night."

Robbie shrugged. He took a sip of his whisky then looked across at her. "Are you thinking that you could make a match? Isn't he too old? Would he want a girl so young and of no position?"

"He is not that old. He is older than Rachel to be sure, and, if she does not like him, I will support her inclination."

"She would be a fool to refuse an offer from a man with Bostock's wealth. I would tell her firmly to take him. But he won't make an offer. He will have trouble finding a decent well brought up young lady to accept him, with his convict past. But, nonetheless, there are better possibilities for him in Sydney than Rachel. You are just a fond mother."

"There may be girls with better positions in society, but she is as beautiful as any."

He shrugged.

Elizabeth wanted to slap him. She missed Rhodes so much at moments like this. Robbie had been sweet to Rachel when she was a child, but now he hardly seemed to take much interest in her. Yet, perhaps she and Rachel were lucky; there were many women she knew who told angry tales of their men grabbing the daughters who were no child of theirs – grabbing them like whores, as if the girls had never been the sweet children they had treated as their own.

She said, "I think Mr Bostock admires Rachel. But I will not push her into any marriage. You are not her father, Robbie. Mr Rhodes is an old friend of Robert Bostock's, you know."

"Rhodes!" Robbie exploded. "When has the great Robert Rhodes ever shown an interest in his daughter?"

Elizabeth said nothing. She had not told Robbie yet of the precious stones. Perhaps she would not.

At the dinner, Rachel was a little overawed at first but soon became animated and spoke with her natural sweetness. Mr Bostock took pains to discover her interest in music and was eager to hear her sing after dinner. Elizabeth watched him gazing at Rachel. He was surely intrigued.

Rachel had not become fond of any of the young men of her acquaintance, Elizabeth was almost sure. Her daughter was not one to keep secrets and talked freely to her mother about the men she met. She found Mr Bostock more interesting, intelligent and considerate than the young officers who danced with her some evenings.

Elizabeth thought she should warn her daughter, even so. "He may be intending to make you an offer of marriage. Perhaps you could think about what you want. Would this be something you could consider? If not, we should try not to see him so often to avoid the embarrassment and to give him an indication of your disposition towards him."

Rachel looked excitedly at her mother. "Would he want to marry me, really, mother? Wouldn't he want someone more important?"

"I think Mr Bostock is quite comfortable with his position in society. He does not need to marry for any other reason than his own wishes. Admittedly, he might want his wife to be a hostess, to entertain his trading partners or to take a prominent place in society."

Her daughter's eyes sparkled. "We might live in a big house and have a large farm or estate. Oh, mother, you could live with us or stay for months each year, and father, too, of course."

"How lovely that sounds, my darling. But you must follow your own wishes and not concern yourself with me. I want you to find contentment with your husband. I think Mr Bostock would treat his wife with consideration, but, even so, if you don't find him pleasing, it would be hard to be a wife to him, to bear his attentions every night and do his bidding."

Rachel's eyes did not lose their sparkle. "I do like him a great deal, mother. He is the most exciting man I have met. And I think he likes me very much. I want to marry a man who has a strong passion for me. Then, even if he becomes weary of me when I get old, I will have been loved."

Elizabeth smiled. "You deserve to be loved, my darling. Many could love you, I am sure. You are right to want your husband to feel strongly for you. It is important for when you weather the hard times that can come with children, and it will lead him to a fondness for you even when you are older."

Rachel listened earnestly but the excitement of a young girl could not be held down for long. "He is so rich, mother. I never thought a rich man would want me. And a gentleman – despite the trouble and the transportation, he is a gentleman, isn't he?"

"In the colony, certainly. I can't say how he would be regarded in England now, but your father supported him."

"Well, I am not going to England, not to live anyway. And he is my father's old friend, isn't he?"

"He is that," said her mother.

*

When Rachel married Mr Bostock in St Philip's some months later, Elizabeth's joy was interrupted by waves of sadness. It was foolish of her to expect the day to be filled with glad relief and triumph, though there was plenty of both: *her* daughter at the altar of St Philip's, with many respectable guests, safely wed to a rich man, almost among the gentry. It was what she had hardly dared dream. And she had helped it to happen. It was a reward for her kindness – and for keeping her wits about her. She was exhilarated for her daughter – to wed for love *and* riches, to a man who loved and cherished her, despite the disadvantage of her birth, despite the position of her mother.

For even as the proud mother of such a bride, how could Elizabeth not feel more intensely the inadequacies of her own situation? Like so many ex-convict women in the colony, she had no husband in name or in church. She had not cared much, especially when Rhodes was with her, but now her station as an unwed wife was another shame in her life. Robbie would never marry her. He might not even stay. When his profits were high enough, he would be off to Scotland with Miss Bellaire, to show her to his family. Rachel, too, would leave Sydney. Elizabeth stood in the English church and shivered.

Robbie gave Elizabeth away and was at his charming best throughout the celebrations. He had been delighted, though a little surprised, when Robert Bostock asked for Rachel's hand. No one told him that Robert had already consulted Elizabeth.

The wedding was lavish. Mr Bostock presented Rachel with a necklace of heavy gold. She wore it and carried the jewel from Rhodes sewn in her gown. Elizabeth feared it might be lost but it was not. The wedding breakfast was at Mr Bostock's new house alongside the harbour. People had thought it an odd place to build a fine mansion, but now that more houses were ringing the shore, it seemed a canny position. Rachel wore a gown made by the colony's best seamstress, from a beautiful, silver-blue fabric that she and Elizabeth had chosen.

The gown Elizabeth chose did not disguise her still slender shape but was not eye-catching; she had no intention of dressing as finely as the bride. She wore her emerald on a simple, thin gold chain. It gave her pale grey gown all the distinction needed. She told Robbie, when he asked, that the jewel was from India – probably true, but she wanted him to assume that she had bought it on her trip to England before they had met.

Robert Bostock had warned Elizabeth that he and Rachel would settle in Van Diemen's Land, where he could seek a large land grant. Robert smarted at the snobbery of the Sydney exclusives: not only he, but Rachel, his angel, would never be good enough for them. He intended to ask in London for his conviction to be expunged and for papers ensuring that he could return to the colony as a free settler. In Hobart, the Bostocks would be accepted everywhere, and there would be none there who had known him as a convict in Sydney.

"You must visit us in Hobart Town, Elizabeth," Robert smiled. "You will enjoy the harbour and the town and the countryside. We will build a large country house with rooms for you and Captain Walker. You could live with us if you wish. We will have invitations everywhere, even to the governor's house."

When she mentioned this to Robbie, he seemed less impressed than she expected. He never said anything complimentary about Hobart Town, she realised, after his many visits there. Was it too full of convicts and ex-convicts for him? He did not seem interested in meeting Lieutenant-Governor Sorell and his wife; he declared they were not made of the same stuff as the Macquaries.

She held her tongue whenever Robbie talked of how his next voyages would earn him a fortune. She did not know enough of trade and the islands to assess his chances of success, although she was becoming worried by the way he always expected that the next voyage would make his name, and, when it did not, he offered many reasons to account for the failure, or the moderate success, and immediately talked of how sure he was about the next voyage.

15 Not Good Enough

Soon after their marriage, Robert Bostock arranged a voyage with Rachel to London. He asked Elizabeth if she would like to accompany them, generously remarking that this would be to Rachel's advantage and be of assistance to him, since his days would sometimes be occupied with business. He extended the invitation to Robbie, too, if his trade would allow the time.

"Rachel and I will go up to Liverpool to visit my relatives," he said. "You could perhaps take a boat from there to Dublin for a few days. Captain Walker could go up to Scotland to see his parents."

She smiled at Mr Bostock's generous invitation. But when she told Robbie of the suggested voyage, he frowned.

"I am not yet ready to return to Scotland."

She sighed; of course, he wished to go as a wealthy man.

He said, "You have your business here and should not go back to England, let alone to Ireland, where things are even worse than when you left. We are both too busy here. I have too many voyages of my own, and I do not wish to come back to an empty house."

So, she would not sail. She would remain to await his pleasure. He often let her come home to an empty house, but she did not ever remark upon it. He had begun taking the children to stay at his large house, where she was told a governess and a nursemaid cared for them. Though he never said so, she had come to the horrid understanding that he feared contamination of his children from her, morally. And perhaps – no, undoubtedly – her manners did not satisfy him anymore. He wanted Helen to learn to be a different sort of woman, a lady. Elizabeth wanted to shout at him that Rachel was a good enough lady, so why did he have such distrust and doubt?

Robbie sometimes took Helen to afternoon concerts held in the homes of gentlemen of his acquaintance – exclusives, free settlers and officers. He did not ask if Elizabeth might like to attend.

When he and Helen returned after the third such concert, Elizabeth waited until the children were in bed, and once she and Robbie had settled in the sitting room with their whisky glasses full, she turned to him.

"Robbie, am I ever to hear some of the fine music that you and Helen like so much? And do you not think that your sons should be introduced to the men of importance you meet on these occasions?"

"Perhaps I will take David soon, though I doubt that he is as musical as Helen."

Elizabeth stared at him, but he was not looking at her. She said, "Do you think I would not like the music? You know how I love your Scottish songs. And, in Ireland, I used to love hearing harpsichords and fiddles and all."

"The music at the soirees is not like anything you would have heard."

She stiffened at the slight sneer in his voice. "When I worked at the big house in Ireland, I heard all manner of genteel music. I liked it."

He did not meet her eyes. "These are events with people you would not find interesting. Much business takes place."

Why is that suitable for our daughter? she felt like asking. She could feel his walls going up against her. With effort, she spoked calmly, "Are there not ladies present?"

"There are a few ladies, the wives and daughters of officers and of my business friends."

He paused, and she stared at him in silence.

He said quietly, "There are only ladies, not shopkeepers or women traders. There are no emancipists. So, you see, it would not be company to your liking."

She struggled to keep anger and anxiety out of her voice. "You mean that I would not be to their liking." How she hoped that he would deny it.

He refilled his glass. Hers was still full.

He glanced at her. "You cannot expect genteel society to accept you, Bess."

"Because I was a convict, or because I am Irish?"

"Being Irish does not recommend you to many here in Sydney Town." He looked a little amused. "The Irish, especially those in the colony, are known mainly for their drinking, fighting and unruliness."

"And what possible reason could they have for unruliness? Who has ruled and fought them for generations? Robbie, you talk of the way the English attacked and overran the Scots; why can't you see how it has been for the Irish?"

He drained his glass. "You cannot expect the gentlemen here to make excuses for the Irish convicts. So many are drunken disgraces, the women, too."

"But I am not. I have nothing to do with those Irish convicts. I have established a respectable business. And I am the owner. Your exclusives own warehouses and stores. Why isn't my business and my property enough to let me listen to music with you and our daughter?"

He poured another glass and sat down. "Bess, you know only too well why not. You are unmarried; you have children from three men, none of them your husband."

"You could have been my husband." Her face felt hot.

He shook his head. She struggled to stop tears from starting.

He said, "I can never be your husband. You know that. I have made my feelings and my principles clear. I cannot marry any ex-convict and least of all you."

She sensed his pride and knew that his principles were the only ones he could hold.

He went on. "You did not merely become a convict; you chose to be a whore on the transport ship. You gave up any hope of reinstatement in society."

"You think us convict girls had a choice?" She was crying now for that lass on the *Britannia* who had tried to catch the eye of an officer, because what other choice had there been?

She had never seen so clearly how much Robbie loathed her connection with Captain Dennett. He seemed to feel there was all the difference in the world between living with Rhodes and being a whore on a convict ship. Had the bequest from Captain Dennett muddled Robbie's judgement for a while?

She spoke as calmly as she was able. "Robbie, I was so young. I knew nothing of men, of the world, of what would happen afterwards."

She had never told him about the master, or the warder at Kilmainham, or her dead first son. She knew that, unlike Captain Dennett or Robert Rhodes, he would not understand, would never forgive, or forget. She knelt by his chair but did not touch him. "Robbie, can you try to imagine what chains feel like on your hands and on your ankles? Heavy iron. Stopping the blood flow. Stopping movement."

His face did not soften.

Her voice came out low and unsteady. "You cannot walk properly in chains, you cannot keep yourself clean, you feel like an animal."

He stared ahead, with an expression of distaste.

"The air in the hold, Robbie, where I was at first – such stale, putrid air, I couldn't breathe. And the dark. Robbie, you haven't understood the fear I had – that I would be taken by the felons, by many of them, one after the other, or all at once. In some ways, I suffered less than women in the hold. Some of them were used bodily more than I was." She heard the begging in her voice. "Why am I not to be forgiven? Why am I lower than them?"

He couldn't see it, couldn't imagine being chained. Or flogged. Or beaten. Or being forced by a man. He had no more understanding of what she and other convict women had faced than the gentlemen at the courthouse or government house - indeed, perhaps less.

He glanced at her and shook his head. She stayed slumped by his chair and heard him leave the house.

When he returned, she was in their bed and awake, but she did not raise her head. He slept as soundly as ever, while she tried to stop remembering the *Britannia*.

1817

She learned from Robbie's careless remarks and from others' pitying gossip that Helen had met Miss Bellaire one day at an afternoon concert, and that their meetings now occurred every week. She tried to ask her daughter for details about Miss Bellaire, but the child was so tight-lipped. It was hard to know what Helen made of the lady. Elizabeth felt an obstinacy and a resistance from Helen that she had not taken seriously before because surely it hadn't been so pronounced. But, in the following months, she noticed other changes in Helen.

Her air was studied; her face became careful. She stopped moving easily alongside her mother. She no longer ran or skipped or shouted. She wanted to wear her hair in a severe, simple style and rejected bright, loose clothes in favour of the most subdued and constricting ones she could get from her mother. This attitude never reverted but became more apparent as the girl grew. Elizabeth mourned the disappearance of the spontaneous, energetic child and in her place, this pale, proper miniature of a church-going lady. For a short time, Elizabeth felt sorry for the girl, for the fun and freedom she had lost.

Then, on more and more occasions, Helen looked in disapproval at her mother's gown and hair or cringed at her speech.

The first few times, Elizabeth checked herself: was she using the wrong words or colourful language, or was it just the Irish way of saying the words that seemed insufferable now to Helen? When Elizabeth lingered to talk to her old friends from the shops and pubs of the district, Helen looked away and did not speak.

Elizabeth's anger at the child flared. How dare she look down her nose at her mother's friends, at women who had always shown her kindness and even love? Several times she spoke harshly to the girl. Twice, she slapped her. After the second time, she was overcome by sadness, looking at the red mark on the child's cheek. She had never been a slapping mother. Her own mother had been gentle, and her Da, too.

She told herself that she would win back Helen's love and rebuild the closeness between them. When her efforts were met with the closed face and averted eyes of her increasingly plain-looking daughter, she found herself reflecting that, really, they had never shared a closeness, that Helen had never been warm and loving or a companion to talk to – she had never been like Rachel.

Elizabeth could see nothing of herself in the stiff, proper girl, but all the worst facets of Robbie – his strict, moralistic attitudes, his unbending pride, his snobbish rejection of convicts and labouring people. Why, it was a wonder he could have lowered himself to live with an Irishwoman. He seemed to have influenced Helen so successfully that she was utterly ashamed of any hint of Irishness in her mother's speech or behaviour.

Elizabeth hardly dared think about what attitudes her daughter held about her mother's convict past. When Rachel was a child, she shouted and fought with anyone who maligned her mother. Helen did not know the whole story but surely the child could see how much her mother had risen, had overcome her beginnings and her convict time?

But, of course, Helen knew that her father had not married her mother, and, now that she was older, she saw that he never would. The child did not question her father's judgement. The might of the Scottish Church stood with him. Elizabeth tried to tell herself it was the church that was the reason, not that Helen saw her mother as not good enough, or evil, not that she hated her. Elizabeth wept more and more in private moments when she thought of Helen's hardness against her. How could Helen see her as a failure, a sinner, a lost woman?

Despite these painful tensions she felt with Robbie and Helen, she was surprised when he announced that the girl was to reside presently with Reverend and Mrs McDonald in Parramatta. She tried to catch his eye, but he turned away. He listed the advantages for Helen, the opportunities for learning, for refinement and for a better class of acquaintance. Elizabeth winced at the word "refinement", but she saw that there was no arguing with him.

"Will she come home regularly, or will you and I visit?"

"It will be easier for her to become accustomed to her new residence if she does not visit."

Elizabeth waited. When he said no more, she said softly, "And so, when will we visit her?"

"I shall see," he said.

She felt herself trembling. Did he mean no? Or that he alone would visit?

The latter, indeed, turned out to be his intention, or at least that was what happened. Over the next two months, she began to fear that Helen would never return, that the child had been entrusted to the Reverend and Mrs McDonald, and that Robbie did not intend to tell Elizabeth the truth. How could he have come to such a decision? It meant that she had lost her two daughters within months.

The only blessing in this torment was that Rachel was already married, that she had not been forced to see her mother humiliated and forsaken, and that she had not been rejected herself. It struck Elizabeth that Robbie had waited until Mr Bostock and Rachel had left for England before he announced his plan for Helen. Rachel had always treated Helen with fond kindness, and Elizabeth had assumed that Helen looked up to her lovely sister. She hoped that at least Helen would be permitted to visit Rachel – her mansion, surely, would be good enough for Robbie?

Their older son, David, was already accompanying his father to the warehouses and shipyards. Elizabeth felt him slipping away, though he was still affectionate and not averse to her hugs and conversation. Their third child, James, her little darling, was still left to her care almost exclusively, except for when Robbie taught him his letters as he had the others. She was glad that their children would read and write. It occurred to her that she should learn too but she didn't dare suggest it for fear that she would be slow or that Robbie would laugh at the idea.

Robbie saw his daughter both at the McDonald residence and at church. To Elizabeth's urgent enquiries, he always reported calmly that the child was in good health and spirits.

Does she not miss me at all then? Elizabeth wondered. *How can that be?* It was so far from her own daily longing and anxiety that it was difficult not to begin resenting the child as well as Robbie and the McDonalds. But she would not blame Helen or let this new arrangement change her feelings for her daughter; not one tiny speck of difference would she feel.

*

Her first visit to Helen at Reverend McDonald's house did not take place until the child had been residing there for three months. The length of their separation was not Elizabeth's choice. She did not dare ask if it was Reverend McDonald's idea or Mrs McDonald's for she feared it was Robbie's.

There was pleasure and trepidation in Elizabeth's anticipation of the visit. How would she stop her tears – not so hard upon arrival, but when departing? If… no, when, anger swelled in her against the reverend, and more against his wife, how would she maintain the expected air of deference? Except for the dealings in her shop, there were few occasions now when she had to face her betters. She avoided ladies – easy if one rarely entered St Philip's – and the exclusive side of society did not request her presence, so she met mostly with folk who were poorer than her and just as humble in background. Apart from Joan, most had arrived in Sydney later than she had. She still occasionally met Mrs Silver, who came to her shop and invited her to visit in the afternoon. Mrs Martin had long since returned to England; this was regrettable, since Robbie could not have scoffed at her.

The McDonalds' house was near the governor's residence in Parramatta, and not far from her son Thomas' farm. Reverend McDonald had been given a moderately large house, more stylish than the farmhouse Elizabeth maintained on the farm. But his house was not in the same class as Robert Bostock's.

Fortunately, Robert had given her the use of his carriage while he was away, and it was comfortable and impressive. She drew up at the McDonald house and hoped that Helen was watching. Not till she approached the front door did uncertainty come upon her: surely, they were expecting her to enter their house that way, not from the servants' entrance? But it crossed her mind. The doubt made it harder for her to set her shoulders back, raise her chin and to glide forward like a lady.

A maid – a convict, English, young and plain – opened the door and showed Elizabeth into a room not at the front but down the corridor. Her heart sank but she rallied herself. No one was in the room to meet her. There were straight chairs with hard seats covered in a cotton print she would scorn to sell, so thin and drab. She sat, her heart pounding. Would Helen have grown, have changed?

A small thin woman appeared, dressed in a dark gown and lace bonnet – Mrs McDonald. Her grave expression did not alter as she faced Elizabeth. Later, Elizabeth could not recall a word the woman said. Disappointment dulled her senses. There was no welcome here, no smile, no sharing in Helen's days or in her accomplishments, no recognition that the polite, sweet girl had inherited or learned anything from her mother.

Helen was ushered in by the maid. She looked at her mother for a second and then at Mrs McDonald.

Elizabeth could have screamed. Instead, she smiled and said in as ladylike and poised a voice as she could muster, "Helen, my dearest, how lovely it is to see you."

She held out her hands and felt them tremble when her daughter looked for permission from Mrs McDonald before coming to her mother. Elizabeth took her child's hands and released one quickly. They sat down. She felt the inertness of the other small hand. She patted it and let it go.

To her dismay, Mrs McDonald stayed with them. Elizabeth tried to address them both at first, and then her daughter only, because Helen said nothing, waiting for the lady to answer. Nonetheless, Helen inspected her mother, her clothes, her posture and her expression. Elizabeth was aware of her daughter's judgement, her disapproval more confident and complete than it had been at home. Elizabeth had chosen her clothing carefully, eschewing fashion and comfort for subdued respectability. Whatever was her daughter critical of?

Was her hair too elaborate, her bonnet too expensive? She tried to concentrate on sending out warmth and fondness to the child. Nothing seemed to come back. She felt herself sliding near to tears, and to an odd, unexpected shame. What kind of woman lost the good opinion of a daughter? What villainess lost the love of her child?

When the maid brought in refreshments, Elizabeth saw her daughter's face become smug; the brief look she gave her mother was sly and superior as if to say, this is how things should be done, not the way an ignorant Irishwoman and ex-convict might think. Elizabeth felt a sad relief that at least Helen showed no hatred, merely spite. But how much distance the child had put between them. She seemed to have no fear of losing her mother's love; it clearly held even less importance for her now than before.

She watched the formal, graceful way her daughter now held a teacup and sipped tea. How fast she learned – like her mother, though perhaps she attributed it only to her father.

"Would you like to show me your room, my dear?" Elizabeth said softly.

Helen's lashes swept down. She did not speak.

Mrs McDonald said quickly, "We should walk in the garden, I think, since the day is quite fine, Mrs Rafferty."

The title hit her. The name – she had been too upset to notice before. How would she get over this? Her daughter did not call her Mrs Walker anymore.

Elizabeth found her voice while she waited for the slow, stiff lady to rise. "I enjoyed establishing my garden in this district. But do you not find the ground hard, Mrs McDonald? It is more so than around the harbour, I find."

She was determined not to take offence or to break her composure. If Helen could not bear to let her mother into her bedchamber or even manage to talk to her, then Elizabeth would talk pleasantly to Mrs McDonald like a lady.

They left the room and entered the passage, passing a grander sitting room on one side and a dining room on the other. Mrs McDonald stopped and knocked at a wooden door. A deep voice answered, and Mrs McDonald opened the door.

"Reverend McDonald, Mrs Rafferty is here."

Elizabeth saw a middle-aged man with no impressive features sitting behind a large wooden table. He was writing but stopped and put down his quill. Elizabeth waited. Mrs McDonald hovered in the doorway till the Reverend beckoned her forward.

Mrs McDonald, in her turn, beckoned Elizabeth, so she entered and stood beside the lady. Helen came in to stand behind Mrs McDonald.

Elizabeth waited. He remained seated. She was only a little surprised. She bowed and half-curtsied. Was it that, or something about her face and air that made him rise and come around the table to acknowledge her? *Do you want a closer look, sir?* she thought, but it was not amusing at all. She saw that he did admire her looks. She gazed solemnly, let him see her eyes, so often praised, and then looked down demurely.

"Well, Mrs Rafferty, your daughter is thriving, is she not?"

Elizabeth could have choked. "Thank you, sir, for your trouble and your care of Helen. She seems to appreciate it very much. I am especially pleased to hear that she is continuing her music lessons. Thank you, sir, and ma'am."

He looked satisfied and he nodded, bringing his hands in front of his plump stomach. "She is a good pupil and a virtuous girl."

And how surprising that is to you, sir, and to you, ma'am, she thought, but she smiled, giving him a look of gratitude. She half-turned to her daughter. "Dear Helen, you have always been a good girl. Your father and I are proud of you."

Helen met her eyes for a second, pleased yet also dismayed and annoyed. Elizabeth could only guess that she did not want her mother's praise or approval. Elizabeth could have sunk to the floor and sobbed. She lowered her face.

The Reverend said, "She is a pious girl and very fond of the scriptures."

Quickly, Elizabeth stopped her face from showing surprise. The scriptures she had heard at Evanton were not words she could love. All she remembered were forbidding words of punishment and fear, no forgiveness.

The garden was small and not well-planted like Elizabeth's; Ben, her convict gardener, had created a haven of peace and beauty. Still, she admired what she could and spoke pleasantly to Mrs McDonald. Helen remained mute. It stabbed at Elizabeth that the girl looked embarrassed as if she couldn't wait for her mother's visit to end.

I do not count with her, Elizabeth thought. *She does not fear that I will stop loving her if she is cold to me. My love, my feelings towards her do not matter to her anymore.*

She felt a rush of pity. Helen had been robbed of love for her mother. Robbie and these people had cut it out of her heart. She felt a pang for the little girl, living day by day with just this dried-up old woman, and with Mary Ann Bellaire swooping in sometimes, probably dominating or resenting her.

She said, "Rachel sends her love, Helen. She has invited you to visit her, if you wish, when she returns from England."

In the past, Helen had worshipped her older sister but now, Elizabeth saw, things sat entirely differently. There was not even any confusion or conflict of feelings: Helen showed no pleasure at the invitation and looked instantly at Mrs McDonald. It was that lady who would decide, and a frown clouded her face. Rachel was a natural daughter, forever unacceptable, even if fathered by a prominent explorer. And married to a man once convicted, even if briefly, who must be shunned, despite his property and wealth.

Mrs McDonald pressed her lips together; a habit Elizabeth had already noticed with irritation. "Reverend McDonald does not wish members of his household to know any persons who benefit from the proceeds of slavery."

Elizabeth gaped and quickly shut her mouth. She felt a wave of shame for Rachel. Had she done the right thing in encouraging her to marry Robert? She wished again that he had done anything rather than buy and sell men, women, and children. But then she stared at Mrs McDonald's smug face. *Did your family never eat sugar, ma'am?* she felt like saying. *We all buy it despite the pain of the slaves. And did your family pay their servants enough – and do you?*

She felt like the card player who has lost and must leave swiftly to avoid complete humiliation. It horrified her that Rachel was unacceptable to them. How they enjoyed their assumption of superiority.

When Elizabeth farewelled her child, she reached out her hand and held Helen's. She moved forward to kiss the girl's cheek and tried not to wince when, as she half expected, the girl stiffly suffered the embrace. Elizabeth stopped herself shuddering as she walked away; the thought came to her again that at least Helen didn't hate her. Even being despised was preferable.

Thank the Lord she had Robert Bostock's carriage. She waved and smiled from inside, but her daughter had averted her face. Elizabeth turned to the front and kept her sobs in until she reached the road.

How she had loved that girl as a baby. Not perhaps the way she had loved her two older ones. Thomas, her first to survive – the joy, the relief, the exultation of watching him grow strong. Rachel, her delight – precious, so wanted, made from pleasure with a man who loved and esteemed her, a blithe, cheery, loving child, as beautiful as her father. But Helen had been wanted, too, and made from love with a man who had loved Elizabeth then and thought highly enough of her. When, how, had he changed the child? How could he be so heartless? How could a child so condemn a loving mother? Thomas had not done so – of course, the only father he knew was Rhodes, but nonetheless there were those in the colony who had made it plain to the boy that his father, Captain Dennett, was a man to respect, but his mother was to be shunned.

Wouldn't Helen grow to accept her mother again? Elizabeth feared the strength and certainty of the McDonalds; Helen might find their self-satisfied assurance irresistible. How would she forego that for the sake of a convict whore, still unwed and liable to produce more bastards? A mother whom her father barely condescended to be seen with around the taverns and certainly not among people he respected.

It would be hard when Robbie next came to her table and her bed. But she could not turn him away and she did not want to. He had lessened her love for him, but he had not killed it. She wanted to cling on to it, and to Helen and their boys. She vowed to live even more like a lady, to curb her drinking, to dress less flashily, to see Joan and the other emancipists only on occasion. But how could she cut them? She would not, for she liked them best, and wouldn't they be the ones standing by her when Robbie flitted off one day?

She could have reeled in someone else; men still nosed about her, and some were rich and pleasant enough. But she would not take another lover; probably, she never would. Robbie became cooler, and dismissive at times. She mourned the loss of their love, the loss of a good, handsome man and the loss of herself as a woman who could keep a man. Though she never had, had she? Rhodes would have let her go sometime, and even without his bankruptcy he would not have returned to Sydney. Lifelong loyalty from a husband was not for the likes of her. When Robbie spent more evenings away in town, she came to feel a relief, a relaxation, even a freedom. She would not live out her days trying to please a man; she would not try again.

She would live a quiet comfortable life in her cottage and would visit Rachel. She would love her children and their children. They would love others more, but she would not mind.

When Robbie next went on a long trading voyage, she would visit Rachel and Robert and see their houses in Van Diemen's Land.

16 Young Thomas

1821

Elizabeth prepared herself for disappointment, humiliation or even rejection when young Thomas Dennett arrived in Sydney. He would hardly rejoice in the connection, especially in front of his fellow officers. For now, she was Mrs Walker to most, and Robbie was respectable, but even so, her story, she was sure, was well known on Thomas's ship.

From her office on the hill, she saw his ship sail in from the heads and glide into Sydney Cove. She saw the harbourmaster and the captain – and then him. In his uniform, a real officer, so proper. Her heart swelled with joy for him, and then with thanks to Captain Dennett.

She could not contain herself. She put on a becoming but simple bonnet and ran down the streets and stairs to the wharf. She paused at the dockside and hovered near Joan's inn, so that she could escape inside if he did not wish to know her.

He stood on the bridge deck and then, with a group of officers, walked down and along the gangplank to the wharf. The group turned sharp right and strode in the direction of the main town and the harbour office. He had not seen her. She sank back against the wall of the inn for a moment, then hurried inside and sat down.

"Did you see him?" said Joan, bringing her a mug of ale. "Was he one of those that just came off the ship?"

"Aye," said Elizabeth. "The young sweet-faced one."

Joan smiled. "He'll come to visit you, won't he, my love? Of course, he will."

"I hope so. I think so."

He appeared the next morning shortly before luncheon. At his smile, she felt her shoulders and back lose their stiffness.

"May I hug you, Thomas lad?"

"Why, of course, Mother. It is so very good to see you."

He spoke like a gentleman. It surprised her how pleased and yet annoyed she was to hear how English he sounded.

"You look well, Tom. Do you love to sail?"

"I always did, Mother, you will recall," he laughed. "You are well? You don't look old like other fellows' mothers, I must say."

She drank in his approving glance at her face and her dress. She had chosen carefully in case he called.

"And Rachel has married Mr Bostock – that is jolly clever of her – and perhaps of you, Mother, I dare say. He is well thought of by many people who do not believe that we can prosper without slaves or cotton or sugar, but not of course by the growing number of Abolitionists. I look forward to seeing Rachel and Mr Bostock next month when I sail down to Van Diemen's Land. I will see their country house, which Rachel told me they have named Vaucluse after our – my – country house here near Sydney Town. She loved it, didn't she, rather more than you did, Mother." He laughed and smiled affectionately.

It warmed her heart to hear him talk of their times at the country house. She had taken him and Rachel there several times in their young years but had rushed back to the comfort and society of Sydney Town after a few days. Children's memories could be formed so quickly. It was true of her own memories of the few years she had known her grandmother.

She asked if he could stay for luncheon and flushed with delight when he said yes. She called for her maid to serve them. Afterwards, she asked when he intended to visit his farm. She did not expect him to ask her to accompany him and so was thrilled to accept his invitation for early in the next week.

Of course, she had no invitations to any of the naval dinners or government receptions. She was eager to hear Robbie read out the reports of them in *The Sydney Gazette*, where Tom's name and rank were mentioned. In some reports, he was called the son of Captain Thomas Dennett.

She looked forward to introducing him to Robbie, and the lad was keen to make her husband's acquaintance, but it did not happen as soon as she would have liked. She hoped Thomas believed her message from Robbie about engagements that he could not postpone.

When they met, she watched Robbie's face constantly. Tom was an accepting lad; he would think Robbie was a proper enough man.

Robbie seemed impressed by Thomas's air and conversation, yet he did not offer the boy any smiles of warmth or approval.

Alas, Tom, you are but the son of a convict whore, whoever your father was. Elizabeth kept her face unperturbed; neither man opposite would see anything but contentment in her countenance.

It was a relief that Robbie was too occupied with his business to accompany them to the farm at Parramatta. Tom was pleased by the carriage Elizabeth borrowed from Mr Bostock and they had a most pleasant journey. She pointed out Mrs Silver's farm, and he recalled his visits there as a boy. She tried to find out about his recent acquaintances or friends. He seemed to keep close to his navy friends. Neither of them mentioned the Dennetts. She guessed they had kept their distance. Then he remarked that Uncle John Dennett had died and had left him some of Captain Dennett's books.

"That is good to hear, Tom."

"The old lady, father's mother, saw me, you know. She asked me to visit with Uncle John."

She smiled, pleased. He told her of his voyages and of Mr Rhodes, now Sir Robert Rhodes, who had visited him several times at the Naval College.

She nodded. "He wrote to tell me that you were becoming a most impressive young man."

At the farm, he showed a serious interest and walked about with the manager and his son. He thanked them, and later thanked her for looking after his land and his interests.

"What else would be my first thought and deed, my dear boy?" she said. "You will be able to build a large house on the land if you wish, and, in any case, it will continue to bring in a good profit for you."

"I should like to build a residence and stay there at times between voyages. And, Mother, there will always be a room for you there."

She never forgot the tender warmth in his eyes.

*

When Robbie came to the shop to tell her, she could not understand at first. She stood stock still and dropped the fine lace she was pricing. Deafness struck her; silence swept over the world. He took her hand, led her to a chair and pushed her stiff body down on it.

"It will be in *The Gazette* tomorrow. The harbour master told me right away so that you would know." His voice sounded faint, but she heard him now. "They think it was a storm coming out of the strait before they reached Van Diemen's Land. The remnants of the ship on the shore are sparse and battered."

She barely recognised the shriek that came out of her.

"Oh, Bess, I am sorry, I didna' mean to speak so plain, but what I am trying to tell you is that not a soul survived. All went down. Thomas could not have suffered long in such seas, in such a wreck. He would have died quick, lassie. He didna' die alone."

Later, she recalled each word, and it was a slight comfort that he had spoken so.

She wondered if her son had tried to swim, as Rhodes had taught him. Had he kept up his swimming? Or was that sea too powerful for any swimmer? Did he try to save himself, or did he fall into the water, helpless and in despair?

For many nights, she woke in sweat and horror, picturing him swimming in a whirlpool of a sea till he grew tired and sank. Some nights she saw him dashed on rocks. Once, she had a half-waking dream that he reached the New South Wales shore and walked along the coast, that he was coming to her, eating shellfish, and finding fresh water. She woke, chilled. Shaking, she huddled into the curve of Robbie's back, sheltering in his warmth.

In the morning, she asked Robbie to write to the Dennetts in England. She hoped that they would put a stone in their graveyard or engrave a line on his father's gravestone. Rhodes had told her of the churchyard and the stone monument. If Robbie would not do it, she would ask Robert Bostock. In any case, she would ask him to tell Rhodes.

When Robbie agreed and wrote the letter, she embraced him, and the tears would not stop. She had cried when news came four years back of her father's death, but he had been old, and his loss did not feel like a part of her had been ripped away. Robbie folded her in his arms and whispered words of comfort in his tongue that sounded like hers. Yet, even in his arms, she kept hearing the roar of the sea, feeling the spray, and shivering in the chill of the waves.

Letters came from Rachel and Robert. Hers was in his perfect handwriting, but they were her words, full of tears.

My childhood play fellow, my protector. One who never shunned me or you, dearest Mother. He welcomed me and Robert with such warmth when we saw him in Greenwich a year ago. I am so thankful that we had that meeting. It would have been unbearable to lose him with only memories of him at twelve. And, Mother, I am thankful that you had the time with him in Sydney. His letters I will cherish. I will forever wish that I had been able to welcome him in our home here. Robert and I wish to build a memorial to him. Perhaps you would like it to be in Sydney. Please, Mother, do come and stay with us if you do not mind leaving Captain Walker. If he is sailing, you must come to us. Or if you cannot, we are able to visit you soon with the children.

Robert's letter was full of comfort and of the sailor's wisdom that he shared with Rhodes.

Thomas's sad death is a fate that threatens every one of us, always. Even those of us who travel at a time of our choice and set out in peaceful weather do not know what may await us on the sea or from the skies. Thomas would have died quickly. He was a contented and impressive young man. He had nothing with which to berate himself.

You may be proud of his unblemished record. May I venture to say, my dear Madam, that your rearing of him provided him with love, health, strong principles, ambition and endurance. May I compliment you on your generosity in allowing him to join the Royal Navy, at a cost to you of never witnessing his growth into a man and never having his support for you in the colony.

I trust it will be of some comfort that several people here and at home will mourn him and remember his name. I will write to tell Rhodes, and if you wish me to write to the Dennett family or to ask Rhodes to do so, please instruct me. As Rachel has told you, we wish to construct a monument to Thomas's memory. Such a monument should be built in Sydney and, may I venture to suggest, also in Hobart Town.

When your grief allows you to consider such matters, please ask Captain Walker or another to write to me with your instructions. In addition, if you wish me to organise a passage for you to Hobart Town, it will please me to do so immediately or at any time of your choosing. Our home is yours, dear Elizabeth, as always. If you wish Rachel and the children to visit you, I can escort them soon. I will be in Sydney in a month, in any case, and request your permission to give you my condolences in person.

He ended with *Your Servant*. No one else in her life had said that, and meant it, without money or business as the motive. After she heard the letters, she held them for a long time and looked forward to the one that would come from Rhodes.

*

Robbie eyed her while they sat on her balcony in the evening breeze. She had stopped expecting his look to be tender, but at this moment it was noticeably cool.

"What happens now to the farm and the land?"

She took a breath. He wanted it. For himself and *his* children, not for Rachel, not for her. "It is mine now, I believe, Robbie. I am his next of kin."

"Didna' the Dennett uncle recognise him?"

"In a way, yes." She studied his face. How far away from her he had gone. She must try harder to accept that he would never be as before.

"Did he no' adopt him, recognise him as the father's heir? I think you may find, Bess, that Mr Dennett might have a claim."

She said quietly, "The family did not adopt him or even accept him. The uncle saw him but twice, I believe."

187

"Then we should see the solicitor and make sure of the property, Bess."

She drew herself up straight and looked out to the waves. "I will go to see him."

"Best if I accompany you, lass."

"But we are not married in law, Robbie, are we? So, I think I shall own the property."

Would this make him marry her? She looked sideways at his face, as he puffed on his pipe, staring fixedly ahead. He did not have an amorous look or even a planning one now. He grunted and poured himself some more whisky. He did not ask her if she wished for any, but she didn't. More than ever, she must keep her head.

The words of the song he used to sing rang in her head. How could he not think of them?

> *What will you do with your towers and your hall,*
> *My son David, oh son David?*

In that song, the mother was the land-hungry villain, but the story's point still held. Robbie couldn't see his greed or his harshness to her; her land was almost all that he wanted from her now.

When she saw the solicitor, it was as she had thought. He drew up papers stating that she was the sole owner of the houses, the shop, and the farm. There was a little money from Thomas and his effects in England, which Rhodes had listed and sent to the London and Sydney lawyers. She would offer the books of Captain Dennett to Rachel and Robert for their sons.

"You are a rich woman, Mrs Walker, by colonial standards," the solicitor said. "May I be so bold as to ask if you are planning to marry?"

She would wager that a lady would not have to answer such a question. "I have no such plan, sir."

"Then you will remain a rich woman. Should you marry, you understand that the land titles and the money would go to your legal husband."

"I understand."

"You should make a will in the not-too-distant future, Mrs Walker, though you appear to be in excellent health. May I inquire if that is so, ma'am?"

She wondered if she should reply. If she were ill, would it benefit her to let him know? Was he thinking about his coming profits and fee?

"I am in perfect health, with no complaints, sir."

She was thankful for it. At forty-one, her body, except for a back tooth or two or three, was as it had always been, though the skin below her eyes would soon start to line and yellow, she feared. Her hair had no silver yet. Her bleeding still happened like clockwork. She was lucky. But her mother and aunts had been strong and good-looking when they were approaching forty, and she had been better fed than they and had avoided hard labour.

She figured she had five or so years yet of good health and pleasant appearance. She should secure her happiness. Robbie had fallen out of love with her, and, once his hopes for controlling her property were quashed, he would probably veer towards a union with Miss Bellaire. She should look further afield, even perhaps in Van Diemen's Land where Robert Bostock's connections would put her in the path of rich pastoralists. But she had no heart for the game, no taste for pursuit, no yen to be pursued.

"I would like to make my will, sir. You are wise to suggest it. For though I plan to live many more years, one can never tell when a carriage accident or a disaster at sea may occur. I wish to leave my wealth to my children. Do they not inherit even without a will?"

"Your... husband, Captain Walker, would be able to contest the inheritance. If it is possible that he might have a mind to do so, then you should have me write a will forthwith."

She caught his serious glance. Why, did he think Robbie might murder her? Surely not! But there were cases now and then in Sydney of spouses dying suddenly, and she could meet with an accident not of his doing.

"I would like to leave a little more to some children than to others. There are some provisions from others for my daughters, you see."

They discussed her wishes, he wrote, and she signed the paper. She had learned to make a rough signature now and it gave her relief and pride not to have to resort to the X of her past. Rachel would receive the treasured emerald from Rhodes as well as Elizabeth's other effects and the shop. Elizabeth knew that the shop would be Robert Bostock's at law, but she had confidence that he would let Rachel make decisions about it if she so wished. It was pleasant to think of Rachel being the one to see the shop succeeding into the future.

Helen would have been embarrassed to be connected to it, despite its sturdy profits. Helen would receive a generous allowance but not the house, because she was now the acknowledged daughter of the McDonalds. The Sydney houses and the Parramatta farm would go to the boys together. Perhaps one or other of them might live on the farm or take management of it; James showed less of a taste for sailing than David and might prefer a life on the land. In any case, both could receive the profits from the produce and enjoy the status of ownership.

The area had become much more prestigious since Governor Macquarie and Mrs Macquarie's interest in the area and Mr and Mrs Macarthur's success there too. The boys might consider building a better house, and she hoped they might avail themselves of Robert Bostock's advice. Robbie would receive some money, but a good deal less if he married. The solicitor accepted her decisions with a nod.

She asked before she signed, "Are my bequests reasonable and just in your opinion, sir?"

"I do not give a judgement on your decisions, Mrs Walker. It is your own right to decide all."

"But what will my children face in terms of public opinion when – if – this will is known when I am gone? I do not wish to embarrass them."

He glanced at her. "Indeed, Mrs Walker, I should think they will be most gratified by your forethought and your consideration for them. Although it is not for me to pass any comment, may I venture to say that if this were a will in my family, I should be well satisfied." He gave her a quick smile and then turned his face back into a dry business-like mask.

She smiled and bowed her head. "Thank you, sir. I appreciate your remarks. I do not have much opportunity to seek advice from gentlemen, except for Mr Bostock, my son-in-law, and he, of course, is generally in Van Diemen's Land."

"Ah, yes. A most successful gentleman. His advice would be worthy of trust." He paused.

She was afraid he would suggest that a query to Mr Bostock should be made forthwith. To her relief, he said no such thing, and they concluded the business. He would keep her will safe and, as she wished, would send a copy to Mr Bostock. She did not want it anywhere near Robbie.

She walked outside into Macquarie Street, down the hill past the governor's gardens and to the shore. She stood where Rhodes had kissed her all those years back. She would ask Robert Bostock if Rhodes were wealthy still or if his wealth were in any danger – if that were so, she should leave him some share of hers, and she would change her will. Not that he would probably outlive her – his daring on the seas and on horseback was enough to suggest the opposite – but she would like to repay him, especially if he should be in need at all in future.

It struck her then that she must leave something to her sister in Ireland, and to her mother, whose health was failing. The lawyer would know who to write to in Dublin. Although she had never heard another word after the news of her father's death, she had continued to send them money, and she could not bear to think of her family not gaining from her fortune. They had surely more need than Rhodes – or than Robbie. Rhodes would think she should leave all she could to them. The news from Dublin in general was of dire poverty for all but the gentry.

She turned and walked back up the hill to the solicitor's office.

17 Stories of a Shipwreck

1822

Robbie's voyages to the islands were often long. He had branched out from his trade with Van Diemen's Land and was bringing goods from the Tahitian islands direct to Sydney. The first such voyage had overshot his estimate by several weeks, so this time Elizabeth was not worried that two months had gone by since he set off. He had taken James with him and left David in Sydney. He held such hopes for this voyage. He had visited the main island once before, but this time he was captain of the ship. The route was not generally one that caused him much concern. It was said that the weather could be changeable, and she wondered if he had sailed too late in the year. At Joan's inn, she had heard sailors talk of huge seas and wild winds in that region at this time.

Another trade ship had sailed for Tahiti just before Robbie's. It was due to return quickly, having no other ports of call, so she awaited word of its arrival, hoping there might be news of Robbie. She did not expect a message from him.

She was sitting with Joan outside the inn in the cool southerly breeze when the trader sailed in. There was the usual bustle of cargo and din of shouts. The captain left the wharf and took a carriage before much of the ship was unloaded. Joan raised her eyebrows. The second mate, when he came over for a tankard, was dour and short of speech. Elizabeth did not know him, but, when Joan introduced her, he gave her an odd dark look.

"Did you meet up with Captain Walker's vessel, Mr Noakes?"

He looked away. "We did not, ma'am."

She shrugged and murmured to Joan that perhaps Captain Walker had remained longer than expected at the other ports.

"Any news?" Joan asked, as she always did, when the sailors burst in shouting for rum.

"Big shipwreck just after we left. We missed the swells, and the wind was pushing us fast the other way, thank God, but you could see the ship strike and go over."

"What ship was that lad?" Joan said, as Elizabeth froze.

"The *Belvedere*."

"Captain Walker's from Sydney?" Elizabeth heard her voice loud and rasping.

"From Sydney. I don't know the cap'n, ma'am."

Joan got the name from other sailors and verified it with the bosun. She sent a boy to ask about survivors while Elizabeth sat like stone.

Joan gripped her hand. "They say maybe no survivors. They didn't meet up with any other ships from there on the way back. It isn't certain, Lizzie."

She did not know if she had drunk too much. Joan sent a serving girl with her to walk up the hill to the house. At her door, she could not even say farewell and waved the child off. The girl ran back down to Joan. *She's afraid of me*, Elizabeth thought. *What, do I have the face now of a witch or a banshee?*

She sat all night at the window: if only another ship would sail into the harbour and take the fear from her. None but fishing boats came in sight.

For the next weeks, she felt numb, not alive. She was waiting for two more deaths that she would not be able to bear. Half her waking hours, over and over, she heard the roar of the sea, felt the sting of its spray, froze in the chill of the waves.

She went out to see Helen, but the Reverend McDonald ushered her into the small side parlour and said coldly that he thought it best not to alarm the girl since the news was not yet clear or certain. She kept her temper and managed not to weep.

At least David, young Davey, was not on the voyage. But sweet James – he must not be lost, he must not.

She sat at her window or at Joan's. Only once did she visit her shop. The farm would flourish without her.

"I have aged twenty years this month," she said to her mirror.

When Robbie had sung his songs to her, she had loved their tunes and stories. Now she kept hearing his voice: he was teaching her their sorrow.

I will love thee still, my dear,
Till all the seas gang dry,
Till all the seas gang dry, my dear,
And the rocks melt with the sun,
And I will love thee still my dear,
While the sands of life shall run.

Rachel sent her comfort. Robert wrote that he had a ship sailing soon to India, and if no news came, he would send it out of its way to enquire.

Then a ship from New Zealand arrived. It had gone up to the islands. Not to Tahiti, but to one nearby. It picked up the cabin boy from Robbie's ship.

His story flew around Sydney in a half-hour.

The ship had been wrecked indeed. All lost but him, the boy thought at first. Then the captain had floated by, clinging to debris, but the boy had lost sight of him. The captain was not seen again. He had gone down with the others.

> *Half owre, half owre to Aberdour,*
> *It's fifty fathom deep:*
> *And there lies good Sir Patrick Spence,*
> *Wi' the Scots lords at his feet.*

> *O long, long may the ladies sit*
> *Wi' their gold combs in their hair,*
> *Waiting for their own dear lords,*
> *For they'll see them na maere.*

The loss struck her anew, even harder. She grieved for Robbie, for his suffering, but more desperately, more desolately, she mourned James. His death was worse than losing Tom, for James was not yet grown, would never be a man. Tom had at least known the joy of fulfilling his goal to be an officer, to sail across the world. James had hardly begun. She had no portrait of him. She held her head in her hands, but never could she drown out the sea's roar, nor stop shivering from the chill of the waves that she felt sweep over her.

She spent days sitting at her office window above the harbour, not seeing the blue water, the curve of sand, the gardens alongside, or the bright sky. She had no heart even to visit Joan.

Late one night, Joan came up to see her, bringing her fresh rock oysters in ice. Everyone was worried about her, Joan said. Elizabeth was poor company, but she gripped her friend's hand and thanked her for the visit.

Elizabeth made plans to visit Rachel and Robert. Before she left, another trader came from Fiji with startling news, both good and bad. James was still lost. The only survivor found was Captain Walker, who was now the honoured guest of the King of Tahiti.

Had he sent a message to her, or to his business partners in Sydney? He had not. When was he coming back? There was no word.

Elizabeth listened to the captain and first mate. She visited Robbie's manager at the warehouse with Davey; he might be assuming the role of owner, so she wanted him to be seen in this capacity, though he was but a lad. The manager seemed to have things in hand, but she asked him to show her and Davey the books and to point out to Davey how the system worked, and where the profits centred, and the areas of loss. She asked about the latter so that Davey could hear the manager's explanations. She had heard Robbie explain them more than once. It disturbed her to hear that the manager was less surprised at the losses; he had doubted some of Robbie's decisions, clearly, and it seemed that he had been proved right. She hoped Davey was taking this in. She would talk to him that night, not to demean his father, for she took pains never to do so, but to ensure that Davey would not back his own judgement willy-nilly against the advice of those with experience. It seemed to her that Davey had not inherited or developed the over-confidence of his father. Her own example, she hoped, with her farm and shop, was giving him a different lesson.

She took him with her to Rachel's. The more he saw of Robert Bostock, the better. And it pleased her that he should know his half-nieces and half-nephews.

Later, she thanked God that she was there when she heard the strange news about Robbie.

18 Stories of Women and Men

1823

When Mr Bostock came in one afternoon surprisingly early, she and Rachel looked up with pleasure until his face made them fear.

"No news of death, my dears," he said quickly.

Elizabeth breathed more easily. "Rhodes?" she said.

He shook his head. "Rhodes is flourishing, according to recent reports. Elizabeth, I have news of Robbie – who is still alive, do not fear."

She put down her embroidery. Why, then, did Robert look so grave and fearful?

"Elizabeth, please prepare yourself for some disappointment and pain. Captain Walker has married the Princess of Tahiti."

After a minute, she heard herself laugh. She felt Rachel's arms around her, felt Robert's hand on her shoulder.

"How shall I tell Davey?" Her tears streamed down. Then she laughed again. "Who will tell Helen? And Miss Bellaire?"

Robert's eyes grew warm. "Ah, yes. Good for you, Elizabeth. Perhaps better a princess than Miss Bellaire? But Davey can visit them when he is a little older if you wish it, and he may well gain some advantage from the connection. All is by no means lost for him. I can assist you in ensuring that he is accompanied by the best assistants and in a ship with a stalwart captain and crew."

"I don't want Davey marrying the princess's sister." She laughed and found that she was crying. "Perhaps the McDonalds will cut Helen off!"

Robert said gently, "I fear they are more likely to offer to adopt her formally. If they can obtain Robbie's agreement, or perhaps even if they cannot. They could probably argue that he has given up his Scottish family and his British identity."

Then he would never return. She sat stock still and stared at Rachel. "Oh, my dear, I wish I had given you better fathers, especially your second one." She turned to Robert. "What do you know of the

Tahitian royal family? Are they not savages? Will they suddenly kill and eat him?"

Robert shook his head but shrugged too. He took a breath. Elizabeth saw that he was troubled, and again she began to fear.

He leaned forward in his chair. "I do not believe they would turn against a man they have accepted and honoured. Presumably, the princess likes him, or the king does, and no doubt Robbie knows not to antagonise them."

Elizabeth shivered. "I hope so. But do you think the marriage is the princess's own choice, or does the king think that a marriage connecting him with a sea captain is of benefit to him? Is it not likely that he will ask a ransom, a price?" She would pay a lot if Robbie wanted to be rescued.

"I do not know much about the Tahitian royal family. In these small societies, the king is usually all-powerful, but one hears that Tahitian women are also powerful and like to choose their husbands."

She recalled hearing tales of the Tahitian women's beauty and forwardness. They bewitched sailors; some European men, even some Englishmen, had abandoned their ships to stay with Tahitian women. Those stories had sounded amusing at the Sailors' Arms, but now they angered and terrified her.

Robert said, "It is not likely that Captain Walker had much choice in the matter. We do not know what his intentions and hopes for the future are, but I very much doubt that he wishes to live out his days there."

She said, "Some sailors thought it was a paradise. It is the land that has stolen more sailors than anywhere. The women there are said to be most beautiful, and charming and forward…" She could not go on.

Robert said quickly, "But Robbie is not a young man. It is the young, mostly, who are led to make such impulsive decisions."

What he said was sensible, yet, to her surprise, his face became troubled. He turned away. She looked at her daughter, but Rachel was bending over the baby in delight and had not noticed her husband's discomfiture.

Elizabeth said, "Yes, I imagine younger men may be more attracted to staying in the islands, but I must admit I don't think it is only younger men who are likely to seek the attentions of a beautiful islander girl." She thought of Captain Dennett for a moment and sat up straighter. "I suppose we must wait to see what news the next ships bring. We cannot tell what the future will be for Robbie, as you say."

Rachel looked up from the baby. "Dear Mother, I am so sorry. You will be alone. You must live with us."

"Indeed," Robert said.

"Thank you. I would like to stay a little longer, but I should also take Davey back to deal with the business soon. And I must tell you – Robbie and I were not as happy in recent times. No, do not feel sad for me. It was bound to happen. He and I are from different worlds, are we not? He cannot help his upbringing, which tells him that he can never marry a convict woman."

Rachel's eyes filled with tears. Robert lowered his face gravely.

Elizabeth said, "For some time now, we have not been the happy pair we once were. I knew I would lose him soon. This is perhaps easier than if he had remained in Sydney and married Miss Bellaire."

*

The next day when Rachel was feeding the baby upstairs, Robert asked Elizabeth to speak to him in his library. She expected some more details about the news of Robbie, something he might not have said in front of Rachel.

They sat in the leather armchairs facing the large window as he said, "I should tell you something that may assist you in understanding the news of Captain Walker. It is something that I tell you in confidence, something I will never tell Rachel." He paused. His face was not only serious but saddened. "I will not burden her with this. She is innocent of the world and its sins and muddles. I love her purity and her high spirits. I would hate to see them diminished, and I would hate such stories to cause her unhappiness. So you must promise not to tell Rachel."

Elizabeth stared at him astonished. "How do I know if I should hide it from her when I do not know what it is?"

"You will see at once that it is not something that is in her interest to know." He sat forward tensely. "I believe it is in your interest to hear now, and I have a hope that you may understand the circumstances. I know you will see its significance. I want to tell you something I learned from my time in Africa."

She nodded. Something about the girls there and Englishmen.

"Most of the traders who worked for me in Africa were quite young. They stayed several months a year in the ports or the villages. They came to know the natives well, especially the chief and his family. As I say, they were young and sometimes, unwisely, they formed too close a friendship with the chief's family." He met Elizabeth's eyes for a moment; she was struck by his nervousness. "One of my company lived with the chief's daughter as his wife and had children with her. He became fond of her and she of him, but he never intended to stay and live with the villagers. It was difficult for him to leave and never go back, but that is what he did. What he had to do."

Elizabeth stared at the pulse beating in his temple and his throat. His colour had deepened.

He went on. "The chief enticed the young man to marry his daughter, and the young man thought he could hardly refuse, for that would give offence and wreck his company's business. It is possible, you see, for Englishmen to become entangled with native chiefs and their women, so that they are no longer in charge."

Elizabeth stared into his darkened eyes. *Was it you, Robert lad? Oh, to be sure, it was.* She almost did not want him to admit it, for Rachel's sake, but she did not blame him much. He clearly expected that she would think less of him if he admitted to having a native wife and children; he feared her for the first time. It was kind of him to tell her even while he was fearful. For he was safe, of course. She would never hurt Rachel with such a story, and no native African woman could follow him here and thrust their children in front of his white family. Indeed, she thought more highly of him in a way: better to be a young man who caressed a native woman with love than one who coldly bound and beat her. She could see the hint of excitement in his eyes and mouth when he mentioned the winning ways of African women, how they came to Englishmen without being coerced. He stressed that in the case he was outlining, there had been no coercion.

She stared out the window at his graceful English trees, just beginning to grow high. She reflected that it would not occur to him to wonder how the young African girl felt – how much her family's need or her own fear led her on, how little she might have felt for the young British man who was enslaving her kind. Only convict women and native women would understand. She thought of how Robert kept quite apart from the local natives on his land. They were not part of his business interests; they were a problem. He sent his men to join the neighbouring squatters in driving them out. There was a lot of shooting going on, and not many natives were to be seen now.

Before this hunting down, white men had used the women, and some had kept a chosen woman for a while. She could never help a grim smile when she saw how acceptable white men found native women to be, if there were no white women at hand, and sometimes even if there were.

The story of Robbie Walker troubled and fascinated her because people spoke as if the princess made the choice. Not the father, but the princess had the power. It seemed wrong to ask how this information had been secured and whether it was reliable; she hoped she would know the truth of it one day. It often came into her mind.

Robert spoke again. "The loss of power would be even more severe for Robbie as a captain who had lost his ship than it was for my traders, who kept their ship and command. But I think the Tahitian family will value him highly and will treat him well. Whether he will try to leave, I cannot know, nor whether the king will permit him to leave. I think that would depend on the wishes of the princess. Whether Robbie will try to escape, I cannot say. That could be dangerous, but I do not think they would kill him."

Elizabeth's secret thoughts had struck her dumb. She could not compose herself to thank him for his reassurances.

He looked at her with trepidation. "You are disappointed, I fear, to learn of such goings-on in my company, among the men I am responsible for. You would have expected my subordinates to behave better and have expected me to ensure that my men did not engage in relations with natives. I wish I had been able to, but, in those places, that trade, the people, one cannot depend on men in those places not to be affected by what they see." He gazed out of the window, across his green lawn and far pastures, and then turned back to her with his usual pleasant, calm manner. "Enough of such sad disappointments. I hope that my words have added to your understanding of how things are for Robbie."

"Yes, indeed. Thank you, Robert. I, too, know that in a confined, secluded society far from home and from the people we are used to, most of us can find nothing certain, and we can find ourselves doing things we never would have countenanced beforehand in our own world."

His jaw clenched. "Exactly. Yes. I thought that you of all people would appreciate how a man might change in different places and circumstances."

She wondered what happened to the African woman and her children. They were saved from ever becoming slaves, she trusted. She said, "Do you think, Robert, that the children of that Englishman have prospered? Have they been protected by their connection with the English masters? They were not thrown onto your slave ships."

Men like Robert did not look at the cargo they traded, did not see them as people, let alone like English people. She had understood this about Captain Dennett, and it was not difficult to understand it about Robert. She added softly, "It was worth it for them."

"Yes, they knew they would be safe in the future." He took a deep breath and stood up. "Elizabeth, I am sorry to have asked you to keep a secret from your daughter, but I am sure you now see why."

She nodded. "I do. If you do not wish to tell her, I will not be the one who does." She hardly dared glance at him but when she did, she saw him looking thoughtful. He had not taken her words as an accusation; he thought she had accepted that the story was about some other young man, not him.

"How could it not distress her? I would not wish to disappoint her." He took a deep breath again and sat down again. "We must hope for the best with Robbie; we must wait and see what happens."

For a moment, Elizabeth could hardly bring her mind back to Robbie and herself. Then she said, "When I heard of that Tahitian princess, such hate boiled in me, it scalded me. And yet today I am thinking that Captain Dennett's wife had just such a hatred for me, and that Captain Rhodes's sweetheart did too, and if Captain Walker's lassie in Scotland knows of me, she despises me too. But all of us women are the same, are we not? We love the men or depend on them – oh, I know not what I am saying. Now I feel like the wife who hates the low loose woman who has taken her husband – except that in my case, the black Indian is not a low, loose woman but a princess, and I am not a wife."

Robert took her hand for a moment and patted it. "My dear Elizabeth, the world is full of puzzles, and we are turned inside out when we go from one place to another – almost like from one world to another, do you not think?"

"Yes, dear Robert. Sure, I seem to have lived in three worlds at least."

"As have I, Elizabeth." He smiled, confident and serene again.

Rachel joined them, and he stood and took her hands in his. She smiled up at him and called for the maid to bring tea.

Elizabeth gazed at her daughter, so happy and secure. *May you always be so, my love*, she prayed, though she never thought about God or the Virgin these days. Neither of them had ever answered, not to save her first wee babe, nor James Brannan, nor Tom, nor young James, nor any doomed convict on the cursed ships, so why ask divine ones for favours?

Later, when she was playing with the older children in the peaceful garden, her mind hovered on Robert Bostock's story. His past had sadness and cruelty in it, yet she hated him no more than she could hate Captain Dennett, and less than she hated Robbie Walker, whom she still loved.

1826, Sydney Town

She wondered if Robbie would come to visit her. He was the talk of Sydney again now that he was back, and the news was that he would wed Mary Ann Bellaire. Elizabeth tried to overcome her jealousy, but how could she? After all this time, to go back to Mary Ann. He acknowledged a child with Mary Ann now – so much for the proper Miss Bellaire. Elizabeth could not sneer; she was the last who would judge, but what would Helen think, and the McDonalds? She almost felt sorry for Robbie having to suffer Helen's disapproval, and sorry for her daughter's disappointment in the only parent she admired. Yet Mary Ann's child wasn't why he chose her; he did so because she had family, respectable, rich connections, or so it appeared.

Who knew, of course, in New South Wales? There were people in the colony who didn't know that Elizabeth had been a convict, a ship wife, a whore and never a wife. If only she had got Robbie to marry her before he went to the islands; it would have been almost worth losing her wealth to him. He wouldn't have been free to think about Mary Ann. But even back when he loved Elizabeth strongly and truly, he never wanted to marry a woman he could not praise to his mother and brothers back in Scotland. A Presbyterian free settler was the only sort of woman he would marry. Elizabeth had been so irritated and scornful when she first realised how he thought – he hadn't a hint of Rhodes's broad-minded views or hard-headed criticism of churchmen, yet it had taken her years to realise that in Robbie's mind, living with her was a forgivable mistake, but marrying her meant his social disgrace and eternal damnation.

He didn't visit, but they came upon each other one afternoon in Gloucester Street. Her heart leapt to see him, for a second anyway. His smile always lifted her spirits. The joy of living was still strong upon him. His face had become crinkly, with that weathered, ruddy look captains had. It took her a minute to see how little she meant to him now, and that was like a punch to her stomach. She asked about the child he had brought with him to Sydney – a pretty, dark girl, she had heard. Were there more, sons perhaps, left on the island? Was his islander wife alive? Both questions were answered with negatives and with shrugs and frowns.

"I am sorry you lost her."

He scowled. "I was glad."

She was puzzled by his harshness. "But the child has lost her mother."

"She is better with the mother I can give her here."

His heart was harder than she remembered. But she needed to speak further with him. She said quickly, "Please, Robbie, do come home – to my house, I should say – so that we may talk without passers-by."

He nodded, and they walked quickly to her parlour. She brought out a good light wine and two glasses, and they sat at the bay window. He showed no emotion about sitting in their old house with her again. It was all she could do not to cry at that coldness, but she kept her countenance pleasant.

"Robbie, I know it must be hard to speak of, but I must ask about James. Did you see him in the waves? Did you – can you tell me how he died? What he suffered?" Her tears streamed down, and she had to restrain herself from falling upon his chest and pulling his arms around her.

His jaw stiffened, and his face darkened with sadness. He looked a different man, an old sailor. "I saw him vanish under the waves."

She met his eyes. "Was he alone? Had he nothing to hold on to? Did he try to live?"

"I am sure he tried. But the waves, Bess, such waves. And such wind. He was swept so far and then under. I saw his head rise but once." He looked away, his eyes brimming.

So, dear James had tried to stay. That was all she could have.

They sat in silence.

She spoke through tears. "He was such a dear lad to me, Robbie. My last babe, my youngest child. I thought he might stay and farm the land in the end." *And not be off to sea all his days, like you and Davey.*

Robbie did not meet her eyes. "There was nothing any of us could do. I was so lucky that the piece of her that I wouldna' let go eventually took me near to shore. Little Jack, the cabin boy, must have been hanging on even harder than I. He was rescued some far miles away by the islanders in their fisheries. He was luckier than I was."

And luckier than James. She did not bother to say it.

He turned and met her eyes for a moment. "I wish more than anything that I could have brought our laddie back to you, Bess. You must wish me dead."

She said quickly, "No, Robbie. I could never wish that. I'm sure you are no more to blame than the captain of young Thomas's ship. It is the sea, the power of it. I was so glad to hear that you were safe, and still glad later even when I heard about your marriage to the island princess."

He drained his glass and said unsteadily, "I can tell you the truth about that, Bessie, and I have told no one else; you will ken why. I was forced to marry the chief's two daughters, one after the other, forced to bed them. I don't mean they weren't smooth-skinned and winsome, but they were natives, pagan heathen black Indians, and I didn't want them, the second girl especially. I was the slave, the man to give them babies, to do their bidding. You know what that gouges out of one's spirit, like breaking a stone that was finely shaped, leaving jagged edges. But it's so much worse for a man."

She saw how his certainty remained unchallenged by her stare. Her hand shook when she re-filled his glass.

He went on. "I know your situation had the added brutality of the law, and of the cruelty of the English to the poorer classes, and to the Irish, but for a man to be forced to be a" – he spat the word – "whore, a breeding stock animal – and for me, raised in a good family, a genteel family, can you believe it? Would you ever have imagined that? And me, the master of ships. Oh, Bessie, it was crushing to be a prisoner, to be ordered about every instant of the day."

"I am sorry for your suffering, Robbie." She lowered her face. To think of a ship's master being treated like that. How thoughtless he seemed, how insensitive to her past story, to the story of so many around him. Her face composed in a sympathetic smile, she saw how he shook, and how not only his spirit was nearly broken. Her fury at Mary Ann vanished: that lady wasn't getting Robbie, nor getting a husband for her old age.

He should have come to *her*. She would have nursed him back to health with the care and persistence that ladies like Mary Ann would never attempt, let alone be capable of maintaining. Only women who had known suffering themselves and witnessed the piteous weakness of others could love with the toil of a servant and the tenderness of a mother. Robbie should have known that, but he had lived a protected life; he had never needed to learn how to choose people, how to tell who would look after him. He had never been alone without a penny or a morsel of food, or with no one to care if he lived or died. Even his native wives had loved him; she would bet her life on it.

"Our children, Robbie, when you marry," she said quietly.

"I'll recognise them in my new will; they'll be my children like the others. You didna' expect I'd abandon them?" His eyes lit with resentment.

She summoned up a grateful look and said she had known he would do right by them, but she had to hear it from his own lips. She no longer wanted to hear how he would talk about Mary Ann or see what his face would show. He downed his wine, and as she expected, soon made his goodbyes.

"I wish you well, Robbie. Health and happiness."

When he had gone, she heard anew the song he used to sing:

How can ye chant, ye little birds,
And I so weary full of care!

Thou'll break my heart, thou warbling bird
That wantons through the flowering thorn:
Thou minds me of departed joys,
Departed never to return.

And that same bird sang of its love,
And fondly so did I of mine.

With lightsome heart I pulled a rose,
Full sweet upon its thorny tree,

And my false lover stole my rose,
But, ah, he left the thorn with me.

The songs she had taken so lightly sounded bitter with sadness, yet their wisdom gave solace. What did it matter with whom Robbie found a little more comfort or pleasure? He had been the last one to give her hope, to sing her love songs, to make her have foolish dreams. She had always known that it was only Rachel and Helen and their children who would have lives of ease and of little fear, only they who had a good chance of finding husbands to love and look after them all their lives, only they who could keep all their children.

Late that night, when she sat alone in her cottage, looking out over the harbour, it consoled her that whatever else happened, Rachel and her children would own beautiful houses they could love, and homes they could live in till they died.

19 Visiting Helen

1830

Helen now lived near the new town of Bathurst with her husband. Elizabeth had never met him. There had been no invitation for her to Helen's wedding, which was organised by the McDonalds and had taken place after Robbie's return. It had crossed her mind to go to the church and stand at the back just to see, but she feared being noticed and causing embarrassment to herself as well as to Helen and the wedding party. Helen's husband was a reverend of the Scottish church. It was a pity that he was a clergyman for Elizabeth feared he would be a strict, severe man and she did not wish such a husband for Helen, whose dependence on her father's Scottish morality seemed damaging enough already. Elizabeth dreaded the severity with which Helen would rear her children, and how rarely she would allow them to see their grandmother.

Her daughter had sent a brief letter of thanks for the wedding gift Elizabeth left for her. The letter seemed completely cold to Elizabeth when she listened to it. She found it difficult not to weep at the formal words.

After Robbie's wedding, she heard the gossip about it from women at her shop and at the Sailors' Arms. Helen had been there, of course. She could not help hoping that Helen might pay her a visit while in Sydney. She did not expect it, and it did not happen.

She resolved to visit her daughter at her country home, and had a letter written and sent to Helen and her husband. Weeks passed and then a grudging reply arrived. It did not forbid her but indicated a preferred time when the Reverend had not many important duties.

It was March when she made the journey, so the weather was rather hot, but at least there would not be much rain to make the roads less safe. Travelling on those rough tracks by carriage would be far from comfortable, but the pleasure of seeing Helen in her own home would make all the discomfort fade from mind.

It was some consolation to Elizabeth that the Reverend was a landowner and sheep farmer as well as a clergyman. He surely could not be puffed up, fat and bookish like some of the clergy in Sydney. Their greatest exercise was to lift a glass of spirits to their lips, or a book off a shelf, or a fork to their mouths. Helen's husband would need to oversee his sheep and his land at least, and most likely would need to take an active role in some of the physical work. For he was not wealthy; indeed, Helen had accepted a substantial sum from Elizabeth as a wedding dowry. It was requested by Robbie, and never mentioned by Helen, even in a letter, for how could the pious, uppity girl speak of money, especially to a mother in trade and a mother whose wealth she considered was not honestly or honourably gained. Elizabeth was delighted to give it, and would have given more, but was told firmly what to do by Robbie. He seemed not to want the Reverend to gain too much of Elizabeth's wealth. For a second, she felt touched, until she understood that he wanted it to go to their son, David. Robbie, who had gained from her wealth in backing his voyages and loans for a ship, nonetheless believed that women should be provided for by the work and resources of their husbands.

The land where Helen and the Reverend had chosen to settle was far from Sydney, almost as far as one could get, over the mountain range that had seemed impenetrable for so long to the residents of Sydney and Parramatta. The land was a grant. As was usual in the colony, settlers of steady character with independent capital were privileged with large tracts of land. Being a clergyman had worked in the Reverend's favour, too, Robbie said, since there was a fear in government and church circles that the outlying new settlements could be overrun with ex-convicts or single ex-soldiers who would not lead respectable family lives.

The talk in Sydney was that the land over the mountains was fertile. Much clearing was to be done, but the trees and vegetation were manageable, and though the natives offered more organised opposition than had happened around Port Jackson or Parramatta, a regiment had been sent to solve the problem, and the residents suffered little further violence. She shuddered when she heard this said by men who seemed undisturbed by the story. She was relieved to hear that Helen's Reverend had hired several servants and had taken guns with him. Apparently, Robbie said, he was acquainted with guns from hunting.

She decided to travel with extra manservants and sought recommendations from Robbie's warehouse manager. He selected two reliable young men who could handle firearms in case of attack. Perhaps there might be roving native tribes along the way, or wild, escaped convicts. Her party would stay at a coach stop on one night but would also need to set up camp on the other nights. She asked her usual driver to give her instruction and to let her take the reins several times around Parramatta, for she had a horror of finding herself the last alive and unable to control the horses to get herself out of trouble. Ever since she had seen an emancipist woman who ran a large grain business drive proudly down Phillip Street, she had longed to try.

But she set out in her carriage as proper as could be. She invited Davey to accompany her and took a maidservant whose manners she had trained for the visit.

The road was alarmingly rough, narrow, and steep once they had climbed and were winding around the mountain range, but the views were striking. Such long vistas into the interior of New South Wales gave an entirely different picture. Up close, the vegetation was dull and scrubby and the trees untidy and irregular, but in the distance, the mountain ridges were softer and the colours richer. The tall blue-green-grey trees became a thick blue shape when far off. Together with the golden rocky cliffs, they formed a grand landscape unlike anything she had ever seen. The peaks and crags were so high, and such singular shapes. It was too wild to be beautiful, to her eye, but it was unforgettable. To her great relief, her party hardly sighted any natives, only two men at a distance who swiftly vanished into the trees.

When she came to Helen's home, she took in a breath. She had not expected any beauty or even a large house, but the rude, wooden structure with its brick chimney was more modest than she had thought any residence of Helen's would be. Helen seemed put out by the size of her mother's party. The men would need to sleep in the barn and the maid in the kitchen. Elizabeth tried to soothe her daughter and said that she was used to country dwellings and that compared to farms in Ireland, it would be most comfortable.

Perhaps it was the mention of Ireland that made Helen's chin rise and her face change from cool to cold.

"This house is only temporary. We will build a large house, of course, when it is time to build our real home." Helen spoke with more condescension than ever, and with the same air of certainty that Elizabeth remembered.

Though Helen was still so young, she had a middle-aged posture and appearance already, to suit the manner she had taken on at six. How Elizabeth yearned to fix her hair in a more becoming style, or to offer her maid as a dresser. She could do no such thing, of course.

When Helen led her mother inside, she showed no more warmth to her than she had at the McDonalds' house, to Elizabeth's disappointment. There was no word of thanks for taking the risky, uncomfortable journey. Elizabeth suspected that Helen wanted no one in the district to see her mother or be reminded of her existence. During the evening, Helen made several references to the prominent settlers and government personages who resided nearby and whom she and her husband visited. The town of Bathurst was well established, she announced; there was a school for young gentlemen in the area. The Reverend had been invited to preside over a literary society. Elizabeth had little idea of what such a society was, but she tried to show admiration.

There was barely a word of welcome for her, merely an acceptance that she had arrived and must be accommodated, fed, and stopped from being an embarrassment or from becoming too close to Helen's children — that last was clear from the outset. It was dusk when Elizabeth arrived, and the baby was asleep. She was overjoyed to see the older two. She held out her arms but was foiled by the prim curtsey of three-year-old Margaret and the stiff, heart-rending bow of two-year-old James. Elizabeth feared that the children had been told unpleasant facts, or stories, about her, and certainly, they had been given instructions. She wondered how they behaved with Mrs McDonald, though no softness seemed to reside in that lady, so surely little affection would be exchanged. Elizabeth gave them the presents she had brought. Helen's mouth grew sterner, but the children showed pleasure and gratitude. Their little faces relaxed and lit up. For a time, there was a happier mood.

The Reverend was less proper and formidable than Elizabeth had feared. He seemed rather dried out and tired by his work or the climate or his harsh beliefs; she could feel only a little sympathy. But he showed care for his children and courtesy to Helen, so Elizabeth found herself relieved and hopeful. Perhaps her daughter's marriage would be satisfying and even make her more generous. The Reverend was cordial to Davey and made plain at once his hopes that the lad might help with the work. It was fortunate that Davey was one for the outdoors and was at the age when demonstrating his capacity for strenuous tasks made him proud.

Elizabeth had brought Helen gifts of linen and bonnets, carefully chosen and of considerable worth. Taking but a moment to open the hat boxes the next morning, Helen showed no pleasure or approval.

"They are too ornate for me and for this district, Mother. You had best take them back to your shop."

"Oh, no, my dear, they are yours, and in future you may find you can wear them with a different trim."

The linen, however, made Helen's mouth tremble as she thanked her mother. Later, when Elizabeth saw the washing on the clothes lines outside, she saw how much the gift was needed.

For the Reverend, she had brought madeira, port, and a good Scots whisky that Robbie loved, and some good writing paper, pens, and India ink. It was a relief to see his face light up at the sight of it all, and particularly at the whisky. For a moment, she had suddenly feared that he was too strict a churchman to drink it. But, indeed, he was delighted to open it that very first night and each one afterwards. It was a great relief, too, that he did not appear to be as harsh and unforgiving as Reverend McDonald to people like Elizabeth. He did not express warmth towards her – she certainly had not been surprised on that account – but he showed less disapproval than her daughter did. He seemed to allow that she had made a success of her business and farm, and he did not refer to her imprisonment or to her lack of husbands. He seemed to value her as a caring female relative and a relative of means.

In the morning, she was delighted to see the baby Amelia, who was not yet trained to avoid hugs from old relatives.

Elizabeth stayed a shorter time than she had planned. Once Davey had cleared the area the Reverend needed, Helen made it plain that her mother's party were outstaying their welcome. Elizabeth did not show her disappointment, even to Davey.

In one regard, she was pleased to leave: she found it hard to sleep in the dusty, thin-walled house. The noises of the bush disturbed her, strange animal noises that she had not encountered even in her early days at Parramatta. And several times, when she needed to walk at night to relieve herself at the outside closet, she heard noises that were surely not animals but humans. There was a native camp at the edge of the Reverend's fields, where she had noticed women and children but no men. She saw some men clad in shirts and breeches coming back from there one night – not native men. She did not peer too hard at their faces. It hardly surprised her that, out here, local men would take their pleasure with native women. In Sydney and Parramatta, it had been common, and in Van Diemen's Land it was customary, though now the natives were being driven out of the farming lands. Robert Bostock was never known to visit the blacks – and she was sure he did not.

Presumably, the Reverend would abstain from such goings-on, though how could she be sure? She saw his shepherd and another assigned man visit the blacks. She did not mention this to Helen; doubtless, the girl was ignorant of it, and what good would it be to her to know? In any case, Helen would probably dismiss such information as the scurrilous, immoral gossip of her embarrassing, low-born mother.

On several nights, while they were sitting inside the house, they could hear sounds of the native women and children. Helen's mouth became pursed, but she said nothing. The Reverend reassured Elizabeth that the attacks of the natives had been successfully stopped a few years back; the men were gone, as he put it. Elizabeth could not dismiss from her mind the shooting that must have taken place – and with Helen and the children so near to it, not enclosed in a large, established estate as Rachel and her family were. How was it that the native women and children survived, or were they but a small remnant? Did all their husbands and fathers die? On several nights, she was startled by the loud banging of sticks that was apparently the natives' music. To Elizabeth, it was harsh, flat and monotonous, yet she noticed how Helen's children liked tapping their hands to the rhythms until their mother stopped them with a slap.

Helen was a severe mother, as Elizabeth had feared, although there were moments of tenderness from both mother and father that made the grandmother smile. *You can't love me, but you can love them, my girl, and thank God for that.* Elizabeth stole every moment she could to speak and play with the children; alas, they were so young they would not remember her. Their current tastes and desires were written on her heart, and she would send gifts for them to enjoy and treasure. But when they grew older, how would she know what they liked?

On the afternoon before she left, when the baby was asleep, the older children were playing outside and her daughter was calmly arranging flowers in a vase, she dared to say, "I am proud of you, Helen. You have risen in society most admirably, and I hope it brings you much happiness and contentment."

Her daughter whipped around. "You know that such approval from you is not welcome to me. I do not look for happiness in this world, Mother, nor do I seek a position of importance."

Elizabeth said nothing. She had taken a risk, but she had hoped that Helen might accept the praise. She did not believe a word of her daughter's other assertions; perhaps Helen told herself such things, but they were far from the truth. Many religious people pretended to care nothing for the social power and riches that they clung to so grimly.

She wondered if her face showed how unconvinced she was. Or perhaps Helen expected subservient agreement from her?

Helen was staring gravely at her mother. Her tone was more heated and confident. "I strive to be virtuous and godly and to raise my family in God's church. I know this means little to you. Do you even believe in God and the final judgement and the hereafter?"

Elizabeth sighed. "I cannot tell about such things. I hope there is a heaven – and a hell, I suppose. If you had seen what I have seen, you might not be so sure, and you might not want to think of a hell. God's ways are not for the likes of me to fathom. My mother and grandmother were devout."

"And your father was a doubter and a mocker; I remember your stories, Mother. But the Roman Catholic Church in Ireland is far from the right doctrine and practices. It is a superstitious peasant church."

"Well, you have certainly got yourself the right husband, then." Elizabeth struggled to speak softly and calmly. "I hope that he brings a little more comfort and financial security to you and the children as they grow up."

Helen stood up straighter. "We will have what we need, and we do not look for more. God and the church will provide."

"That is fine for some, isn't it?" Elizabeth could not stop her retort. Helen had no notion of the suffering of Sydney's poor, let alone Ireland's. As her Da used to say, the bishops stayed stout while their flock scratched and starved, and no one gave a thought to those not in their flock.

Helen leaned forward. "You pride yourself on having found a wonderful husband for my half-sister – a godless, ex-convict slave trader. Oh, a man accepted by the rich and powerful, a man with piles of money – but such ill-gotten, sinful money, the spoils of slavery and brutality. One might have thought that your own incarceration would have given you some sympathy for the poor wretches that men like Bostock capture and sell."

"How can you think that I don't have sympathy for them?" Elizabeth could barely control her anger. "I was chained and owned. I saw floggings and killings. The ship I sailed in was not as bad as a slave ship, but I could not bear more than one night in the hold. I wager I have more sympathy than your church folk. But everyone wants sugar and cotton and prosperity, even you." She managed to soften her tone. "Rachel was married in the Church of England, and her children were christened there. I'd wager that Robert Bostock and his family consider themselves Christians."

Helen turned aside. "What is the good of us conversing, Mother? I cannot comprehend a woman like you. All you care about is wealth and comfort. You always take the easy road. You grabbed the first wealthy man who came your way when you were but a girl, the very man who was oppressing your cousin and your friends. You continued to grab wealthy captains, even as a woman of middle age. One might wonder if you only like men who are masters of ships." Mockery played around her eyes, but there was shame there, too.

Elizabeth was torn between tears and rage. She wished she could say, *yes, my choices were not wise, but nor were they free. And they were not easy. But you are like me, Helen, don't you see? You found the way to get on with those in charge of you; you pleased and obeyed, first your father, then a reverend. You got where you are today by grabbing your man, the top man. But unlike me, you have let them rule your every thought.* She almost laughed. But she grieved, too. Like her, Helen had given up so much to get where she wanted and needed to be.

A moment later, she thanked God she hadn't said any of it. From the inner room came the baby's cry as she woke from a sleep. Both mother and grandmother went to her. Elizabeth waited while Helen picked up the child. She was grateful when her offer to change the infant was accepted with a nod and Amelia was in her arms.

When she farewelled Helen, a chill swept over her. When would they meet again? She would not repeat this journey. But Helen and her family would visit Port Jackson to see Robbie or the McDonalds or the other churchmen. She *would* see her grandchildren, even if she had to barge into the horrid McDonald house or into Mary Ann Bellaire's.

20 In Van Diemen's Land

1831

Robbie died only four years after his marriage. At the funeral service for him, she stood at the back of the church and saw Helen next to Mary Ann and Davey. Helen did not look in her direction when the funeral procession left the church. Only Davey waved and bowed to her.

Of course, she was not invited to the wake, or whatever Mary Ann called it. Elizabeth sent a girl around to the kitchen to ask if the grandchildren from the country were staying there or at the McDonalds'. They weren't, so she did not try to call upon Helen. She sent a wreath to her instead. A short note came in due course. Elizabeth did not bother to have it read to her. She pored over it but could see no word that began with "L", no word that looked like "love".

She called in on Joan and had a good gossip. She saw Davey every day since he was still living in her house. She looked in at her old shop, now leased to a woman who was keeping up its profits, if not quite its quality. She visited Robbie's grave with Davey and then again on her own. She stood for a long time and remembered Robbie in London, on the ship and in their early years when he loved her.

Two months later, when she disembarked in Hobart, she hoped that she would never board a ship again. She had offered her Sydney house to Davey and sold the property in the district known as Vaucluse, since he had no future interest in a house so far from the trading district and wharves. She would still see him often for he came regularly to Hobart; he was working for Robert Bostock now. He was as warm to her as ever and friendly to Rachel, but he was reserved, it seemed, with everyone else. He never saw Helen and never mentioned women friends. He loved the sea and ships. She was learning to accept him as he was and to stop worrying that the losses and divisions in their family had closed him off from people. He was still young, after all. There was no one to draw her back to Port

Jackson. Only memories were there, of young Thomas, young James, Rhodes, the swimming in the harbour coves, Robbie – and Helen. All gone. She would continue to send presents to Helen's family, and she treasured the secret hope that the children might come to visit their Aunt Rachel and their grandmother one day, even if only when they were grown. She thought she might miss the sparkle of the harbour's waves in the sun, but the smaller harbour in Hobart Town was pretty enough and held no pain for her.

Rachel was overjoyed at Elizabeth's wish to live with them. Robert was most welcoming; he even convinced Elizabeth that he preferred to have her with them rather than in Sydney. He appreciated the support she gave to his wife and the love she showed his children; he valued having another family member with him. He had wanted to bring his sister from England to reside with him, but her frail health stopped her from risking the voyage.

Vaucluse, the Bostock family estate on the South Esk River, and their house in Hobart Town became Elizabeth's world. She learned each room, each wall, each piece of furniture, each view outside, every garden, and almost every paddock, stream, tree, and hill. She came to love them.

Robert Bostock introduced her everywhere in Van Diemen's Land as the successful business lady whom he had met in London when she was married to his friend, Sir Robert Rhodes. The first time he said it, she laughed inside at the lie, but she realised it was a kindness to Rachel to conceal the story of her birth and to make her mother sound more impressive. She kept the name Mrs Walker for Rachel's sake. And what was the alternative? She had no claim to be Mrs Rhodes and did not want to dishonour Rhodes or his wife, Lady Rhodes. Someone might still recognise the name, Elizabeth Rafferty, and despise it. Perhaps a few of their Van Diemen's Land acquaintances knew Walker as Rachel's maiden name, though probably not. The folk of Van Diemen's Land were a mixed crew and often vague about their pasts. She could not look down on them for that. Indeed, it was far preferable to the Sydney exclusives' concentration on everyone's lineage and past achievements, a posture she was all too familiar with from Robbie. Most Van Diemen Landers were happy to meet a well-dressed woman who knew how to behave.

Soon after she came to stay, she was included in the Bostock's invitation to Government House in Hobart. It was a large reception with music afterwards. If only Robbie could see her now, she thought, when she climbed the steps to the imposing front entrance and enjoyed the view down over the river and along to the town on one side and the wooded hills on the other.

The inside rooms were pleasant, but she had seen more style and expense in Sydney. Governor Arthur and his wife spoke briefly and politely to Rachel and Robert and were civil to her, with no discernible sniffs or shudders of disapproval. She was a little afraid since the governor was said to be such a churchman and to disapprove of emancipists. The governor's wife had an air of dignity, but her dress was plain and uninteresting. Elizabeth kept thinking of the previous governor's lady; *her* story was unforgettable. Her title of Mrs Sorell was as false as Elizabeth's Mrs Walker or Mrs Rhodes; she was really Mrs Kent. She had left her officer husband years back to live with the governor, who had a wife and children himself in England. Elizabeth wished she could have met Mrs Sorell. What an adventurous or alluring woman she must have been, or lucky, perhaps, though what had she been forced to suffer for the sake of success or love? Rachel and Robert had liked her and Governor Sorell, finding them friendly, amusing and high-spirited. Governor Arthur's lady, though capable and confident, did not seem charming or interesting. The other ladies Elizabeth met at the reception were varied. Some were overdressed; some laughed loudly; a few were genteel in manner and speech. None said anything that she found entertaining or remembered afterwards.

She found herself seated next to a merchant and ship owner who knew Robert and apparently considered himself on a similar level of wealth, success, and respectability.

"You will love the countryside," he said. "Hobart Town is improving, much more bearable than in former years. The countryside is very pleasant now that the blacks have been cleared and there are few convicts roaming about."

She knew not how to answer, so she bowed her head and looked aside. It always gave her a shock the way gentlemen spoke of convicts as only a notch above the natives, especially when in the same breath they boasted of killing blacks.

She had noticed since her return to Van Diemen's Land that there were no blacks to be seen. At Robert and Rachel's, she heard talk of plans to keep them on a nearby island – a gaol, really. It was a mournful thought; as Rhodes had remarked, they had seemed so free. She recalled them swimming, rowing their small boats or sitting outside around their fires with their children; she hoped they could still do those things. At dinner at Robert's house, she heard men scoff at the Van Diemen's Land Indians, at how their king and queen had no finery, no army, no lands with crops and no animals the English wanted. Their land was now pasture, owned by the colonists. That was the way of the English. And of the so-called civilised world, of course, as even Rhodes would have to agree, despite his sympathy for all races and his old French ideas of liberty, equality and fraternity, which nobody else accepted.

Her companion continued speaking, taking her agreement for granted. "It was a wild place a few years back until Governor Sorell organised the convicts properly. They far outnumbered the free settlers. There are still too many of them, aren't there! But do not be alarmed, madam; the bad ones are far away in Macquarie Harbour prison so they can't bother us in Hobart Town."

"That is fortunate, indeed," she said. It had horrified her to see the chain gangs in the street and at road making on the way to Robert's country house. The clanking sound, the stooping, bruised figures sickened her. It put her off Hobart Town – but not in the same way that convicts put off the man next to her. She added, "I understand that most of the convict women are in private assignment."

"Quite so. And except for runaways, it works excellently. We had a notorious runaway female a few years back, joined some cut-throats, including a native boy – can you imagine?" He raised his eyebrows. "They caused a terror of thefts and even murder, but they were caught pretty smartly."

She met his eye, shocked, but pushing down scenes from long ago. "And did they face the gallows?"

"Not the girl, but the men did. The black was shot at the arrest, naturally, no trusting such savages. The girl is in the gaol. She won't get out on assignment." He gave a short laugh. "She was from London. At first, when we heard the story, we assumed she was an Irish girl. The poorer ones from Ireland are hard to civilise. Though they are rarely enterprising enough to escape, I must say. It's the men of the Irish race that are truly wild. Not the women – more biddable, the biddies."

To break the silence that followed, she said, "In Sydney, I had English servants and employees, but a friend had a most reliable Irishwoman for some years."

He nodded, with a friendly glance. Clearly, her Irish accent did not cause him to think twice about mouthing such attitudes towards Irish convicts. Her clothes and connections erased her past. To the people sitting about her, it was inconceivable to have sympathy with a convict. They could not see that a girl like Polly would never be a threat. Elizabeth gripped her glass and saw again the captain's cabin, the hold below, and the tormented face of the girl Captain Dennett had lashed. She was glad that the escaping girl had lived. What had she been running from that led her to cast her lot with a native? What were others of the gang running from? What did they hope to find? She could guess, but the man sitting next to her hadn't the slightest understanding of the true story. Probably, it would never be known, except by a few convicts.

She turned to Rachel on her other side. There were such horrors where Rachel and her children lived, but it was changing. She lifted her glass, held its fine stem and watched the candlelight sparkle on the crystal.

One or two government house receptions were enough for her. She did not belong; she did not seek such company. Most of the folk weren't real gentry at all, and the airs they put on!

The wives of landowners in the country were less prone to posing as great gentry, but they either were ladies or tried hard to be, and Elizabeth could not feel close to them. She had no heart to trust new acquaintance and no wish to tell her secrets to anyone again. She enjoyed a few visits to the nearest neighbours in the South Esk district; she especially liked to see their houses and their drawing rooms and to walk in their gardens. But regular visits were not for her. Rachel had friendships with the younger women, and that was enough. Elizabeth relished her afternoons spent with her grandchildren when Rachel returned visits to the other large homes.

Occasionally, she had a wish to be in her old house in Sydney Town, staring down at the bright blue harbour. There, she could be her own boss – drink as much as she liked, eat as much or as little as she wanted, wander down to the Sailors' Arms and have a gossip with Joan if she was still there. But, though it had been her haven at times, she knew that it wasn't what she really wanted; in such a life, she could end up a sad old crone in the corner. Rachel, the grandchildren, and Robert were more important and, mostly, were better company.

Yet, at times, their words, or the tone of what their guests said took her breath away. At a dinner Rachel and Robert hosted with the Fords and Wilsons from neighbouring estates, Mr Wilson remarked that his overseer had not been hard enough on the new convict labourers.

"He is not a natural disciplinarian," he said, smiling broadly.

"It takes some strength," said Mr Ford. "I saw a guard at the Hobart Town barracks flog the villains. By the time their bodies drooped, he had broken quite a sweat."

He laughed and Mr Wilson joined him, to an amused titter from some others around the table. He would have said more, Elizabeth assumed, but for the presence of the ladies. She could not look at Robert for fear that she might see approval or tolerance. She heard again the screams from the triangle, heard the prayers in Irish, the calls for mothers. She saw the vision that never left her: James in the dungeon of the *Britannia,* the white lines in the blood on his back, flogged down to the bones.

Mrs Wilson murmured, "The girls have to be trained for weeks before the washing is even passable."

These smug people had not known hunger. Or fear of masters. They could barely see the convicts who surrounded them in service, or in town. They could not recognise those convicts as men and women, sons and daughters, parents, and lovers. She had to hide her eyes. It was some relief that they could not identify her with the convicts. But why were those who lived in the most comfort also the most hard-hearted? How could they not see, hear, or feel the suffering? Yet she knew how; Captain Dennett had shown her.

She sat among these cheerful settlers and thought again of the one gentleman she knew who did see the suffering – Rhodes, whom she might never have met if she hadn't been Captain Dennett's ship wife and set up her shop. Rhodes's old ideas of liberty and the progress of humankind had seemed outlandish, but she saw now what he meant, though of course, it would never be. And yet she had to hope – when more convicts served out their terms and found work or land, wouldn't their children do better? It didn't seem to occur to these landowners sitting around the table. But Rhodes believed that, just like Rachel, the children of convicts would become a strong new breed.

She felt glad again that Helen's children were respectable and far removed from their grandmother's past. She didn't mind anymore that Helen would keep it all secret from them, though it still hurt that Helen hardly deigned to remember the outlines of her mother's story, let alone try to understand the unjust causes of Elizabeth's imprisonment or to ponder the sufferings of any convicts. Helen's children would be accepted everywhere and might become prosperous if their parents' church allowed such ambitions. They would have book learning, like Robbie. She hoped they would love old and new poems as he did.

Rachel's children were rich already, without any efforts of their own. But they showed energy, and the boys would carry on Robert's shipping and trading business and also his pastoral property. Their daughters would probably marry pastoralists.

She liked to think of how life would be for their generation and the next. Wouldn't they feel they owned their homeland; wouldn't they feel at home amid equals? She hoped they would not imprison or drive out or kill off the natives. But she feared that the custom of the colony would continue: the natives would suffer more than the African slaves – killed, not just enslaved. How she wished she could talk to Rhodes about this. She could only hope that her descendants would be kind masters to whoever worked for them. Why would they have cause to be otherwise?

1837

Elizabeth backed out of the room with the new-born in her arms. When she turned and walked to the cradle, she heard Robert's cry. Never had she heard a man make such a sound, not even in the gaols or on the ship. Pity swept over her. He loved her daughter so.

The birthing had been the hardest of Rachel's eleven childbed times. Elizabeth had stood by her bed, held her hand, wiped her brow, talked with her, prayed with her – and all the time, fear was mounting in her, in both of them. Rachel's labouring went on all day and all night. Too long. The doctor from Launceston arrived. He put in his hands, but the baby did not come; he gave Rachel some liquid, but it did not bring ease. How could Rachel keep working so, heaving, gasping, and hurting? Elizabeth struggled to keep back her tears as she dampened her daughter's brow. When Elizabeth locked eyes with her, it was as if the two of them were outside the panting, groaning body. Rachel's eyes were full of love and patience but then, all at once, full of fear.

Later, Elizabeth asked herself if there had been a moment when Rachel knew, just before her back arched, her eyes rolled, and her skin burned hot. *No, no, God*, Elizabeth pleaded, *not my daughter, not my darling, not Rhodes's child. Don't take her, not from Robert, not from this baby, not from me.* But Rachel screeched and was not herself any longer. Elizabeth knew; the fits would come next – and death. *Please God, swiftly*, she prayed. *But not yet, oh not yet.* There was nothing the doctor could do; she knew that before she heard him telling Robert to farewell Rachel. Then the doctor came close with his large tongs and motioned to Robert and her. Robert left, but she shook her head fiercely.

"I am not afeared. I will stay with her." She pressed the wet cloth to her daughter's face and held the hand that was now stiffening into a claw.

After a startled pause, the doctor ignored her and pulled the baby out.

Elizabeth could not leave her child yet for this new baby. She called out for the nursemaid to come, take it and wash it. The doctor cut the cord and eased out the afterbirth. Could that help Rachel? Elizabeth feared not.

She spoke softly to her darling girl. The words came in the old tongue that she had taught Rachel a little of in the early years. In the old words, with the old tunes, she sang her dear girl to her rest. The body contorted. It was not Rachel now. The sickness had won. The power of death was sweeping over her. Then she was gone.

With the doctor, Elizabeth stretched her out, stroked her mouth to its real shape, smoothed down her hair and her hands. "I will wash my daughter after you go," she said.

Robert ran in. She left him with his love and carried out the baby. After he had left the room and looked with grief yet love at the child, Elizabeth returned to the bedside with water, herbs, and cloth. She had watched her mother, grandmother and aunts do this; she had not forgotten.

*

After Rachel's death, Robert offered her a house of her own, and for a moment her heart sank. Did he hate her hanging about in Vaucluse, his country house? Was she now the old unwanted hag, embarrassing everyone?

He said quickly that he only wondered if she might prefer to be in her own residence and mistress of it, perhaps in Hobart Town or on the estate where the grandchildren could visit.

"But the easiest arrangement for me is to keep things as they are, my dear Elizabeth. We all love to have you with us. I will never forget our dearest Rachel's promise that you will always have your rooms here."

She would be a mother to this last one of Rachel's children, would hold him at night as Rachel would have done, would love him best of all, this tiny motherless one. She was needed to bring up this child, to watch over him, to tell him of his mother, of his mother's father, of his lost uncles; to tell him the old stories and sing to him the Irish and Scottish songs.

And, though they were older, the other grandchildren needed her too, needed a kinswoman to care for them, watch over them and take pride in them. Rachael needed help in planning her wedding. Margaret needed a chaperone while she was courting. Elizabeth loved to praise Charles, Robert and Thomas who were learning their father's merchant and pastoral business.

In 1839, when her grandson George was fourteen, he went to the mainland to work on the coast, in the new Port Philip district. She was glad to think of him striking out, independent of his father. Eliza, Augustus, and Ernest studied well at their schools, and when home, enjoyed their grandmother's attention and her stories. Elizabeth silently promised Rachel to keep watch over the hearts of all her children. She was not needed to run the house and would not have felt able to do so. The older granddaughters and the housekeeper had it all in hand.

No one could know how much she loved living in this big house, like a lady almost – and to the young servants that was perhaps what she seemed, though that was just their ignorance. She tried to remember the servants' names, to know a little about their background and possible difficulties and to treat them with more kindness than Milady had shown to her. She relished the size of the place; she could live relaxed and independent in her part of it, and yet out of her window she could watch the young grandsons riding off and the granddaughters walking in the garden, graceful and nearly carefree. She loved the distant sound of the servants keeping everything clean, and the sounds of the barn and of the sheep when they were brought near. The fragrance of the flowers in her room and in all the rooms and gardens was enough to make her smile.

She kept herself apart from the young grandchildren's social evenings. Though the young people were always pleasant to her, she began to feel herself an old relic, and feared someone would see that she was nought but a disreputable Irishwoman. She could eat with the family most nights if she wished or take a meal in her sitting room; it was a delight to eat at the big dining table with Robert and the children. If they were entertaining, she would go up to her rooms straight after the meal. If not, she would sit in her comfortable chair near the fire and listen to their talk of the estate and the town and their friends. If there was a big party, she stayed in her room, happy to know that Robert and the children and the servants were about.

It was not just the most luxurious home she had ever had, but the safest; she returned to a long-lost freedom and innocence when she did not have to think of how to survive or get on; for the first time that she could remember since the early days with Rhodes, she did not worry herself to sleep. She could die here, at peace.

Sometimes, Robert talked to her after dinner almost as he must have talked to his family, perhaps to his sister. Elizabeth enjoyed hearing what he had to say about the colony and the news from England. He began to gather news from Ireland to tell her. She found herself able to reminisce a little. He told her more about his own family. There was an ease between them. They never spoke of her convict time, or of his. They never talked of Captain Dennett or of Robert's – or his colleague's – African wife. Yet what they had lived through gave them a bond which they felt always. They knew things that their fellow settlers and genteel acquaintances would never know: the shock of lost liberty, the ache of injustice, the cut of cruelty.

They had lost the people they loved most and were learning how to survive sadness. They wanted to go on living, for their children, and she for her grandchildren, too. They shared memories of Rachel and of Rhodes. He read aloud the letters that came to them from Rhodes every so often. They marvelled at his travels, his maps, his fame. They confessed to each other how much they missed him. Robert was the only person who understood how she mourned Rhodes. She and Robert had each passed beyond romance and passion and the need to be one of a pair. They asked nothing of each other but listening, understanding and sympathy. He had probably known other such companions, but she had never had such a friend. There had been

James Brannan, but he had been more like a father, and she had been too young and unhappy.

She and Robert had another bond: they knew shame. They had done things they could never speak of to their children. She never spoke of gaols to the grandchildren, and their knowledge of her past was left deliberately vague. Robert never spoke to his children of his conviction or pardon. She wondered if the children knew much about his slave trading; she never heard the subject mentioned. He did not speak of it to her, but he remarked that his business life was much easier now and that he had no wish to board a ship again. Sometimes his face showed melancholy. She hoped he might be reviewing his slaving days, but he never uttered a word of regret or remorse. More and more, she found herself regretting how much she and Robert and all the colonies and British peoples gained their comfort and luxury from trade in sugar and slaves. She shuddered to think of all that selling and crushing of bodies and souls.

1847

The grave Robert erected for Rachel was of pure marble. The church had no graveyard yet, so the grave was in a cemetery in nearby Campbell Town. It was a grand monument to her beautiful girl, to Robert's beautiful girl, though not a girl – a woman at the end of her childbearing. But a beauty even then, her hair still raven-black like her father's, her skin firm and clear.

Elizabeth came home one day from visiting Rachel's grave with her youngest grandsons, Ernest and James, and saw herself in the glass in the entrance hall – a grim old face; she would not have guessed she looked so. She smiled quickly, lest the children should shrink from her. She checked her reflection again. That was better; she still had a spark of life and softness, thank the Lord, and she must keep it till she dropped.

They sat down for tea in the garden, as it was a warm summer day. Here, the heat was less intense and the air less dry than in New South Wales. The settlers enjoyed comparing the weather of Van Dieman's Land to England's. There were parks now, like Robert's here, that had some English trees and many English flowers, but even though the light was not nearly as dazzlingly bright as Sydney's, she could not say it was the same as that of England or Ireland. The children liked to ask their father and her about London. They had not yet been back "home", as they called it. She found herself telling them of Ireland again while she poured the tea – how it was so much greener and prettier than England or here, and how some houses were fine, not the vast palaces of London, yet very grand.

James leaned against her shoulder. "Granny, you miss Dublin Town and the countryside. You remember it so well. You talk of it as if you were there yesterday. Do you want to go back?"

She caught her breath. "Of course, I miss it, my boy." She stroked his hair, so like Rachel's and Rhodes'. She met the child's gaze. "If I were younger and could take you lads there, and, if your father or your Uncle David wished to travel with us, it would be grand to show you both the Great Sugarloaf Mountain."

James sat up. "I'd love to see it. And Dublin Town too. Do you wish you lived there again?"

Elizabeth gazed at them. "No, I am happy here with you."

The boys smiled. "We know you are," James said, with his ten-year old's confidence. "And that's good, Granny. I'd hate it if you lived somewhere else. Who would tell us stories of ships and fairy creatures and far-off lands? Who would sing to us?"

Elizabeth smiled. "Exactly. And I am expecting you both to know all the songs by heart soon."

Her memories of her homeland were enough. It had been so long – she would not go back. She could not bring herself to tell James and Ernest how poor her family was, how desperate everyone was. She would never tell them. It was not shame that stopped her, for the shame was not her family's, since like most poor folk, their poverty was not of their own making; rather, what stopped her was the sadness. Should she hand on Ireland's old and current sorrows to these children?

When her heart was sore some nights, it comforted her that she had supported her sisters' families for years and did so still. In the dark of night, memories often haunted her, but now, gazing at her two dear boys, their hair shining in the sun, their clear, confident eyes, she told them that she had been the luckiest of her family in the end, to leave Ireland and come to the colony, and they smiled, though they could not quite understand.

Author's Note

I first heard of Elizabeth Rafferty in 2011. I found her story – and the gaps in it – intriguing and challenging. Elizabeth's life and the issues she faced did not let me go.

Most of this remarkable story is true, historical fact. The motives and conversations of the characters in this novel are products of my imagination. For those who want to know what is truth and what is invention, the following facts are documented:

- Elizabeth's date of trial, 1795 (no detailed trial records remain for her. The burning of the Irish Records Office in 1922 destroyed court and legal records.)
- Her imprisonment in Dublin (in the New Prison, later called Kilmainham, and called Kilmainham in the novel, for clarity) and Cork.
- Men and women were unsegregated in the Dublin County New Prison.
- Elizabeth's presence on the *Britannia II* transport ship, 1797 (there were two transports named *Britannia*).
- The presence of Meg Rafferty and James Brannan on the *Britannia* voyage.
- The large number of alleged Defenders among the convicts on board.
- The use of leg and hand irons on men and women convicts.
- Elizabeth's relationship with the *Britannia's* captain, Thomas Dennett.
- The separation of the convicts from the officers in Rio de Janeiro.
- The escape of three convicts in Rio de Janeiro.
- The punishment of a female in the stocks on the ship.
- The suicide leap overboard by a female convict.
- The allegations of mutiny, the floggings and convict deaths on the Britannia.

- The flogging and death of James Brannan, who denied the charge of mutiny.
- Captain Dennett's harsh threats issued to Brannan and prisoners.
- Elizabeth's arrival in New South Wales.
- The enquiry by Governor Hunter into Captain Dennett's and the surgeon's treatment of convicts resulting in the appointment of Crown officials to manage the convicts on future transport ships.
- The criticism of Captain Dennett by Governor Hunter's enquiry and his return to England as captain of the *Britannia*; he did not captain any more convict ships.
- The birth of Captain Dennett's son, Thomas Dennett, the day before Captain Dennett sailed from Sydney.
- Elizabeth's pardon including the words, 'for good behaviour'. Her properties, including the site of the later famous Vaucluse House, and her shop.
- The successful reputation of Captain Dennett as an East India trader, and his publications of shipping routes.
- The will of Captain Dennett acknowledging his child with Elizabeth and bequeathing her an income for life with the proviso that she must live in New South Wales.
- Elizabeth's relationship with whaler-explorer Robert Rhodes.
- Her journey to India and England.
- Rhodes' imprisonment in the King's Bench, London, his exploration, and later publications, trade in America.
- Rachel Rhodes' baptism in Sydney.
- The conviction for slavery and later pardon of Robert Bostock after a successful appeal to the Privy Council.
- Bostock's receipt of an invitation from the Colonial Office as a free settler to Van Diemen's Land, erasing his convict past.
- Bostock's earlier 'wife' in Africa.
- Rachel's marriage to Robert Bostock and the children they had.
- Elizabeth's relationship with Captain Robert Stewart Walker.
- Captain Walker's respectable Scottish background.

- The birth of male and female children to Elizabeth and Walker.
- Helen's marriage to a clergyman farmer.
- The imprisonment of Captain Walker on Tahiti.
- Captain Walker's marriage to the Princess of Tahiti; their child.
- The birth of an illegitimate child to Miss Bellaire, fathered by Captain Walker.
- The marriage of Miss Bellaire to Captain Walker.
- Captain Walker's death: there are conflicting documents for that name.
- The return of Thomas Dennett junior to Sydney.
- Thomas Dennett junior's death on the ship to Van Diemen's Land, though not death by drowning.
- Elizabeth's journey to Hobart Town, 1822.
- Rachel's death in 1837 in childbirth.
- Bostock's son George's settlement in Port Phillip in 1839.
- The presence on the *Britannia* of Mrs Silver (Silk). The presence of Mr and Mrs Silver in the colony.
- The emergence of the Defenders in the early 1790s.
- Their attacks on Church of Ireland landowners in 1795 in the counties of Dublin, Kildare, Wicklow, Longford, Meath and Westmeath.
- The numerous arrests, trials and sentences of Defenders and the raising of militias by the landowning gentry to counter the Defenders.
- Peter Rafferty's ownership of a shop in Dublin in 1790s, and his connections to gentry and the Church of Ireland. Due to the lack of Irish records, there is no documented evidence that he was Elizabeth's uncle.

Readers can find traces of Elizabeth's story in Sydney, Tasmania, London and Dublin.

Though Elizabeth's shop in Sydney has vanished, there was a facsimile built for a time at Old Sydney Town, a tourist site. The Rocks district in Sydney contains restored buildings which give a flavour of Elizabeth's times. A portrait of Rachel survives and can be seen in Thelma Birrell's or Les Watters' books (see Bibliography).

The tourist brochure for Vaucluse House, Sydney, originally the site of one of Elizabeth's farms, mentions Elizabeth, though its claims are not all verified.

In Tasmania, Vaucluse in Hobart has become a retirement home, but Vaucluse on the Esk is still a large property and mansion recently on the market for millions.

In Victoria, Elizabeth's grandchildren are honoured at private schools, where they funded Houses, and at pastoral properties and in municipal libraries and council buildings in the Western District.

In London, one can visit the East India warehouses and the Slavery Museum in the Canary Wharf docklands area.

In Dublin, one can stroll along Baggott Street, see the river and the Green and the Cathedral, and linger in a pub by the Canal. In Wicklow, one can visit mansions and see the Great Sugarloaf Mountain.

Bibliography

Albiston, Jordie, *Botany Bay Document: A poetic History of the Women of Botany Bay*, St. Kilda: John Leonard Press, 1996.

Alexander, Alison, *Governors' Ladies*, Sandy Bay, Tasmania: Tasmanian Historical Research Association Inc., 1987.

Alexander, Alison, *The Ambitions of Jane Franklin*, Crow's Nest, NSW: Allen and Unwin, 2013.

Atkinson, Alan, *The Europeans in Australia, Volume One, The Beginning*, Sydney: NewSouth Publishing, 2016.

Atkinson, Alan, *Elizabeth and John, The Macarthurs of Elizabeth Farm*, Sydney: NewSouth, 2022.

Atwood, Margaret, *Alias Grace*, Soho Square, London: Bloomsbury Publishing, 1996.

Atwood Margaret, *The Handmaid's Tale*, Toronto: McClelland and Stewart, 1985.

Atwood, Margaret, *The Testaments*, London: Penguin-Random House, 2019.

Australian Council of National Trusts, *Historic Houses of Australia*, Melbourne: Cassell Australia Limited, 1974.

Australian Dictionary of Biography, Vols 1-8, Melbourne: Melbourne University Publishing, 1966-79.

Barker, Pat, *The Silence of the Girls*, London: Penguin-Random House, 2018.

Bateson, Robert, *The Convict Ships*, Frenchs Forest, NSW: A.H. and A.W. Reed, 1974.

Boochani, Behrouz, translated by Omid Tofighian, *No Friend But The Mountains*, Melbourne: Picador, 2018.

Bradshaw, Delia, *With Love, Delia: Letters to an Irish Grandmother*, Melbourne: Blurb, 2012.

Birrell, Thelma, *Mariners, Merchants – Then Pioneers*, Brisbane: Birrell, 1993, 2006.

Bishop, Patrick, *The Irish Empire, the Story of the Irish Abroad*, London: Boxtree, 1999.

Bradbury, Bettina, *Caroline's Dilemma, A Colonial Inheritance Saga*, Sydney: NewSouth Publishing, 2019.

Carey, Peter, *Jack Maggs*, St Lucia: University of Queensland Press, 1997.

Christopher, Emma, *Slave Ship Sailors and their Captive Cargoes, 1730-1807*, Cambridge, UK: Cambridge University Press, 2006.

Christopher, Emma, *Freedom in White and Black, A Lost Story of the Illegal Slave Trade and Its Global Legacy*, Madison: University of Wisconsin Press, 2018.

Clark, C. M. H. *A History of Australia*, Vols 1-6, Melbourne: Melbourne University Publishing, 1981.

Cloche, Danielle, *Voyages to the South Seas*, Melbourne: Melbourne University Publishing, 2007.

Clune, Frank, *The Viking of Van Diemen's Land*, Sydney: Angus and Robertson, 1949, 1954.

Cochrane, Peter, *The Making of Martin Sparrow*, North Sydney: Penguin, Viking, 2018

Collins, David, *An Account of the English Colony in New South Wales, [Volume 1]*, London: A. H. and A.W. Reed reprint, 1975.

Collnett, Captain James, R. N., *A Voyage to New Holland and Round the World*, ed. G. A. Mawer, Sydney: Rosenberg Publishing, , 2016.

Cook, Judith, *To Brave Every Danger: the Epic Life of Mary Bryant*, London: MacMillan, 1997.

Cossu, Anna, *A Place in the Rocks*, Sydney: Historic Houses Trust of New South Wales, 2008.

Council of the Library of New South Wales, *Our Origins, From Penal Camp to Parliament*, Sydney: Mitchell and Dixon Galleries, 1973.

Dark, Eleanor, *Storm of Time*, Sydney: Harper Collins, 2013.

De Breffny, Brian, ed., *The Irish World, The History and Cultural Achievements of the Irish People*, London: Thames and Hudson, 1977.

De Vries-Evans, Susanna, *Pioneer Women ... Pioneer Land*, Sydney: Angus & Robertson, 1987.

Donahue, Emma, *The Wonder*, London: Picador, 2016.

Erikson, Carolly, *The Girl from Botany Bay*, Melbourne: John Wiley and Sons, 2004.

Flannery, Tim, ed. *The Birth of Sydney*, Melbourne: Text, 2000.

Flinders, Matthew, *Terra Australis*, Melbourne: Text, 2012.

Frost, Lucy, *No Place for a Nervous Lady*, Melbourne: McPhee Gribble, 1984.

Graeme-Evans, Eleanor, *From Sarah to Sara*, Launceston, TAS: Regal Press, 2010.

Grenville, Kate, *The Secret River*, Melbourne: Text, 2005.

Grenville, Kate, *Searching for the Secret River*, Melbourne: Text, 2006.

Grenville, Kate, *The Lieutenant*, Melbourne: Text, 2010.

Grenville, Kate, *Sarah Thornhill*, Melbourne: Text, 2011.

Grenville, Kate, *A Room Made of Leaves*, Melbourne: Text, 2020.

Hall, Barbara, *Death or Liberty*, Sydney: Hall, 2006.

Hill, David, *Convict Colony*, Sydney: Angus and Robertson, 2019.

Hill, David, *First Fleet Surgeon*, Canberra: National Library of Australia, 2015.

Historic Houses Trust of NSW, *Vaucluse House*, Sydney: Historic Houses Trust of NSW, 1982.

Historic Houses Trust of NSW, *Susannah Place 1844*, Sydney: Historic Houses Trust of NSW, 1993.

Hughes, Robert, *The Fatal Shore*, London: Pan Books, 1988.

Irving, R. and Chisholm, P. ed. *Old Sydney Town*, Somersby NSW: Old Sydney Town Pty. Ltd., 1974.

Karskens, Grace, *The Colony, A History of Early Sydney*, Crows Nest, NSW: Allen and Unwin, 2010.

Keneally, Thomas, *Bring Larks and Heroes*, Melbourne: Cassell, Australia, 1967.

Keneally, Tom, *The Commonwealth of Thieves*, Random House, 2005.

Keneally, Thomas, *The Great Shame*, Milsons Point, NSW: Vintage, Penguin, 1999.

Keneally, Meg, *Fled*, Crows Nest, NSW: Allen and Unwin, 2019.

Kent, Hannah, *The Good People*, Sydney: Picador, 2016.

Kent, Hannah, *Burial Rites*, Sydney: Picador, 2013.

King, Jonathan, *Mary Bryant, Her Life and Escape from Botany Bay*, Cammeray, NSW: Simon and Schuster, 2005.

Koch, Christopher, *The Many Coloured Land*, Sydney: Penguin, 2002.

Koch, Christopher, *Out of Ireland*, Sydney: Penguin, 1999.

Leahy, Cathy and Ryan, Judith, ed. *Colony Australia 1770–1861/Frontier Wars*, Melbourne: National Gallery of Victoria, 2018.

Leary, Rachel, *Bridget Crack*, Crows Nest, NSW: Allen and Unwin, 2017.

Livett, Jennifer, *Wild Island*, Crows Nest, NSW: Allen and Unwin, 2016.

McKinnon, Catherine, *Storyland*, Sydney: 4th Estate, 2017.

Mitchell and Dixon Galleries, Library of New South Wales, *Our Origins, From Penal Camp to Parliament*, Sydney: Library of NSW, 2000.

Mundle, Rob, *First Fleet*, Sydney: ABC Books/Harper Collins, 2015.

Munro, Alice, *The View from Castle Rock*, Toronto: Vintage, 2006.

New South Wales Pocket Almanac and Colonial Remembrancer, 1806, Sydney: Trove.

Newton, John, *A Savage History, Whaling in the Pacific and Southern Oceans*, Sydney: NewSouth Publishing, 2013.

Niall, Brenda, *The Boyds*, Melbourne: Melbourne University Press, 2002.

Niall, Brenda, *Can You Hear the Sea?* Melbourne: Text, 2017.

Nicol, John, *Life and Adventures of John Nicol, Mariner*, Melbourne: Text Classics, 1997.

Nicholls, Mary, ed., *The Diary of the Reverend Robert Knopwood, 1803-1838*, Hobart: Tasmanian Historical Research Association.

North, Jessica, *Esther*, Crows Nest, NSW: Allen and Unwin, 2019.

O'Brian, Patrick, *The Nutmeg of Consolation*, London: Harper Collins, 1997.

Pembroke, Michael, *Arthur Phillip, Sailor, Mercenary, Governor, Spy*, Melbourne: Hardie Grant, 2014.

Pownall, Eve, *Australian Pioneer Women*, Melbourne: Penguin, 1988.

Rees, Sian, *The Floating Brothel*, Sydney: Hodder Australia, 2001.

Reynolds, Henry, *The Other Side of the Frontier*, Sydney: NewSouth Publishing, 1981.

Reynolds, Henry, *Forgotten War*, Sydney: NewSouth Publishing, 2013.

Robinson, Portia, *The Women of Botany Bay*, Sydney: Macquarie Library, 1988.

Ross, James, *The Settler in Van Diemen's Land*, Melbourne: Marsh Walsh Publishing, 1975.

Seal, Graham, *Great Convict Stories*, Crows Nest, NSW: Allen and Unwin, 2017.

Seal, Graham, *The Savage Shore*, Crows Nest, NSW: Allen and Unwin, 2015.

Serong, Jock, *Preservation*, Melbourne: Text, 2018.

Scott Tucker, Michelle, *Elizabeth Macarthur*, Melbourne: Text, 2019.

Slattery, Luke, *Mrs M*, Sydney: 4th Estate, 2017.

Smith, Babette, *A Cargo of Women*, Crows Nest, NSW: Allen and Unwin, 2008.

Sproud, Dan, *The Usurper*, Hobart: Blubber Head Press, 2001.

Swiss, Deborah J, *The Tin Ticket*, Sydney: Penguin/Berkley, 2010.

Stallard, Avan Jedd, *Antipodes, In Search of the Southern Continent*, Melbourne: Monash University Publishing, 2016.

Tardiff, Phillip, *Notorious Strumpets and Dangerous Girls*, Sydney: Angus and Robertson, 1991.

Tench, Watkin, *1788*, ed. Flannery, Tim, Melbourne: Text, 2009.

The Victorian Writer *History*, (now Writers Victoria), Melbourne: Victorian Writers' Centre, June 2014.

Tipping, Marjorie, *Convicts Unbound*, South Yarra, VIC: Viking O'Neill, 1988.

Treloar, Lucy, *Salt Creek*, Sydney: Pan Macmillan, 2015.

Vaucluse House Trust, *Vaucluse House*, Sydney: Vaucluse House Trust, 1959.

Watters, Leslie, *Elizabeth Rafferty in Sydney's The Rocks and her Bostock Legacy; convict, settler, shopkeeper, 1795-1822*, Canberra: Watters, 2014.

Williams, Sue, *Elizabeth and Elizabeth*, Crows Nest, NSW: Allen and Unwin, 2021.

Wood, Charlotte, *The Natural Way of Things*, Crows Nest, NSW: Allen and Unwin, 2015.

Wright, Alexis, et al., *Telling Someone Else's Story*, *Meanjin Quarterly*, Summer, 2016, Melbourne: Melbourne University Press, 2016.

www.ingramcontent.com/pod-product-compliance
Lightning Source LLC
Chambersburg PA
CBHW061438030726
47503CB00005B/1469